37

D1070915

Trail Driver Texas Joe Shipman was tall, lean—and tough.

He could ride, rope, curse, brand, and fan a six gun at high speeds. His goal was to get 4,500 cattle safely to market —and then to get himself dangerously drunk. It was a scheme that could only lead to trouble.

Joe Shipman was the kind who could drift from good to bad to worse. But there was one thing stopping him. Her name was Reddie Bayne, a hard-riding lady with red-gold hair. Could she get her man before it was too late—before one of Texas Joe's wild escapades sent him on a one-way trip to Boot Hill?

Books by Zane Grey

Published by POCKET BOOKS

THE TRAIL
DRIVER

PUBLISHED BY POCKET BOOKS NEW YORK

515998
F
GRÉ
90/91
7.32

POCKET BOOKS, a division of Simon & Schuster, Inc.
1230 Avenue of the Americas, New York, N.Y. 10020

Copyright 1931, 1936 by Zane Grey; copyright renewed 1959, 1964 by
Romer Zane Grey, Elizabeth Zane Grosso and Loren Zane Grey

Published by arrangement with Harper & Row, Publishers, Inc.

ISBN: 0-671-50169-0

First Pocket Books printing April 1959

20   19   18   17   16

POCKET and colophon are registered trademarks
of Simon & Schuster, Inc.

Printed in the U.S.A.

THE TRAIL
DRIVER

CHAPTER 1

THAT HOT SUMMER day in June the Texas town of San Antonio was humming like a drowsy beehive. The year 1871 appeared destined to be the greatest for cattle-drives north since the first one inaugurated by Jesse Chisholm in 1868. During the Civil War cattle had multiplied on the vast Texas ranges by the hundreds of thousands. There was no market. Ranches were few and far between, and the inhabitants very poor. Chisholm conceived the daring idea of driving a herd north to find a market. Despite the interminable distance, the hardships and perils, his venture turned out a success. It changed the history of Texas.

By the spring of 1871 the Chisholm Trail had become a deciding factor in the recovery of Texas. The hoofs of Texas long-horns and Spanish mustangs had worn a mile-wide trail across the undulating steppes of the Lone Star State.

Adam Brite had already made one trip this year. Starting in March with twenty-five hundred head of cattle and seven drivers, he had beat the Indians and floods in his most profitable venture. He had started too early for both. The misfortunes of trail drivers following him that year could not dampen his ardor for a second drive. Perhaps he might make three drives this auspicious year. Buying cattle right and left for cash, he had in sight a herd of four thousand five hundred. This would be by far the largest number of long-horns ever collected, let alone driven north. And Brite's immediate and vital problem was trail drivers.

Five boys were on the way to San Antonio from Uvalde

1

Ranch with a herd, and their services had been secured in the sale. Brite did not care to undertake so big a job without at least ten of the hardest-riding and hardest-shooting drivers on the ranges. To this end he had been a busy man for the single day that he had been back in San Antonio. At Dodge his seven drivers had seemed to vanish as if by magic in the smoke and dust of that wildest of frontier posts. But Brite felt himself particularly fortunate in having secured one of Chisholm's right-hand drivers for his foreman.

Brite waited for this man, eager and hopeful. His life-long friend, the cattleman Colonel Eb Blanchard, had recommended Texas Joe Shipman, and promised to find him and fetch him around. The afternoon was waning now. Lines of dusty riders were off to the range; the lobby of the Alamo Hotel was thinning out of its booted, spurred, and belted cattlemen; the saloon inside had lost something of its roar. Sloe-eyed Mexicans in colorful garb passed down the street. Brite was about to give up waiting when Colonel Blanchard entered with a young man who would have stood out paramount even among a host of rangy, still-faced, clear-eyed Texans.

"Heah yu air, Adam," called out Blanchard, cheerily, as he dragged up the tall rider. "Tex, meet my old partner, Adam Brite, the whitest stockman in this State. . . . Adam, this is Joe Shipman. He rode on my ootfit longer than I can recollect, an' has made two trips up the Trail. Little the wuss for likker at this time. But never yu mind thet. I vouch for Tex."

"Hod do, Shipman," replied Brite, shortly, extending his hand. This rider was tall, wide-shouldered, small-hipped, lithe, and erect. His boldly cut features were handsome. He had tawny hair, eyes of clear amber, singularly direct, and a lazy, cool, little smile. He looked about twenty-four years old.

"Howdy, Mistah Brite," he replied. "I'm shore sorry I'm drunk. Yu shee, I met old pard—Less Holden—an' dog-gone him—he hawg-tied me an' poured aboot a barrel of applejack down me."

Brite knew Texans. He required no second look at this stalwart rider to like him, to accept him even without Colonel Blanchard's recommendation.

"I'll leave yu to talk it over," went on Blanchard. "Reckon yu'd do wal to take Tex on right heah."

"All right, Colonel. Much obliged," replied Brite. "Come, Shipman, let's set down. . . . Have a cigar. . . . What wages do yu want to be foreman for me on my next drive?"

"Wal, what'll yu pay?" inquired Shipman, and it was easy to see that he did not care what he got.

"Forty a month, considerin' we'll drive forty-five hundred haid."

"Whew! . . . An' how many drivers, boss?"

"Ten, at least, an' fifteen if we can get them."

"Wal, we cain't never make it with only ten. There'll be hell shore up the Trail this summer."

"Will yu take the job?"

"I reckon so," drawled the rider. "Shore swore I'd never go again. I've been up three times. Had a Comanche arrer in my shoulder. An' I'm packin' lead in my hip."

"I seen yu walked with a limp. Hurt yore ridin' any?"

"Wal, nobody ever said nothin' aboot it if it did."

"Ahuh. Do yu know any riders yu can hire?"

"I might get my old pard, Less Holden," replied Shipman, brightening. "No better ever forked a hawse. But Less is the wildest hombre."

"Thet's no matter. Get him, an' half a dozen more. Also a cook. I'll go oot an' buy a new chuck-wagon. The last one went to pieces on us. We lost time. I'll buy supplies, too."

"When yu aim to hit the Trail, boss?"

"Soon as thet Uvalde ootfit comes in. Expect them today. We ought to get away day after tomorrow."

"Dog-gone! I had a gurl somewhere heah in this town. I cain't find her. . . . Wal, it's a dog's life. . . . Reckon with such a big herd yu'll want a real ootfit."

"Hardest riders on the range."

"Wal, thet ain't a-goin' to be easy. Drivers shore as scarce as hen teeth. Boss, there's fifty thousand haid due to leave this month."

"All the more reason for us to get the jump on them."

"Wal, I'd just as lief there was half a dozen herds ahaid of us."

"Shipman, grass an' water good only in spots this spring."

"All right, boss. I'll do my best," replied the rider, rising.

"Report to me heah after supper," concluded Brite, and watched the Texan move leisurely away. His limp was not pronounced and it did not detract from his striking appearance. Brite thought that he would have liked to call him son. After all, he was a lonely old cattleman. And more than once he had felt a strange melancholy, almost a presentiment, in regard to this trail driving. It had developed into a dangerous business. Storm, flood, drought and cold, lightning and the extremely strenuous nature of the work, were bad enough. But of late the Comanches and Kiowas had gone on the warpath. There had always been Indian depredations in Texas; however, nothing so serious as threatened now. Brite concluded that buffalo meat and hide hunters were responsible. The time would come when the Indians would no longer stand for the slaughter of the buffalo. And when that time arrived all the hunters and trail drivers as well as settlers would be forced to unite for war against the redskin. The wild young Texans scouted this idea, but all the old timers like Brite knew its truth.

Brite had to shoulder his way into Hitwell's merchandise store. Three months before he had bought supplies here and had the place to himself. A motley horde of *vaqueros*, soldiers, cattlemen, drivers, Indians, and loungers now filled the big place. Brite finally got Hitwell's ear. They had been in the cattle business together before the war. "Sam, what's all this aboot?"

"Wal, it's shore a rush," replied Hitwell, rubbing his hands. "If old Jesse Chisholm had foreseen this he'd have gone in the supply business."

"Reckon yu better duplicate thet order I gave yu in March an' add a third more to it."

"When yu leavin', Adam?"

"Day after tomorrow."

"Be all packed for yu. Fresh supplies just in from New Orleans."

"How aboot a chuck-wagon?"

"Sold oot, Adam. Haven't got any kind of a wagon left."

"Cain't yu get me one?"

"Wal, I'll try, Adam, but chances air slim."

"Hell! I'd better go rustlin' aboot."

He visited other stores without avail. It was long after sunset when he got back to the hotel. Brite had supper and then went out to look for Shipman. The heat of day had passed and it was pleasant sitting out in front. Across the street stood a saloon which evidently rivaled the merchandise store for visitors. A tall gambler leaned against the door. He wore a long black coat and a flowered vest and a wide-brimmed black sombrero. Booted, spurred, gun-packing trail drivers passed in and out, noisy and gay. Riders passed to and fro against the lighted windows.

Soft steps and clinking spurs behind Brite drew his attention.

"Wal, boss, I shore been lucky," drawled the voice of Shipman.

Brite turned to see the trail driver, accompanied by a flaming-faced youth under twenty. He had eyes of blue fire and an air of reckless insouciance.

"Hullo, Shipman. Shore glad yu had some luck. It's more than I had. Couldn't buy any kind of a wagon."

"Boss, this heah's my pard, Less Holden. . . . Less, shake with Mr. Brite."

"Where yu hail from?" queried Brite, after the introduction, bending keen eyes on the stripling.

"Dallas. I was born there."

"Wal, yu didn't need to tell me yu was a Texan. Who yu been ridin' for?"

"Dave Slaughter. Goin' on three years. But I've never been up the Trail."

"Holden, if yu've rode for Dave Slaughter yu're good enough for me. . . . Shipman, what's the other good luck?"

"Boss, I corralled a boy named Whittaker. Couldn't be no

better. An' I talked with a chap from Pennsylvania. Tenderfoot, all right, but husky. Says he can ride. Reckon yu better let me hire him, boss. Santone is shore full of riders, but they've got jobs."

"Yes, by all means," replied Brite. "Looks like we'll be delayed findin' an ootfit. I'm stumped aboot a chuck-wagon, too."

"Wal, Less an' me will look around for a secondhand wagon."

"Don't overlook a cook. . . . Hullo! did I heah my name called?"

"Shore did. Thet boy who just limped off his hawse there," returned Shipman, pointing.

Turning, Brite espied a mustang and rider that had arrived in front of the hotel. He was in the act of dropping his bridle and evidently had just addressed one of the men present.

"Brite? Shore, he's around somewheres."

"Heah I am," called Brite, stepping along the curb, followed by the two drivers. The rider was young, dark as a Mexican, ragged and soiled, and he smelled of dust.

"Air yu Mr. Adam Brite?" he asked, when Brite strode up.

"Yes, I'm Brite. Yu must be one of my boys with the Uvalde herd?"

"Shore am, boss, an' glad to report we got in without losin' a steer."

"What's yore name?"

"Ackerman, sir."

"Meet my foreman, Shipman, an' his pard, Holden."

"Howdy, Deuce," drawled Shipman, extending a hand.

"Dog-gone if it ain't Texas Joe," burst out the rider, with a delighted grin. They gripped hands warmly.

"Whar yu beddin' the herd, Deuce?" asked Shipman, when the greetings were over.

"Aboot five miles oot in the creek bottom. Not much grass, but plenty of water. Stock all fine an' fat as pigeons. We moseyed along slow."

"Have yu got a wagon?"

"Shore, an' a good cook. He's a niggah, but he shore is a white one. An' how he can cook!"

"Wal, Mr. Brite, this sounds like music to me," said Shipman, turning to his employer. "Whar's the stock yu had heah already?"

"I've two thousand haid in three pastures just oot of town. We can bunch them on the Trail in no time an' work along slow while Ackerman catches up."

"Shore, boss, but we gotta have drivers," protested the foreman.

"There's eight of us now, includin' myself. I'd risk it with two more good men."

"Wal, we'll find them, somewhares. . . . An', boss, how aboot grub?"

"Ordered at Hitwell's. . . . Let's see, Ackerman. Send yore wagon in early mawnin' tomorrow. An' after loadin' supplies have it catch up oot on the Trail."

"Deuce, cain't yu stay in town an' see the sights?" queried Shipman, his eyes kindly on the weary, dusty rider.

"Wisht I could. But two of the boys air all in, an' I gotta rustle back." With that he stepped astride, and bidding them good-by, he trotted away.

"Wal, boss, we'll comb Santone for a couple of drivers. An' in the mawnin' I'll be heah to help load thet chuck-wagon."

"All right. I'll meet yu oot at the pastures. Good night."

Brite headed back toward the lobby of the hotel to be confronted by a man he well knew, yet on the moment could not place. The blond, cold-faced, tight-lipped, gimlet-eyed Texan certainly recognized him. "Howdy, Brite. Don't yu-all know me?" he drawled.

"Shore I know yu. But I don't recollect yore handle," replied Brite, slowly drawing back his half-extended hand.

"Wal, stick a pan on thet handle an' yu'll have me pat."

"Hell yes! Pan Handle Smith!" exclaimed Brite, and this time shot out his hand. The other met it with his, and the steely grip of that soft, ungloved member thrilled Brite to his marrow. "How'd yu turn up heah?"

"Just rode in. From the river. An' I'm rustlin' north pronto."

"Wal, Pan Handle, yu always was on the move. I hope it's not the same old—"

"Shore is, Brite. By ——! I cain't have any peace. I dropped into a little game of draw below an' got fleeced. Thet riled me. I hung on an' caught a caird-sharp at his tricks. Wal, I called him an' his pard. They'd been workin' the buffalo camps. Didn't know me. Drawed on me—settin' at table at thet—the damn fools! I had to shoot my way oot, which is why I left my money. Been ridin' hard an' just got in. I'm hungry, Brite, an' haven't a dollar."

"Easy. Glad yu bumped into me," replied Brite, handing him a greenback. An idea flashed into his mind simultaneously with the action. And it chased away the cold little chill Smith's story had given him. "On the dodge, eh?"

"Wal, it might be hot for me heah till thet fracas is forgotten."

"Pan Handle, if I recollect right, yu used to drive cattle?"

"Wal, I reckon," replied Smith, with a far-away look in his eyes and a wistful smile.

"How'd yu like to help me drive a big herd north to Dodge?"

"Brite, I'd like it a heap. I don't want no wages. I can get a stake at Dodge," returned the other, keenly.

"You're on. For wages, of course. What ootfit have yu?"

"Not much. A fine hawse. But he needs a rest. A saddle, blanket, an' Winchester. An' all the rest of my worldly goods is on my back."

"An' on yore hips, too, I notice," drawled Brite, his glance taking in the gray travel-worn figure and the gun butts, protruding from sheath, significantly low. "Go get a good feed, Smith. Yu shore look peaked. An' meet me heah in an hour or so. Yu'll need to stock up heavy on ammunition. An' yu'll need a change of duds."

"Wal, I appreciate this more than I can say, Brite," replied Smith, and strode away.

Brite watched him out of sight. And not until then did he realize what he had done. Hired one of the most notorious of Texas gun-fighters to be a trail driver! The fact was that he was actually harboring an outlaw on the dodge. It shocked Brite a little—the bare fact. But on second thought he laughed. This was frontier Texas. And every community had a gunman of whom it was inordinately proud. Wess Hardin, Buck Duane, King Fisher, and a host of lesser lights were as representative of Texas as Crockett and Travis and Bowie. On the other hand, there were men noted for fast and deadly trigger work who put themselves outside the pale. They were robbers, bandits, desperadoes, sheriffs with an itch to kill instead of arrest, cowboys on the rampage, gamblers who shot to hide their cheating. Pan Handle Smith had been outlawed, but he had really been more sinned against than sinning. Brite concluded that he was fortunate to engage the outlaw for his second drive north. Something presaged a tremendous ordeal. Forty-five hundred long-horns! Too late now to undo this rash deal! He would go through with it. Still, old Texan that he was, he experienced a cold tight contraction of skin at the thought of possibilities. Many a driver had failed to reach the end of the long Trail.

CHAPTER **2** BRITE'S FIRST CAMP was Pecan Swale, some twelve or more miles out of San Antonio. Grass had been scarce until the drivers reached this creek bottom. The gigantic herd had drifted faster than usual, arriving at the Swale before sunset.

Shipman, with the chuck-wagon, and Ackerman, with the second herd, rolled in together.

"Any drive close behind?" called Brite, from his resting-spot in the shade. He was tired. Tough as he was, it took several days to break him in to saddle and trail.

"Nope, boss. Henderson is startin' next with two herds. But he won't be ready for days. Then the herds will come a-whoopin'," returned the rider.

"Wal, thet's good. Shipman, I reckon yu better take charge now."

"Then we'll all lay off till after supper. Looks like a mighty good place for cattle to hang."

The location was a most satisfactory one, and would be hard to leave, at least for those drivers who had been up the Trail. A grove of pecan and walnut trees and blackberry bushes choked the upper end of the valley with green and yellow verdure. Below it a lazy shallow stream meandered between its borders of willow. Grass grew luxuriantly all through the bottomlands, and up the gentle slopes. Dust clouds were lifting here and there where the mustangs were rolling. The drivers threw saddles, blankets, and bridles to the ground, and flopped down after them. Gloves, sombreros, chaps, and boots likewise went flying. The boys were disposed to be merry and to look each other over and take stock of the whistling cook. Alabama Moze, they called him, and he was a prepossessing Negro, baffling as to age. His chuck-wagon was a huge affair, with hoops for canvas, and a boarded contraption at the rear. Moze was in the act of letting down a wide door which served as a table. He reached for an ax and sallied forth for firewood. That article appeared scarce, except for the green standing trees.

From his lounging-spot Brite studied his outfit of men, including the cook. Shipman had not been able to secure any more drivers. Brite thought it well indeed that he had taken on Pan Handle Smith. That worthy followed Moze out into the grove. Divested of coat and chaps, he made a fine figure of a man. Even on the Texas border, where striking men were common, Smith would have drawn more than one glance. In fact, he earned more than that from Joe Shipman. But no remarks were made about Smith.

Bender, the tenderfoot from Pennsylvania, appeared to be a hulking youth, good natured and friendly, though rather shy before these still-faced, intent-eyed Texans. He had heavy, stolid features that fitted his bulky shoulders. His hair was the color of tow and resembled a mop. He had frank, eager blue eyes. Whittaker was a red-faced, sleepy-eyed young rider of twenty-two, notable for his superb physique.

The Uvalde quintet mostly interested Brite. In a land where

young, fierce, rollicking devils were the rule rather than the exception this aggregation would not have attracted any particular attention in a crowd of drivers. But Adam Brite loved Texas and Texans, and as he studied these boys he conceived the impression that they had a shade on the average trail driver. Not one of them had yet reached twenty years of age. The dark, slim, bow-legged Deuce Ackerman appeared to be the most forceful personality. The youth who answered to the name San Sabe had Indian or Mexican blood, and his lean shape wore the stamp of *vaquero*. Rolly Little's name suited him. He was small and round. He had yellow hair, a freckled face, and flashing brown eyes, as sharp as daggers. Ben Chandler was a typical Texas youth, long, rangy, loose-jointed, of sandy complexion and hair, and eyes of clear, light blue. The last of the five, Roy Hallett, seemed just to be a member of the group—a quiet, somber, negative youth.

Preparations for supper proceeded leisurely. Brite marked that Pan Handle helped the Negro in more ways than packing in firewood. The drivers noted it, too, with significant stares. On the Trail it was not usual for any rider to share the tasks of a Negro. Manifestly Pan Handle Smith was a law unto himself. The interest in him increased, but it did not seem likely that anyone would question his pleasure.

Texas Joe left camp to climb the ridge from which he surveyed the valley. Evidently he was satisfied with what he saw. Brite's opinion was that the cattle would not stray. It was unusual, however, to leave them unguarded for even a moment. Presently Smith appeared to be studying the land to the north. Upon his return to camp he announced: "Trail riders haided for Santone. An' there's a lone hawseman ridin' in from 'cross country."

"Wal, Shipman, we'll shore see more riders than we want on this trip," said Brite.

"Ahuh, I reckon."

"Boss, yu mean painted riders?" spoke up Ackerman.

"Not particular, if we're lucky. I had to feed a lot of Comanches last trip. But they made no trouble. I reckon the riders thet bother me most are the drifters an' trail dodgers."

"Boss, mebbe we'll be an ootfit thet breed had better pass up," drawled Shipman.

"Wal, I hope so. Yu cain't never tell what yore ootfit is until it's tried."

"Tried by what, Mr. Brite?" asked the tenderfoot Bender, with great curiosity.

The boss laughed at this query. Before he could reply Shipman spoke up: "Boy, it's jest what happens along."

"Nothing happened today in all that nice long ride. I've an idea these trail dangers are exaggerated."

Suddenly one of Ackerman's boys let out a stentorian: "*Hawl Hawl*" This would probably have started something but for the cook's yell following and almost as loud: "Yo-all come an' git it!"

There ensued a merry scramble, and then a sudden silence. Hungry boys seldom wasted time to talk. Brite called for Moze to fetch his dinner over under the tree. It took no second glance for the boss to be assured that this cook was a treasure.

The sun set in a cloudless, golden sky. An occasional bawl of a cow from the stream bottom broke the silence. A cooling zephyr of wind came through the grove, rustling the leaves, wafting the camp-fire smoke away. Brite had a sense of satisfaction at being on the Trail again and out in the open. Much of his life had been spent that way.

"Moze, where yu from?" asked Shipman, as he arose.

"I'se a Alabama niggah, sah," replied Moze, with a grin. "Thet's what they calls me. Alabama."

"Wal, so long's yu feed me like this I'll shore keep the redskins from scalpin' yu."

"Den I'll be awful sho to feed yu dat way."

"Wal, boys, I hate to say it, but we gotta get on guard," went on Shipman, addressing the outfit. "There's ten of us. Four on till midnight, three till three o'clock, an' three till mawnin'. Who goes on duty with me now?"

They all united in a choice of this early-night duty.

"Shipman, I'll take my turn," added Brite.

"Wal, I'll be dog-goned," drawled the foreman. "What kind

of an ootfit is this heah? Yu all want to work. An' the boss, too!"

"Fust night oot," said someone.

"I reckon I gotta make myself disliked," returned Shipman, resignedly. "Bender, yu saddle yore hawse. Lester, same for yu. An', Smith, I reckon I'd feel kinda safe with yu oot there."

"Suits me fine. I never sleep, anyhow," replied the outlaw, rising with alacrity.

"Deuce, I'll wake yu at midnight or thereabouts. Yu pick yore two guards. . . . An' say, boss, I 'most forgot. Who's gonna wrangle the hawses? Thet's a big drove we got."

"Shore, but they're not wild. Herd them on good grass with the cattle."

"All right, we'll round them up. But we ought to have someone regular on thet job. . . . Wal, so long. It's a lucky start."

Brite agreed with this last statement of his foreman, despite the strange presentiment that came vaguely at odd moments. The Brite herd of forty-five hundred head, trail-branded with three brands before they had been bought, had a good start on the herds behind, and full three weeks after the last one that had gone north. Grass and water should be abundant, except in spots. Cattle could go days without grass, if they had plenty of water. It had been rather a backward spring, retarding the buffalo on their annual migration north. Brite concluded they would run into buffalo somewhere north of the Red River.

"Moze, couldya use some fresh meat?" called Deuce Ackerman.

"I'se got a whole quarter of beef," replied Moze. "An' yo knows, Mars Ackerman, I'se a economical cook."

"I saw a bunch of deer. Some venison shore would go good. Come on, Ben. We've a half-hour more of daylight yet."

The two drivers secured rifles and disappeared in the grove. Hallett impressively acquainted Little with the fact that he was going to take a bath. That worthy expressed amaze and consternation. "My Gawd! Roy, what ails yu? We'll be fordin' rivers an' creeks every day pronto. Ain't thet so, boss?"

"It shore is, an' if they're high an' cold yu'll get all the water yu want for ten years," returned Brite.

"I'm gonna, anyway," said Hallett.

"Roy, I'll go if yu'll pull off my boots. They ain't been off for a week."

"Shore. Come on."

Soon the camp was deserted save for the whistling Moze and Brite, who took pains about unrolling his canvas and spreading his blanket. A good bed was what a trail driver yearned for and seldom got. At least, mostly he did not get to lie in it long at a stretch. That done, Brite filled his pipe for a smoke. The afterglow burned in the west and against that gold a solitary rider on a black horse stood silhouetted dark and wild. A second glance assured Brite that it was not an Indian. Presently he headed the horse down into the Swale and disappeared among the trees. Brite expected this stranger to ride into camp. Strangers, unfortunately many of them undesirable, were common along the Chisholm Trail. This one emerged from the brush, having evidently crossed the stream farther above, and rode up, heading for the chuck-wagon. Before the rider stopped Brite answered to a presagement not at all rare in him—that there were meetings and meetings along the trail. This one was an event.

"Howdy, cook. Will yu give me a bite of grub before yu throw it oot?" the rider asked, in a youthful, resonant voice.

"Sho I will, boy. But I'se tellin' yo nuthin' ever gits throwed away wid dis chile cookin'. Jus' yo git down an' come in."

Brite observed that the horse was not a mustang, but a larger and finer breed than the tough little Spanish species. Moreover, he was a magnificent animal, black as coal, clean-limbed and heavy-chested, with the head of a racer. His rider appeared to be a mere boy, who, when he wearily slid off, showed to be slight of stature, though evidently round and strong of limb. He sat down cross-legged with the pan of food Moze gave him. Brite strolled over with the hope that he might secure another trail driver.

"Howdy, cowboy. All alone?" he said, genially.

"Yes, sir," replied the boy, looking up and as quickly looking down again. The act, however, gave Brite time to see a handsome face, tanned darkly gold, and big, dark, deep eyes that had a furtive, if not a hunted, look.

"Whar yu from?"

"Nowhere, I reckon."

"Lone cowboy, eh? Wal, thet's interestin' to me. I'm short on riders. Do yu want a job? My name's Brite an' I'm drivin' forty-five hundred haid north to Dodge. Ever do any trail drivin'?"

"No, sir. But I've rode cattle all my life."

"Ahuh. Wal, thet cain't be a very long while, son. Aboot how old air yu?"

"Sixteen. But I feel a hundred."

"Whar's yore home?"

"I haven't any."

"No? Wal, yu don't say? Whar's yore folks, then?"

"I haven't any, Mr. Brite. . . . My dad an' mom were killed by Indians when I was a kid."

"Aw, too bad, son. Thet's happened to so many Texas lads. . . . What yu been doin' since?"

"Ridin' from one ranch to another. I cain't hold a job long."

"Why not? Yu're a likely-lookin' youngster."

"Reckon I don't stand up good under the hardest ridin'. . . . An' there's other reasons."

"How aboot hawse-wranglin'?"

"Thet'd suit me fine. . . . Would yu give me a job?"

"Wal, I don't see why not. Finish yore supper, lad. Then come have a talk with me."

All this while Brite stood gazing down at the youth, changing from curiosity to sympathy and interest. Not once after the first time did the boy look up. There were holes in his battered old black sombrero, through one of which peeped a short curl of red-gold hair. He had shapely brown hands, rather small, but supple and strong. The end of a heavy gun-sheath protruded from his jacket on the left side. He wore overalls, high-top Mexican boots, and huge spurs, all the worse for long service.

Brite went back to his comfortable seat under the pecan

tree. From there his second glance at the horse discovered a canvas pack behind the saddle. The old cattleman mused that it was only necessary to get out over this wild, broad Texas range to meet with sad and strange and tragic experiences. How many, many Texas sons were like this youth! The vast range exacted a hard and bloody toll from the pioneers.

Dusk had fallen when the boy came over to present himself before the cattleman.

"My name is Bayne—Reddie Bayne," he announced, almost shyly.

"Red-haided, eh?"

"Not exactly. But I wasn't named for my hair. Reddie is my real given name."

"Wal, no matter. Any handle is good enough in Texas. Did yu ever heah of Liver-eatin' Kennedy or Dirty-face Jones or Pan Handle Smith?"

"I've heahed of the last, shore."

"Wal, yu'll see him pronto. He's ridin' for me this trip. . . . Air yu goin' to accept my offer?"

"I'll take the job. Yes, sir. Thanks."

"What wages?"

"Mr. Brite, I'll ride for my keep."

"No, I cain't take yu up on thet. It's a tough job up the Trail. Say thirty dollars a month?"

"Thet's more than I ever earned. . . . When do I begin?"

"Mawnin' will be time enough, son. Shipman an' the boys have bunched the hawses for the night."

"How many haid in yore *remuda?*"

"Nigh on to two hundred. More'n we need, shore. But they're all broke an' won't give much trouble. Yu see, when we get to Dodge I sell cattle, hawses, wagon, everythin'."

"I've heahed so much aboot this Chisholm Trail. I rode 'cross country clear from Bendera, hopin' to catch on with a trail-drive."

"Wal, yu've ketched on, Reddie, an' I shore hope yu don't regret it."

"Gosh! I'm glad. . . . An' if I have, I'd better unsaddle Sam."

Bayne led the black under an adjoining pecan, and slipping saddle, bridle, and pack, turned him loose. Presently the lad returned to sit down in the shadow.

"How many in yore ootfit, Mr. Brite?"

"An even dozen now, countin' yu."

"Regular Texas ootfit?"

"Shore. It's Texas, all right. But new to me. I've got a hunch it'll turn oot regular Texas an' then some. Texas Joe Shipman is my Trail boss. He's been up three times, an' thet shore makes him an old-stager. Lucky for me. The rest is a mixed bunch except five Uvalde boys. Fire-eatin' kids, I'll bet! There's a tenderfoot from Pennsylvania, Bender by name. Shipman's pard, Less Holden. A Carolinian named Whittaker. If he's as good as he looks he couldn't be no better. An' last Pan Handle Smith. He's a gunman an' outlaw, Bayne. But like some of his class he's shore salt of the earth."

"Ten. Countin' yu an' me an' the cook makes thirteen. Thet's unlucky, Mr. Brite."

"Thirteen. So 'tis."

"Perhaps I'd better ride on. I don't want to bring yu bad luck."

"Boy, yu'll be good luck."

"Oh, I hope so. I've been bad luck to so many ootfits," replied the youth, with a sigh.

Brite was struck at the oddity of that reply, but thought better of added curiosity. Then Deuce Ackerman and Chandler came rustling out of the shadow, coincident with the return of Little and Hallett.

"Boss, I seen a dog-gone fine black hawse oot heah. No pony. Big thoroughbred. I didn't see him in our *remuda*," declared Ackerman.

"Belongs to Reddie Bayne heah. He just rode up an' threw in with us. . . . Bayne, heah's four of the Uvalde boys."

"Howdy, all," rejoined the rider.

"Howdy yoreself, cowboy," said Ackerman, stepping forward to peer down. "I cain't see yu, but I'm dog-gone glad to meet yu. . . . Boys, Reddie Bayne sounds like a Texas handle."

The other Uvalde boys called welcome greetings. Some one threw brush on the fire, which blazed up cheerily. It was noticeable, however, that Bayne did not approach the camp fire.

"Boss, did yu heah me shoot?" queried Ackerman.

"No. Did yu?"

"I shore did. Had an easy shot at a buck. But the light was bad an' I missed. I'll plug one in the mawnin'."

"Deuce, if yu'd let me have the rifle we'd got the deer meat all right," declared Ben.

"Is thet so? I'll bet yu I can beat yu any old day!"

"What'll yu bet?"

"Wal, I hate to take yore money, but—"

"Sssssh! Riders comin'," interrupted Ackerman, in a sharp whisper.

Brite heard the thud of hoofs off under the trees. Horses were descending the road from above.

"Cain't be any of our ootfit," went on Ackerman, peering into the darkness. "Fellars, we may as wal be ready for anythin'."

Dark forms of horses and riders loomed in the outer circle of camp-fire light. They halted.

"Who comes?" called out Ackerman, and his young voice had a steely ring.

"Friends," came a gruff reply.

"Wal, advance, friends, an' let's see yu."

Just then a hard little hand clutched Brite's arm. He turned to see Reddie Bayne kneeling beside him. The lad's sombrero was off, exposing his face. It was pale, and the big dark eyes burned.

"Wallen! He's after me," whispered Bayne, hoarsely. "Don't let him—"

Brite gripped the lad and gave him a little shake. "Keep still."

The riders approached the camp fire, but did not come close enough to be distinctly seen. The leader appeared to be of stalwart frame, dark of face, somehow forceful and forbidding. Brite had seen a hundred men like him ride into Texas camps.

"Trail drivers, huh?" he queried, with gleaming eyes taking in the boys round the camp fire.

"Wal, we ain't Comanche Injuns," retorted Deuce, curtly.

"Whose ootfit?"

"Brite, of Santone. We got four thousand haid an' twenty drivers. Any more yu want to know?"

"Reckon yu took on a new rider lately, huh?"

"Wal, if we did—"

Brite rose to stride out into the firelight.

"Who're yu an' what's yore business heah?"

"My name's Wallen. From Braseda. We tracked a—a young —wal, a fellar whose handle was Reddie Bayne."

"Reddie Bayne. So thet was thet rider's name? What yu trackin' him for?"

"Thet's my business. Is he heah?"

"No, he isn't."

"Wal then, he was heah, Brite."

"Shore. Had supper with us. An' then he cut oot for Santone. Reckon he's there by now. What yu say, Deuce?"

"Reddie was forkin' a fast hawse," replied Ackerman, casually.

"Any camps between heah an' Santone?" went on the rider.

"Not when we passed along. May be by this time."

"Brite, if yu don't mind we'll spend the night heah," said Wallen, speculatively.

"Wal, stranger, I'm sorry. One of my rules is not to be too hospitable on the old Trail," drawled Brite. "Yu see thet sort of thing has cost me too much."

"Air yu handin' me a slap?" queried Wallen, roughly.

"No offense. Just my rule, thet's all."

"Ahuh. Wal, it's a damn pore rule for a Texan."

"Shore," agreed Brite, coolly.

The rider wheeled, cursing under his breath, and, accompanied by his silent companion, thudded off into the darkness. Brite waited until he could make sure they took the road, then he returned to the spot where he had left the lad.

Bayne sat against the tree. By the dim light Brite saw the gleam of a gun in his hand.

"Wal, I steered them off, Bayne," said Brite. "Hope I did yu a good turn."

"Yu bet yu did. . . . Thank yu—Mr. Brite," replied the lad in a low voice.

Deuce Ackerman had followed Brite under the tree. "Boss, thet Wallen shore didn't get nowheres with me. Strikes me I'd seen him some place."

"Who is Wallen, son?"

"Rancher I rode for over Braseda way."

"What's he got against yu?"

There was no reply. Ackerman bent over to peer down. "Throwed yore hardware, hey, Reddie? Wal, I don't blame yu. Now, cowboy, come clean if yu want to, or keep mum. It's all the same to us."

"Thank yu. . . . I'm no rustler—or thief—or anythin' bad. . . . It was just . . . Oh, I cain't tell yu," replied the lad, with emotion.

"Ahuh. Wal, then it must be somethin' to do aboot a gurl?"

"Yes . . . Somethin' aboot a gurl," hurriedly replied Bayne.

"I've been there, cowboy. . . . But I hope thet hombre wasn't her dad. 'Cause she's liable to be an orphan."

Ackerman returned to the camp fire, calling out: "Roll in, fellers. Yu're a-gonna need sleep this heah trip."

"Bayne, I'm shore glad it wasn't anythin' bad," said Brite, in a kindly tone.

One of the boys rekindled the fire, which burned up brightly. By its light the old cattleman had a better view of young Bayne's face. The hard and bitter expression appeared softening. He made a forlorn little figure that touched Brite.

"I—I'll tell yu—sometime—if yu won't give me away," whispered the lad, and then hurried off into the darkness.

Brite sought his own blankets and lay thinking of the lad's confession—something about a girl! That had been true of him once, long ago, and to it could be traced the fact of his lonely years. He warmed to this orphaned lad. The old Trail was a tough and bloody proposition; but anything might be met with upon it.

CHAPTER 3   BRITE OPENED HIS EYES to gray dawn. A rifle-shot had awakened him. Moze was singing about darkies and cotton, which argued that the camp had not been attacked by Indians. Brite crawled out of his blankets, stiff and sore, to pull on his boots and don his vest, which simple actions left him dressed for the day. He rolled his bed. Then securing a towel, he made through camp for the creek. Texas Joe was in the act of getting up. Three other boys lay prone, quiet, youthful, hard faces clear in the gray light.

"Boss, it's sho turrible gittin' oot in de mawnin'," was Moze's laconic greeting.

"Moze, I reckon I'm not so young as I was."

Down by the stream Brite encountered Reddie Bayne busy with his ablutions. "Howdy, son. I see yu're up an' doin'."

"Mawnin', Mr. Brite," replied the youth as he turned on his knees to show a wet and shining face as comely as a girl's. Brite thought the lad rather hurriedly got into his jacket and covered his red-gold curly hair with the battered old sombrero. Then he wiped face and hands with his scarf.

"I'll rustle my hawse before breakfast."

The water was cold and clear. Brite drank and washed with the pleasure of a trail driver who valued this privilege. At most places the water was muddy, or stinking and warm, or there was none at all. Upon his return up to the level bank he heard the lowing of cattle. Daylight had come. The eastern sky was ruddy. Mocking birds were making melody in the grove. Rabbits scurried away into the willows. Across the wide shallow stream deer stood on the opposite bank, with long ears erect. A fragrance of wood smoke assailed Brite's keen nostrils. There seemed to be something singularly full and rich in the moment.

Brite got back to camp in time to hear an interesting colloquy.

"Say, boy, who'n hell air yu?" Texas Joe was asking, in genuine surprise. "I cain't recollect seein' yu before."

"My name's Reddie Bayne," replied the lad. "I rode in last night. The boss gave me a job."

"He did? Packin' water, or what?" went on Shipman.

"Hawse-wranglin'," said Reddie, shortly.

"Humph! Yu're pretty much of a kid, ain't yu?"

"I cain't help it if I'm not an old geezer like—"

"Like who? Me? Say, youngster, I'm cantankerous early in the mawnin'."

"So it would seem," dryly responded Bayne.

"What yu packin' thet big gun on yore left hip for?"

"Kind of a protection against mean cusses."

"Heah, I didn't mean was yu wearin' it ornamental. But what for on the left side?"

"I'm left-handed."

"Aw, I see. Gun-slinger from the left hip, huh? Wal, I reckon yu got a lot of notches on the handle."

Bayne did not deign to make a reply to this, but it was evident that he was a little upset by the cool and sarcastic foreman. As Brite came on he saw the lad's fine eyes flash.

"Mawnin', boss. I see yu have gone an' hired another gunman," drawled Texas Joe.

"Who? Reddie Bayne, heah?"

"Shore. No one else. What's Texas comin' to thet boys who ought to be home a milkin' cows rustle oot on bloody trails packin' big guns?"

"I haven't any home," retorted Bayne, with spirit.

"Reddie, shake hands with my foreman, Texas Joe Shipman," said Brite.

"Howdy, Mr. Shipman," rejoined Bayne, resentfully, with emphasis on the prefix, and he did not offer his hand.

"Howdy, Girlie Boy," drawled Joe. "Suppose yu rustle yore hawse an' let me see him an' yore ootfit."

Bayne's face flamed red and he trotted off into the grove, whereupon Brite took occasion to acquaint Shipman with the incident that had made Bayne one of the outfit.

"Hell yu say! Wal! Pore kid! . . . Wallen, now I just wonder where I've heahed thet name. Odd sort of handle. I'll bet my spurs he's no good. It's the no-good fellars' names thet stick in yore craw."

"Yu cow-tail twisters, come an' git it," sang out Moze.

San Sabe romped into camp with a string of mustangs which the men had to dodge or catch.

"Boots an' saddles heah, my tenderfoot Hal from Pennsylvania," yelled Texas Joe to the slow-moving Bender. "Thet's for all of yu. Rustle. An' get ootside some chuck. This's our busy day, mixin' a wild herd of long-horns with a tame one."

Strong brown hands flashed and tugged. As if by magic the restless ponies were bridled and saddled. The trail drivers ate standing. Texas Joe was the first to mount.

"Fork yore hawses, boys," he called, vibrantly. "Boss, I'll point the herd, then send Ackerman in with his guard to eat. Follow along, an' don't forget yore new hawse-wrangler, young Bayne."

In a few moments Brite was left alone with Moze. The red sun peeped over the eastern rim and the world of rolling ranges changed. The grove appeared full of bird melody. Far out the bawl of new-born calves attested to the night's addition to the herd. A black steed came flashing under the pecans. Bayne rode into camp and leaped off.

"All bunched an' ready, boss," he said, in keen pleasure. "Gee! thet's a *remuda*. Finest I ever seen. I can wrangle thet ootfit all by myself."

"Wal, son, if yu do yu'll earn Texas Joe's praise," returned Brite.

"Pooh for thet cowboy! I'd like to earn yores, though, Mr. Brite."

"Fall to, son, an' eat."

Brite bestrode his horse on the top of the slope and

watched the riders point the herd and start the drive up out of the creek bottom.

Used as he was to all things pertaining to cattle, he could not but admit to himself that this was a magnificent spectacle. The sun had just come up red and glorious, spreading a wonderful light over the leagues of range; the air was cool, fresh, sweet, with a promise of warmth for midday; flocks of blackbirds rose like clouds over the cattle, and from the grove of pecans a chorus of mocking-bird melody floated to his ears; the shining creek was blocked by a mile-wide bar of massed cattle, splashing and plowing across; shots pealed above the bawl and trample, attesting to the fact that the drivers were shooting new-born calves that could not keep up with their mothers.

Like a colossal triangle the wedge-shaped herd, with the apex to the fore, laboriously worked up out of the valley. Ackerman's Uvalde herd had the lead, and that appeared well, for they had become used to the Trail, and Brite's second and third herds, massing in behind were as wild a bunch of long-horns as he had ever seen. Their wide-spread horns, gray and white and black, resembled an endless mass of uprooted stumps of trees, milling, eddying, streaming across the flat and up the green slope. The movement was processional, rhythmic, steady as a whole, though irregular in spots, and gave an impression of irresistible power. To Brite it represented the great cattle movement now in full momentum, the swing of Texas toward an Empire, the epic of the herds and the trail drivers that was to make history of the West. Never before had the old cattleman realized the tremendous significance of the colorful scene he was watching. Behind it seemed to ride and yell and sing all the stalwart sons of Texas. It was their chance after the Civil War that had left so many of them orphaned and all of them penniless. Brite's heart thrilled and swelled to those lithe riders. He alone had a thought of the true nature of this undertaking, and the uplift of his heart was followed by a pang. They had no thought of the morrow. The moment sufficed for them. To drive the herd, to stick to the task, to reach their objective—that was an unalterable obligation assumed when they started. Right then Brite conceived his ultimate appreciation of the trail driver.

At last the wide base of the herd cleared the stream bed, leaving it like a wet plowed field. Then the *remuda* in orderly bunch crossed behind. Brite recognized Reddie Bayne on his spirited black mount. The lad was at home with horses. Moze, driving the chuck-wagon, passed up the road behind Brite and out on the level range.

Then the sharp point of the herd, with Texas Joe on the left and Less Holden on the right, passed out of sight over the hill. Farther down the widening wedge, two other riders performed a like guard. The rest held no stable position. They flanked the sides and flashed along the rear wherever an outcropping of unruly long-horns raised a trampling roar and a cloud of dust. Each rider appeared to have his own yell, which Brite felt assured he would learn to recognize in time. And these yells rang out like bells or shrilled aloft or pealed across the valley.

Brite watched the dashing drivers, the puffs of dust rising pink in the sunrise flush, the surging body of long-horns crowding up the slope. A forest of spear-pointed horns pierced the sky line. And when the last third of the herd got up out of the valley, on the wide slope, the effect was something to daunt even old Adam Brite. Half that number of cattle, without the wilder element, would have been more than enough to drive to Dodge. Brite realized this now. But there could not be any turning back. He wondered how many head of stock, and how many drivers, would never get to Dodge.

Brite turned away to ride to the highest ridge above the valley, from which he scanned the Trail to the south. For a trail drive what was coming behind was as important almost as what lay to the fore. To mix a herd with that of a following trail driver's was bad business. It made extra toil and lost cattle. To his relief, the road and the range southward were barren of moving objects. A haze of dust marked where San Antonio lay. To the north the purple, rolling prairieland spread for leagues, marked in the distance by black dots and patches and dark lines of trees. It resembled an undulating sea of rosy grass. Only the unknown dim horizon held any menace.

The great herd had topped the slope below and now showed in its entirety, an arrow-headed mass assuming proper perspective. It had looked too big for the valley; here up on the range it seemed to lengthen and spread and find room. The herd began its slow, easy, grazing march northward, at the most eight or ten miles a day. In fine weather and if nothing molested the cattle, this leisurely travel was joy for the drivers. The infernal paradox of the trail driver's life was that a herd might be driven north wholly under such comfortable circumstances, and again the journey might be fraught with terrific hardship and peril. Brite had never experienced one of the extreme adventures, such as he had heard of, but the ordinary trip had been strenuous and hazardous enough for him.

Brite caught up with the chuck-wagon and walked his horse alongside it for a while, conversing with the genial Negro. From queries about the Rio Grande country and the Uvalde cattlemen, Brite progressed to interest in the quintet of riders who had brought the southern herd up. Moze was loquacious and soon divulged all his knowledge of Deuce Ackerman and his comrades. "Yas, suh, dey's de finest an' fightin'est boys I ever seen, dat's shore," concluded Moze. "I ben cookin' fer two-t'ree years fer de U-V ootfit. Kurnel Miller ran dat ootfit fust, an' den sold oot to Jones. An' yo bet Jones was sho glad to git rid of dem five boys. What wid shootin' up de towns every pay day an' sparkin' Miss Molly, de Kurnel's dotter, why, dat gennelman led a turrible life."

"Wal, I reckon they weren't no different from other boys where a pretty girl was concerned."

"Yas, suh, dere wuz a difference, 'cause dese boys wuz like twin brothers, an' Miss Molly jes' couldn't choose among 'em. She sho wanted 'em all, so Mars Jones had to sell 'em to yo along wid de cattle."

"Wal, Moze, we shore might run into anythin' along the old Trail," replied Brite, with a laugh. "But it's reasonable to hope there won't be any girls till we reach Dodge."

"Dat's a hot ole town dese days, I heah, boss."

"Haw! Haw! Just yu wait, Moze. . . . Wal, we're catchin' up with the herd, an' from now it'll be lazy driftin' along."

Soon Brite came up with the uneven, mile-wide rear of the herd. Four riders were in sight, and the first he reached was Hallett, who sat cross-legged in his saddle and let his pony graze along.

"How're yu boys makin' oot, Roy?"

"Jes' like pie, boss, since we got up on the range," was the reply. "There's some mean old mossy-horns an' some twisters in thet second herd of yores. Texas Joe shot two bulls before we got 'em leavin' thet valley."

"Bad luck to shoot cattle," replied Brite, seriously.

"Wal, we're short-handed an' we gotta get there, which I think we never will."

"Shore we will. . . . Where's Reddie Bayne with the *remuda?*"

"Aboot a half over, I reckon. Thet's Rolly next in line. He's been helpin' the kid with the *remuda.*"

"Ahuh. How's Reddie drivin'?"

"Fine, boss. But thet's a sight of hawses for one boy. Reckon he could wrangle them alone but fer them damn old mossy-horns."

Brite passed along. Rolly Little was the next rider in line, and he appeared to be raising the dust after some refractory steers. Cows were bellowing and charging back, evidently wanting to return to calves left behind.

"Hey, boss, we got some ornery old drags in this herd," he sang out.

"Wal, have patience, Little, but don't wear it oot," called Brite.

The horses were grazing along in a wide straggling drove, some hundred yards or more behind the herd. Reddie Bayne on the moment was bending over the neck of his black, letting him graze. Brite trotted over to join him.

"Howdy, Reddie."

"Howdy, Mr. Brite."

"Wal, I'll ride along with yu an' do my share. Everythin' goin' good?"

"Oh yes, sir. I'm havin' the time of my life," rejoined the youth. He looked the truth of that enthusiastic assertion. What a singularly handsome lad! He looked younger than the sixteen years he had confessed to. His cheeks were not full, by any means, but they glowed rosily through the tan. In the broad sunlight his face shone clear cut, fresh and winning. Perhaps his lips were too red and curved for a boy. But his eyes were his most marked feature—a keen, flashing purple, indicative of an intense and vital personality.

"Thet's good. I was some worried aboot yu last night," returned the cattleman, conscious of gladness at having befriended this lonely lad. "Have my boys been friendly?"

"Shore they have, sir. I feel more at home. They're the— the nicest boys I ever rode with. . . . All except Texas Joe."

"Wal, now, thet's better. But what's Joe done?"

"Oh, he—he just took a—a dislike to me," replied the lad, hurriedly, with a marked contrast to his former tone. "It always happens, Mr. Brite, wherever I go. Somebody— usually the rancher or trail boss or foreman—has to dislike me—an' run me off."

"But why, Reddie? Air yu shore yu're reasonable? Texas Joe is aboot as wonderful a fellar as they come."

"Is he?—I hadn't noticed it. . . . He—he cussed me oot this mawnin'."

"He did? Wal, thet's nothin', boy. He's my Trail boss, an' shore it's a responsibility. What'd he cuss yu aboot?"

"Not a thing. I can wrangle these hawses as good as he can. He's just taken a dislike to me."

"Reddie, he may be teasin' yu. Don't forget yu're the kid of the ootfit. Yu'll shore catch hell."

"Oh, Mr. Brite, I don't mind atall—so long's they're decent. An' I do so want to keep this job. I'll love it. I'm shore I can fill the bill."

"Wal, yu'll keep the job, Reddie, if thet's what's worryin' yu. I'll guarantee it."

"Thank yu. . . . An', Mr. Brite, since yu are so good I—I think I ought to confess—"

"Now see heah, lad," interrupted Brite. "Yu needn't make no more confessions. I reckon yu're all right an' thet's enough."

"But I—I'm not all right," returned the lad, bravely, turning away his face. They were now walking their mounts some rods behind the *remuda*.

"Not all right? . . . Nonsense!" replied Brite, sharply. He had caught a glimpse of quivering lips, and that jarred him.

"Somethin' tells me I ought to trust yu—before—"

"Before what?" queried Brite, curiously.

"Before they find me oot."

"Lad, yu got me buffaloed. I'll say, though, thet yu can trust me. I dare say yu're makin' a mountain oot of a mole hill. So come on, lad, an' get it over."

"Mr. Brite, I—I'm not what I—I look—atall."

"No? Wal, as yu're a likely-lookin' youngster, I'm sorry to heah it. Why ain't yu?"

"Because I'm a girl."

Brite wheeled so suddenly that his horse jumped. He thought he had not heard the lad correctly. But Bayne's face was turned and his head drooped.

"Wha-at?" he exclaimed, startled out of his usual composure.

Bayne faced him then, snatching the old sombrero off. Brite found himself gazing into dark, violet, troubled eyes.

"I'm a girl," confessed Reddie, hurriedly. "Everywhere I've worked I've tried to keep my secret. But always it was found oot. Then I suffered worse. So I'm tellin' yu, trustin' yu—an' if—or when I *am* found oot—maybe yu'll be my friend."

"Wal, I'm a son-of-a-gun!" burst out Brite. "Yu're a girl! . . . Shore I see thet now. . . . Why, Reddie, yu pore kid—yu can just bet yore life I'll keep yore secret, an' be yore friend, too, if it's found oot."

"Oh, I felt yu would," replied Reddie, and replaced the wide sombrero. With the sunlight off those big eyes and the flushed face, and especially the rebellious red-gold curls she reverted again to her disguise. "Somehow yu remind me of my dad."

"Wal now, lass, thet's sweet for me to heah. I never had a girl, or a boy, either, an' God knows I've missed a lot. . . . Won't yu tell me yore story?"

"Yes, sometime. It's a pretty long an' sad one."

"Reddie, how long have yu been masqueradin' as a boy rider?"

"Three years an' more. Yu see, I had to earn my livin'. An' bein' a girl made it hard. I tried everythin' an' I shore hated bein' a servant. But when I grew up—then it was worse. 'Most always boys an' men treated me fine—as yu know Texans do. There was always some, though, who—who wanted me. An' they wouldn't leave me free an' alone. So I'd ride on. An' I got the idee pretendin' to be a boy would make it easier. Thet helped a lot. But I'd always get found oot. An' I'm scared to death thet hawk-eyed Texas Joe suspects me already."

"Aw no—no! Reddie, I'm shore an' certain not."

"But he calls me Girlie Boy!" ejaculated Reddie, tragically.

"Thet's only 'cause yu're so—so nice-lookin'. Land sakes! If Texas really suspected he'd act different. All these boys would. They'd be as shy as sheep. . . . Come to think of thet, Reddie, wouldn't it be better to tell Texas Joe an' all of them?"

"Oh, for Heaven's sake!—please—please, don't, Mr. Brite. . . . Honest, we'd never get to Dodge!"

Brite greeted this appeal with a hearty laugh. Then he recalled Moze's talk about the Uvalde boys. "Wal, maybe yu're right. . . . Reddie, I've a hunch now thet hombre Wallen knows yu air a girl."

"Yu bet he does. Thet's the trouble."

"In love with yu?"

"Him! . . . Why, Wallen's too low to love anyone, even his own kin, if he ever had any. . . . He hails from the Big Bend country, an' I've heahed it said he wasn't liked around Braseda. He claims he bought me with a bunch of cattle. Same as a nigger slave! I was ridin' for John Clay, an' he did let me go with the deal. Wallen made thet deal 'cause he'd found oot I was a girl. So I ran off an' he trailed me."

"Reddie, he'd better not follow yore trail up this way."

"Would yu save me?" asked the girl, softly.

"Wal, I reckon, but Texas Joe or Pan Handle would have thet hombre shot before I could wink," declared the cattle-man, in grim humor.

The girl turned an agitated face to him. "Mr. Brite, yu make me hope my dream'll come true—some day."

"An' how, Reddie?"

"I've dreamed some good rancher—some real Texan—would adopt me—so I could wear girl's clothes once more an' have a home an'—an'—"

Her voice trailed away and broke.

"Wal, wal! Stranger things than thet have happened, Reddie," replied Brite, strangely stirred. On the moment he might have committed himself to much but for an interruption in the way of distant gun shots.

"Rumpus over there, Mr. Brite," suddenly called Reddie, pointing to a huge cloud of dust over the west end of the herd. "Yu better ride over. I'll take care of the hawses."

Putting spurs to his mount, Brite galloped in the direction indicated. Hallett and Little were not in sight, and probably had been obscured by the dust. A low roar of trampling hoofs filled his ears. The great body of the herd appeared intact, although there were twisting *mêlées* of cattle over toward the left on the edge of the dust line. Brite got around the left wing to see a stream of long-horns pouring out of the main herd at right angles. The spur was nearly a mile long, and bore the ear marks of a stampede. With too few drivers the danger lay in the possibility of the main herd bolting in the opposite direction. Except in spots, however, they were acting rationally. Then Brite observed that already the forward drivers had the stream curving back to the north. He became conscious of relief, and slowed up to take his place behind the most exposed section of the herd. All across the line the cattle were moving too fast. A restlessness had passed through the mass. It was like a wave. Gradually they returned to the former leisurely gait and all appeared well again. Little rode past at a gallop and yelled something which Brite did not distinguish.

The drive proceeded then in its slow, orderly procession, a time-swallower, if no more. Hours passed. The warm sun began its westering slant, which grew apace, as did all the details of driving, the rest and walk and jog, the incessant stir of cattle, the murmur of hoofs, the bawl of cows, the never-failing smell of dust, manure, and heated bodies, and ever the solemn sky above and the beckoning hills, the dim purple in the north.

In another hour the great herd had surrounded a little lake in the center of an immense shallow bowl of range land. Trees were conspicuous for their absence. Moze had wisely hauled firewood, otherwise he would have had to burn buffalo chips for fuel. Brite walked his horse a mile along the left flank before he reached the chuck-wagon and camp. These were at the head of the lake, from which slight eminence the whole center of the depression could be seen. Gramma grass was fair, though not abundant. The cattle would need to be herded this night.

Reddie Bayne came swinging along on the beautiful black, always a delight to a rider's eye. Reddie reined in to accommodate Brite's pace.

"Heah we air, the long day gone an' camp once more. Oh, Mr. Brite, I am almost happy," declared Reddie.

"There shore is somethin' sweet aboot it. Make the best of it, Reddie, for God only knows what'll come."

"Ah! There's thet Texas Joe!" exclaimed Reddie as they neared camp. "Looks mighty pert now. I reckon he's pleased with himself for turnin' thet break back. . . . Boss, what'll I do when he—he gets after me again?"

"Reddie, don't be mealy-mouthed," advised Brite, low-voiced and earnest. "Talk back. Be spunky. An' if yu could manage a cuss word or two it'd help a lot."

"Lord knows I've heahed enough," replied Reddie.

They rode into camp. Texas Joe had thrown off sombrero, vest, and chaps, and gun-belt as well. It occurred to Brite that the tall amber-eyed, tawny-haired young giant might well play havoc with the heart of any fancy-free girl.

"Wal, heah yu air, boss," he drawled, with his winning smile. "Fust I've seen yu since mawnin'. Reckoned yu'd rode back to Santone. . . . It shore was a good drive. Fifteen miles, an' the herd will bed down heah fine."

"Texas, I got sort of nervous back there," replied Brite as he dismounted.

"Nothin' atall, boss, nothin' atall. I'd like to inform yu, though, thet this heah Pan Handle Smith might have rode up this Trail with Jesse Chisholm an' been doin' it ever since."

"Thanks, Joe. I hardly deserve thet," rejoined the outlaw, who appeared to be getting rid of the dust and dirt of the ride.

Lester Holden was the only other driver present, and he squatted on a stone, loading his gun.

"I had fo' shots at thet slate-colored old mossy-horn. Bullets jest bounced off his haid."

"Boys, don't shoot the devils, no matter how mean they air. Save yore lead for Comanches."

"Wal, if there ain't our Reddie," drawled Texas Joe, with a dancing devil in his eye. "How many hawses did yu lose, kid?"

"I didn't count 'em," replied Reddie, sarcastically.

"Wal, I'll count 'em, an' if there's not jest one hundred an' eighty-nine yu're gonna ride some more."

"Ahuh. Then I'll ride, 'cause yu couldn't count more'n up to ten."

"Say, yu're powerful pert this evenin'. I reckon I'll have to give yu night guard."

"Shore. I'd like thet. But no more'n my turn, Mister Texas Jack."

"Right. I'm mister to yu. But it's Joe, not Jack."

"Same thing to me," returned Reddie, who on the moment was brushing the dust off his horse.

"Fellars, look how the kid babies that hawse," declared Shipman. "No wonder the animal is pretty. . . . Dog-gone me, I'll shore have to ride him tomorrow."

"Like bob yu will," retorted Reddie.

"Say, I was only foolin', yu darned little pepper-pot. Nobody but a hawse thief ever takes another fellar's hawse."

"I don't know yu very well, Mister Shipman."

"Wal, you're durned liable to before this drive is much older."

Somehow, Brite reflected, these two young people rubbed each other the wrong way. Reddie was quite a match for Texas Joe in quick retort, but she was careful to keep her face half averted or her head lowered.

"Reckon we'll all know each other before we get to Dodge."

"Ahuh. An' thet's a dig at me," replied Texas Joe, peevishly. "Dog-gone yu, anyhow."

"Wal, haven't yu been diggin' me?" demanded Reddie, spiritedly.

"Sonny, I'm Brite's Trail boss an' yu're the waterboy."

"I am nothin' of the sort. I'm the hawse-wrangler of this ootfit."

"Aw, yu couldn't wrangle a bunch of hawg-tied suckin' pigs. Yu shore got powerful testy aboot yoreself, all of a sudden. Yu was meek enough this mawnin'."

"Go to hell, Texas Jack!" sang out Reddie, with most exasperating flippancy.

"What'd yu say?" blustered Texas, passing from jest to earnest.

"I said yu was a great big, sore-haided, conceited giraffe of a trail-drivin' bully," declared Reddie, in a very clear voice.

"Aw! Is thet all?" queried Texas, suddenly cool and devilish. Quick as a cat he leaped to snatch Reddie's gun and pitch it away. Reddie, who was kneeling with his back turned, felt the action and let out a strange little cry. Then

Texas fastened a powerful hand in the back of Reddie's blouse, at the neck, and lifted him off his feet. Whereupon Texas plumped down to draw Reddie over his knees.

"Boss, yu heahed this disrespectful kid," drawled Texas. "Somethin' shore has got to be done aboot it."

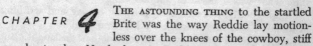

CHAPTER 4 THE ASTOUNDING THING to the startled Brite was the way Reddie lay motionless over the knees of the cowboy, stiff as a bent poker. No doubt poor Reddie was petrified with expectation and horror. Brite tried to blurt out with a command for Texas to stop. But sight of that worthy's face of fiendish glee completely robbed the cattleman of vocal powers.

"Pan Handle, do you approve of chastisement for unruly youngsters?" queried Texas.

"Shore, on general principles," drawled Smith. "But I reckon I cain't see thet Reddie has been more than sassy."

"Wal, thet's it. If we don't nip him in the bud we jest won't be able to drive cattle with him babblin' aboot."

"Lam him a couple, Tex," spoke up Lester. "Reddie's all right, I reckon, only turrible spoiled."

Texas raised high a broad, brown, powerful hand.

"Shipman—don't yu—dare—smack me!" cried Reddie, in a strangled voice.

But the blow fell with a resounding whack. Dust puffed up from Reddie's trousers. Both her head and feet jerked up with the force of the blow. She let out a piercing yell of rage and pain, then began to wrestle like a lassoed wildcat. But Texas Joe got in three more sounding smacks before his victim tore free to roll over and bound erect. If Brite had been petrified before, he was now electrified. Reddie personified a fury that was beautiful and thrilling to see. It seemed to Brite that anyone but these thick-headed, haw-

hawing drivers would have seen that Reddie Bayne was an outraged girl.

"Oh-h-h! Yu devil!" she screamed, and jerked for the gun that had been on her hip. But it was gone, and Lester had discreetly picked it up.

"Ump-umm, kid. No gun-play. This heah is fun," said Lester.

"Fun—hell!" Then quick as a flash Reddie leaped to deal the mirth-convulsed Texas a tremendous kick on the shin. That was a horse of another color.

"Aggh-gh-gh!" roared Texas, clasping his leg and writhing in agony. "Aw, my Gawd! . . . My sore laig!"

Reddie poised a wicked boot for another onslaught. But she desisted and slowly settled back on both feet.

"Huh! So *yu* got feelin's?"

"Feelin's? Say, I'll—be—daid in a minnit," groaned Texas. "Kid, thet laig's full of lead bullets."

"If yu ever touch me again I'll—I'll fill the rest of yore carcass with lead."

"Cain't yu take a little joke? . . . Shore I was only in fun. The youngest driver always gets joked."

"Wal, Texas Jack, if thet's a sample of yore trail-drivin' jokes, I pass for the rest of the trip."

"But, say, yu ain't no better than anybody else," protested Texas, in a grieved tone. "Ask the boss. Yu wasn't a good fellar—to get so mad."

Reddie appealed voicelessly to the old cattleman.

"Wal, yu're both right," declared Brite, anxious to conciliate. "Tex, yu hit too darned hard for it to be fun. Yu see Reddie's no big, husky, raw-boned man."

"So I noticed. He certainly felt soft for a rider. . . . Kid, do yu want to shake an' call it square? I reckon I got the wust of it at thet. Right this minnit I've sixteen jumpin' toothaches in my laig."

"I'd die before I'd shake hands with yu," rejoined Reddie, and snatching up her sombrero, and taking her gun from the reluctant Lester, she flounced away.

"Dog-gone!" ejaculated Texas, ruefully. "Who'd took thet

kid for such a spitfire? Now I've gone an' made another enemy."

"Tex, yu shore was rough," admonished Brite.

"Rough? Why, I got mine from a pair of cowhide hobbles," growled Texas, and getting up, he limped about his tasks.

Presently Moze called them to supper, after which they rode out on fresh horses to relieve the guard. Deuce Ackerman reported an uneasy herd, owing to the presence of a pack of wolves. Brite went on guard, taking a rifle with him. He passed Bayne's black horse. The *remuda* had bunched some distance from the herd. It was still warm, though the fiery-red sun had gone down behind the range. Brite took up his post between the horses and cattle, and settled to a task he had never liked.

The long-horns had not quieted down for the night. Distant rumblings attested to restlessness at the other end of the herd. Brite patrolled a long beat, rifle across his pommel, keeping a sharp lookout for wolves. He saw coyotes, jack-rabbits, and far away over the grass, a few scattered deer. Before dusk settled thick Reddie Bayne appeared with the *remuda*, working them off to the eastward, toward a sheltered cove half a mile beyond Brite. Twilight stole on them down in the bowl, and over the western horizon gold rays flushed and faded.

Before dark Reddie rode up to Brite.

"Hawses all right, boss. I reckon I'll hang around yore end. We all got orders to stand guard till called off."

"Maybe somethin' brewin'. Maybe not. *Quién sabe?*"

"I reckon what's brewin' is in thet hombre's mind."

"Which hombre, Reddie?"

"Yu know. . . . Wasn't it perfectly awful—what he did to me, Mr. Brite?"

"Wal, it was kinda tough," agreed Brite. "Tex got in action so quick I just was too flabbergasted."

"Yu shore wasn't very chivalrous," rejoined Reddie, dubiously. "I've my doubts aboot *yu* now."

"It sort of paralyzed me 'cause I knowed yu was a girl."

"I'll bet *thet* would paralyze him, too," retorted Reddie,

darkly. "Boss, I could get even with Texas by tellin' him thet he had insulted a lady."

"By thunder! yu could. But don't do it, Reddie. He might shake the ootfit."

"I'd hate to have *him* know I—I'm a girl," replied Reddie, musingly.

"Let's hope none of them will find oot."

"Mr. Brite, I'd never forgive myself if I brought yu bad luck."

"Yu won't, Reddie."

"Listen," she whispered, suddenly.

A weird chanting music came on the warm air, from the darkness. Brite recognized the Spanish song of a *vaquero*.

"San Sabe singin' to the herd, Reddie."

"Oh—how pretty! He shore can sing."

Then from another quarter came a quaint cowboy song, and when that ceased a faint mellow voice pealed from far over the herd. The rumblings of hoofs ceased, and only an occasional bawl of a cow broke the silence. San Sabe began again his haunting love song, and then all around the herd pealed out the melancholy refrains. That was the magic by which the trail drivers soothed the restless long-horns.

The moon came up and silvered the vast bowl, lending enchantment to the hour. Reddie passed to and fro, lilting a Dixie tune, lost in the beauty and serenity of the night. From a ridge pealed forth the long, desolate, blood-curdling moan of a prairie wolf. That brought the ghastly reminder that this moment was real—that there was death waiting just beyond.

The cowboys smoked and sang, the cattle slept or rested, the balmy night wind rustled the grass, the ducks whirred to and fro over the lake. The stars paled before the full moon.

Texas Joe came trotting up. "Boss, yu an' Reddie go to bed. Two hours off an' then two on, for five of us. I ain't shore yet thet all is wal."

Reddie never stopped singing the sweet ditty.

"Gosh, Tex, it cain't be midnight yet!" exclaimed Brite.

"It cain't be, but it shore is. Go along with yu. . . . Reddie, yu got a sweet voice for a boy. I shore am a-wonderin' aboot yu."

"Boss, yu see?" whispered Reddie, fiercely, clutching Brite's arm. "Thet hombre suspects me."

"Let him—the son-of-a-gun! Then if he finds yu oot it'll be all the wuss."

"For him or me?"

"For him, shore."

"How yu mean, boss, wuss?"

"Wal, it'd serve him right to fall so dinged in love with yu thet—"

"O my Gawd!" cried Reddie, in faint, wild tones, and spurred ahead to vanish in the shadows.

"Wall" quoth Brite, amazed. It was evident that he had said something amiss. "Thet was an idee. Didn't she fly up an' vamoose?"

Brite made his way slowly into camp. Hallett and Ackerman were already in by the fire, drinking coffee. San Sabe came riding up, still with the remnants of song on his lips. Reddie's horse was haltered out in the moonlight and something prone and dark showed beside a low bush. Brite sought his own blankets.

Next morning, when Brite presented himself for breakfast, Whittaker and Pan Handle were the only drivers in camp. They were eating in a hurry.

"Herd movin', boss," announced Smith. "We been called."

Brite answered their greetings, while his ears attuned themselves to the distant sound of hoofs. The hour was early, as the sun had not yet risen. A cloudless sky and balmy air attested to promising weather.

"Where's Reddie?"

"Off with the hawses. When he heahed Joe yell he quit eatin' like a scared jack rabbit. I called for fresh hawses."

"Must be somethin' up," muttered Brite. "Wal, it's aboot time."

"I don't care much aboot this heah trail drivin'," drawled Whittaker. "Too slow. I hired oot for action."

"Humph! Son, yu'll get yore belly full of action," declared Brite, grimly.

"Heah comes Red with hawses," announced Pan Handle. "Boss, I shore like thet kid. Nice quiet lad. Rides like a *vaquero* an' shore knows hawses."

"Hey, men, ketch yore ponies," shrilled Reddie, and flashed away out of sight.

It was everybody for himself. Fortunately, a rope corral aided the drivers in catching the fresh, unwilling horses. Brite haltered his, a ragged little bay, and returned to finish his meal. Soon the others were off.

"Moze, what started the herd so pronto?" queried Brite.

"I dunno, boss. Jes' started themselves, I reckon. Cattle is sho pustiferous annimiles. De Lawd Hisself nebber knows what dey'll do."

"Right. . . . Pack without washin' up, Moze. An' move right along."

"Ise a-movin', sah."

Brite climbed aboard the little bay. He, like all the drivers, had to ride what horses Reddie could fetch in promptly, and in this case he realized at once that he was in for tricks. The bay showed every indication of bucking, but by spurring him off over the prairie Brite wore off his mean edge. A red disc of sun peeped up over the eastern rim. The day had begun. Flocks of black birds wheeled from the water in the direction of the cattle. A distant low cloud of dust moved to the northward. Brite caught up with it to find the cattle slowing down and spreading out. Bayne had the *remuda* in order on the right, and half a mile behind.

Ackerman sat his mustang, waiting for Brite, whom evidently he had seen following.

"Boss, did yu run acrost thet daid steer back a ways?" he queried.

"No, I didn't."

"Wal, I did. An' I had to shoot it."

"What for?"

"Somebody had crippled it. Laig broke by a needle-gun slug."

"Yu don't say! We haven't any buffalo guns in this ootfit."

"Looks queer to me. Must have been done jest before daylight."

"Does Texas know aboot it?"

"Cain't say. Reckon not. He was off guard. Went on at dawn. Same for me. But one of the boys must have heahed thet big gun."

"Ahuh. Plenty of thick brush around thet lake. There might have been a camp somewhere. Somebody wantin' beef, mebbe."

Brite rode on to fill in a wide breach behind the herd, and there he walked his horse, and rested, and watched the horizon to the rear, and found the long hours pleasant. By mid-afternoon the endless, long slope, almost imperceptible until it had been surmounted, lay behind the herd and in front the land dropped to a creek bottom. Wide white bars of sand hemmed in a winding sheet of water. Across on the far bank dark green groves of timber and light green levels of grass invited camp and rest for that night. Four drivers, one after the other, pealed back the foreman's order: "Cross above. Keep movin'. Push the drags."

Brite saw the head of the great herd swerve to the west along the bank. Seven riders congregated on that side. The cattle wanted to drink, and after drinking they would cross. The danger evidently lay in stragglers working off the bars into bad places. Gunshots attested to hard practice in turning stock. Brite could not recall just where the trail did cross, but he calculated anywhere along there. Smith waved a red scarf from a high bank. He alone rode on the west of the herd. Then he disappeared, and the cattle appeared to roll in a bobbing stream down the incline. The after mass of longhorns crowded those in front, and the knocking of horns and bellowing of cows grew incessant. Brite saw that he was needed more around on the right flank, to help keep the stragglers in line, and the slow ones from dropping back. When the red and white front of the herd appeared wading and wallowing across, then the difficulty of holding back the rear grew greater, and passed from hard riding to hazardous toil. Seven riders on that side had their work cut out for them. Reddie Bayne got the *remuda* in line to the left, then joined the drivers on the right. Brite yelled for the youngster to keep out from in front of those ugly old mossy-horns. Some of these charged, kicked their heels like mules, and wickedly shook their heads. When at length the wide ragged rear end of the herd passed on into the shallow water they left a number mired in the quicksand. These were mostly the unruly cattle that had run too soon off the bank. Some of them were floundering; some were sinking; all were bellowing lustily.

Texas Joe came galloping back from upstream.

"Reddie, what'n hell yu mean layin' off yore *remuda?*" he shouted, his amber eyes flashing. "Git oot of heah!"

Reddie took to the shallow water with his horse on the run. Then Joe sent Whittaker, Bender, and Smith across.

"Boss, yu ain't needed heah. Go along," he concluded.

"Let 'em alone, Tex. There's only twenty-one haid," replied Brite.

"Hell no!" rang out the foreman, untying his lasso. "We ain't lettin' nuthin' go. . . . Pile in, boys, an' stretch hemp. Keep away from thet ooze an' drag 'em upstream."

Whereupon Shipman rode off the bar, swinging the loop of his rope around his head. His horse sank up to his fetlocks, but kept moving. Texas cast a long loop and snared a bull that had only horns and head above the mire. Then spurring and yelling, the driver set to the task of dragging the longhorn out. The other boys followed suit, and there ensued a scene of strenuous noisy activity. They all got fast to a cow or steer, and put spurs to their mounts. Some of the cattle were dragged out easily. Others came but slowly and by dint of tremendous effort on the part of horse and rider. Texas could not budge the big bull, and Brite yelled to let that one go. Then the foreman's horse bogged down to his flanks. Like a flash Texas was off to loosen his cinch and tear his saddle free. Thus encumbered, with the rope still fast to the pommel and the bull at the other end, he bogged down himself. His horse floundered out to safety, but Texas had to yell for help. Ackerman and San Sabe rode to his assistance.

"Cut free," yelled Ackerman as he pitched an open loop to Texas.

"San, go below an' sling yore rope over thet damn bull," ordered Texas, and catching Ackerman's rope, he fastened it over the pommel of his saddle. He was half way up to his thighs in the quicksand and perceptibly sinking.

"I'm fast, Deuce," called out San Sabe, wheeling his horse. "Now drag'em oot!"

The horses plunged, the ropes twanged. Texas was pulled over on his side, but clinging to the rope he held on. The two riders broke the bull loose from the anchoring mire and began to drag him upstream. Presently he let go and found his footing, to crawl out like a giant mud-turtle. A third rider swung in to catch the bull, and then with three ropes on him he was literally dragged out of the quicksand. Texas cursed the old mossy-horn as if he were human.

Brite reveled in this scene, and only once thought it necessary to lend a hand, and then he was not wanted. Like Comanche Indians these young riders yelled and rode, with fierce flashing eyes and many a ringing shout. Their profanity and grim humor seemed to fit their actions—all so hard, primitive, and inevitable.

The last unfortunate cow appeared to be too far out and too deeply sunk to be extricated. But these boys labored on. They did all save get off and wade. The lassoes were too short. Only one caught over a horn and it slipped off.

"Boys, she's gone. Stranglin' now," called Brite. "Come off an' let well enough alone."

"Aw, put her oot of her misery," called one of them.

Guns boomed. One bullet whizzed off the skull of the cow.

"Hey, I thought yu fellars from down Uvalde way could shoot," drawled Texas, pulling his gun. He took deliberate aim. There was a significance in his posture. At the discharge the rolling eye of the animal went out. She laid her head over, and it sank until only the tip of a long horn stuck up.

"Aw, hell!" laughed Deuce Ackerman, sheathing his gun.

"Tex, I shore hope yu hit plumb center like thet when some redskin is aboot to peel my hair," said Less Holden.

Texas made no further comment. Dragging his saddle out of the mud, he shook the blanket and flopped it over his horse. The saddle went on, dripping water and sand. Soon Texas mounted to ride after the boys, now splashing across the shallow stream. Brite followed, careful to go briskly and let his horse pick the way. He had been in quicksand before.

They drove the twenty rescued cattle across the broadly marked sand bar and up into the timber. Beyond the strip of trees the great herd had stopped to graze on the green level, now contented with their lot.

"Right heah is good enough," said Texas, wearily. "Deuce, keep an eye open for Moze. He'll need some direction an' mebbe help comin' across. . . . Gosh! I'm as tired as if I'd done a day's work. An' wet. Sand in my boots! — the luck! Nice new boots! . . . Heah, Red, pull'em off for me. Thet's a good kid."

"Who was yore nigger this time last year?" asked Reddie, coolly.

"Never mind who, darn yu. . . ." Then Texas subtly changed. "Say, I asked yu a favor. My hands air all skinned."

"Shore," agreed Reddie, hastily, and with good grace he pulled off Shipman's boots.

Deuce Ackerman sat his horse, peering back through the thin strip of trees to the river.

"Tex, did yu see thet crippled steer this mawnin'?" he asked.

"No. How crippled?"

"By a big buffalo gun. Laig broke. I shot it."

"Buffalo gun! Who's got one in this ootfit?"

"Nobody."

"Deuce, air yu shore?" queried Texas, suddenly interested.

"Shore. I know needle guns. An' the holes they make."

"What's on yore mind? . . . Hey, boss, yu heah him?"

"Yes. He told me this mawnin'," replied Brite.

Pan Handle Smith knelt on one knee, after the manner of riders, and he looked keenly at Ackerman.

"Somebody not in our ootfit shot thet steer this mawnin' aboot daylight," returned the rider.

"Texas, I heahed thet gun," put in Smith. "It woke me up."

"Ahuh. There was a camp near us, then. I reckoned I smelled smoke when we rode down to the lake."

"Shore. I seen smoke way down to the west. Made a little stringy cloud ag'in thet gold sunset."

"Campers wantin' meat, I reckon," spoke up Brite. He suggested what he wanted to believe.

"Ump-umm," responded Deuce, pondering. "Thet was a tough old steer. An' he'd been shot from far off. Somebody took a pot shot at thet herd. But not for meat."

"What for, then?" demanded Texas, sharply.

Nobody replied to that. Brite knew that the three men were thinking the same as he was, and did not readily voice their suspicions.

"Wal, heah comes Moze," went on Ackerman. "Come on, Reddie. Yu got a big hawse. We'll lend Moze a drag."

The two rode off under the trees out upon the bar. Moze had halted the chuck-wagon on the opposite bank, where evidently he was looking for a safe place to drive across.

Texas looked from Pan Handle to Brite, and the curious, cold little gleam in his amber eyes was something to see.

"Do you reckon we're bein' follered?" he queried.

"Like as not," returned Brite.

"What'd the idee be, if we was?" asked Smith. "We're a dozen strong. Thet'd be a fool trick."

"Smith, it looks bad. Tex has been up the Trail before. He knows an' I know thet the chances air stampeders air on our track. My herd is too big. An' my ootfit too small."

"Stampeders, eh? I sabe."

"Never had any trouble before," went on Brite. "Fact is I've been amazin' lucky. But I've heahed of the hell other herd-owners have had. There's a regular drain on herds. Most of it comes from two-bit stampeders who collect a few haid heah an' there an' finally get enough to drive to Dodge on their own hook. An' again jealous drivers hire some of the trail-dodgers to stampede the herd ahaid of them. It's a dirty bizness."

"Say, it's a shootin' bizness," declared Texas, with fire in his eyes. "Boss, will we do a little scoutin' back tonight, or wait an' see if—"

"Let's wait," interrupted Brite. "If we air trailed we'll shore find it oot soon enough. An' if we're not it's no matter. . . . Ask Moze if he seen any riders back along the Trail."

During the night Brite was awakened by he knew not what. The three belted stars he knew were sloping to the west, so the hour was late. It was also very still. No sound from the herd! No sing-song of lonely cowboys on duty! The insects had thinned down their melancholy dirge to a faint ghost of its earlier strength. The fire had burned down low. Coyotes wailed piercingly off to the north, no doubt on the edge of the herd.

Then a ringing shot cracked the silence. Brite sat up, fully awake.

"Forty-five," he soliloquized, and peered around in the darkness to see who lay near him. Three sleeping drivers never stirred. Then heavier shots boomed out, reports that Brite recognized as belonging to buffalo guns. One of the cowboys stalked erect like a specter. Texas Joe! He turned his ear to the south. The biting ring of a .45 brought a sharp command from Shipman.

"Out of heah, men! Grab yore rifles an' rustle!"

Two of the drivers moved in concert. They sat up, looked, dove for rifles, to leap up and follow the stalking Texas, now already in shadow. The third rider awoke slowly, bewildered. It was Hal Bender.

"Get up, Bender," called Brite, rising himself.

"What's up, boss?" queried the tenderfoot, aghast, as he pulled on his boots.

"Somethin', I don't know what. Heahed shootin' oot there. Fetch yore guns."

"Ah! What's that?"

A low rolling rumble off to the south smote Brite's keen ears.

"Hawses. Rustlers after our *remuda*, I'll bet," declared Brite, quickening his stride to a trot. His gun barrel clinked on a sapling. He had to go slower or risk knocking himself on trees in the darkness. Bender panted closely behind him. Twice Brite halted to listen, each time getting the direction by sound. Then they emerged from the timber into the open—a gray level under the wan stars. Sharp voices drew Brite farther to the left. He ran, careful not to trip in the grass, holding his rifle forward and peering keenly ahead.

"Who comes?" rasped from the opaque gloom. That was Texas' voice.

"Brite. Where air yu?"

"This way. Look oot for a hole."

Brite and Bender soon joined a group of four, one of whom was mounted. This rider was talking: ". . . don't know nothin' 'cept what I heahed. Hawses runnin' wild. Then shots. Two big buffalo guns an' a forty-five."

"Ahuh. Which way, San?"

The *vaquero* stretched his arm to the south.

"Everybody listen," ordered Texas, and he for one got down to lay his ear to the ground.

The silence was vibrant, intense. Nothing disturbed it. Texas stood up.

"Hawses movin' somewhere. Just restless. No more runnin'. . . . Now, listen some more."

Texas cupped his hands around his mouth. A whistling intake of air attested to his purpose. Suddenly he exploded: "HEY, REDDIE!"

The stentorian yell split the silence and rolled away across the level, strange and wild. At once came an answer, faint but unmistakable, from the south.

"There! Sounds like . . ."

"Ssshh! Listen hard," interrupted Texas. Another reply came from the opposite direction, and then a very distant cry from the west. Lastly a nearer voice concluded the location of the herd.

"Spread oot, fellars, an' run this way," ordered Texas. "Stop every hundred yards or so, an' look sharp for the hawses. Hell to pay, I reckon."

San Sabe took the lead on his horse and was soon out of

sight. Brite worked to the right and obeyed orders. He must have halted a dozen times before he was rewarded by any sound, and then he heard horses that he could not see. After this he walked, out of breath, and strung with eagerness. Texas Joe had not reacted quietly to this midnight disturbance. Shrill neigh of horses swerved Brite back to the left. Soon a compact black patch stood out against the gray.

"Where'n hell air yu, Reddie?" called Shipman.

"Heah I'm comin'," came in the high-pitched voice Brite had learned to know. Presently he ran into the waiting group just as Reddie Bayne's big black loomed out of the gray.

"What yu doin' oot heah at this hour?" demanded Texas, peremptorily.

"I didn't go to camp," replied Bayne.

"Ahuh. An' why didn't yu obey orders?"

"I got suspicious, Shipman. An' I stayed with the hawses. I heahed voices an' I seen lights. Then I bunched the *remuda* an' worked them toward camp away from the herd. Pretty soon I heahed poundin' hoofs. Then a string of riders showed comin' fast. I shot at the leader an' hit him or his hawse. But he kept right on. He an' the riders with him piled right into my *remuda*. When they began to shoot I savvied what they were up to. They cut oot some of my hawses an' drove them away. I shot at them an' they shot back. . . . Reckon thet's aboot all."

"Stampeders! . . . Wal, Deuce had it figgered," declared Texas.

"Let's fork our hawses an' hunt 'em up," suggested Holden.

Brite did not think this advisable, but he held his tongue.

"How many'd they run off, Reddie?" queried Texas.

"I cain't tell. Not many, though."

"Wal, we'll wait till mawnin', anyhow. . . . Reddie, go to camp an' get some sleep. It's most daybreak."

"If yu don't mind, I'd as lief hang oot heah," returned Bayne.

"Mebbe thet's just as wal. . . . Spread oot, boys, an' surround the *remuda* loose like. Yell if yu heah any hawses comin'."

Silence once more settled down over the prairie. The riders vanished one by one. Brite patrolled a beat that eventually fetched him close to Texas Joe.

"What yu make of this, Joe?"

"Wal, we oughta expected it. I reckon we're in for rough sleddin'. Too many haid of stock an' too few drivers."

"Thet's how I figger it," rejoined the boss, thoughtfully. "But I'll tell yu, Shipman. If we get to Dodge with half our stock I'll still make a big stake. An' shore I won't forget yu boys."

"Boss, I ain't carin' a damn how many haid we lose. But I won't give up one single damn old long-horn without a fight. But hawse-stealin'! Thet riles me. . . . Say, Brite, did it strike yu—how game thet kid Bayne was, stayin' oot heah all alone? Dog-gone him! He rubs me the wrong way, but somehow I gotta like him."

"So do I. Tex, I wish yu'd treat Reddie a—a bit better."

"Ahuh. I seen thet. Wal, I ain't a-goin' to have any favorites this drive. Why, the whole ootfit will hate my guts before we reach Dodge! . . . At thet, the whole ootfit never will make it, Brite."

"Got a hunch, hey?" queried the boss, gloomily.

"So bad it hurts. . . . Wal, the east is grayin'. Wonder what this *heah* day will bring forth."

Brite plodded back to his beat, and watched the stars pale and die, the east kindle, the gray steal away as if by magic, and the horses and cattle and land take shape.

Presently Texas Joe waved him campward. The herd appeared to be up and on the slow move north. And again the day promised fine. As Brite trudged into camp he espied San Sabe, Bender, Ackerman, standing, cups in hand, around Alabama Moze.

Then Texas came striding in on foot, his hawk eyes narrowed and his handsome lips tight.

"Deuce, yu point the herd an' get goin'," he said, tersely. "Send Pan Handle back shore with the others."

"Air yu goin' to rustle?"

"Yu bet. Reddie's drivin' in some hawses. I reckon I'll take a look at them tracks south. . . . Boss, we lost upward of twenty-five haid of hawses."

"Small loss, if it ends there."

"Ahuh. Say, for an old Texan yu're nice disposed toward these stampeders."

"Tex, I'll bet he'll rave one of these days," laughed Deuce.

Reddie came loping in behind half a dozen ragged mustangs. The drivers spread and waved arms and ropes to corral them in a corner. Soon, then, only Brite, Texas Joe, Reddie, and the Negro were left in camp. Texas appeared taciturn, as well as hungry. He was in a hurry, too. Reddie received his pan of food and cup from Moze, and repaired to an improvised seat, where he devoted himself assiduously to his meal.

The sun peeped up red over the purple horizon, and all the range land took on a rosy sheen. Even the birds heralded that transformation. Brite paused to take in the fresh radiance of the dawn. The long gramma grass shone bright as silver, and the flowers stood up with pale beautiful faces toward the east.

All of a sudden Texas Joe got up, cursing inaudibly. His lean head stuck out like that of a hawk as he peered to the south.

"What yu heah, Tex?" queried Brite, sharply.

"Hawses."

Brite soon had to confess that Texas was correct.

"What of thet?" went on the boss.

"Wal, nothin'. Only couplin' it with what come off this mawnin' it ain't so good."

Presently a group of riders appeared at the far corner of timber. Brite counted seven or eight, all dark figures, coming at a brisk trot. Texas gave one long look, then turned to Brite.

"Boss, thet bunch has been watchin' us," he said, his eyes gleaming. "Timed us nice. Our boys just left an' the guard not in sight."

Suddenly Reddie Bayne leaped up, letting his pan clang to the ground.

"Wallen an' his ootfit!" cried Reddie, startled.

"Shore aboot thet, boy?" asked Texas, darkly.

"Yes, shore. I know *him*. . . . I'll bet they stampeded my *remuda*. . . . An' now they're after me."

"Wal, keep back an' be careful what yu say. . . . Brite, have yore Winchester handy. Let me do the talkin'. . . . This heah's a time we may need yore Pan Handle Smith."

The dark compact bunch of riders closed the gap quickly and drew up in a semicircle just opposite the fire and chuck-wagon. Brite did not need to question their character and intent—not this time! He recognized the swarthy Wallen, whose big bold eyes swept the camp, and the range beyond. Foremost of the other riders was a more striking individual even than Wallen—a man of about fifty years, with a visage like a bleak stone bluff and eyes like fiery cracks. Brite had seen this same man somewhere. The five others were a likely crew for these leaders—all young, lean, unkempt cowboys.

"Wal, heah's our Reddie Bayne," spoke up Wallen, gruffly, pointing a heavy hand at Reddie.

"Shore an' proper, Wal," replied his lieutenant, in a dry, crisp voice.

Whereupon Wallen turned his rolling eyes upon Brite. "Lied to me back on the trail a ways—hey, Brite?"

"If I did I'll stick to it," retorted Brite, his blood leaping.

Texas Joe strode forward and to one side, getting out of line of the chuck-wagon with a significance that no Texan could have mistaken.

"Wallen, I see some of yore outfit packin' needle guns on their saddles," he said, with biting sarcasm.

"What if they air? We're huntin' buffalo."

"Ahuh. Thet what *yu* say."

"I'll talk to Brite, an' not to yu, cowboy," declared Wallen, aggressively.

"Yu talk to Texas Joe," interposed Brite, caustically.

"Brite, we want thet youngster yu kidnapped. Reddie Bayne," declared the leader of the visitors.

"Wallen, I ain't used to palaverin' with men like yu," re-joined Texas, bitingly. It struck Brite that his foreman was playing for time to let Pan Handle Smith and the others reach camp. Brite flashed a furtive glance across the rosy grassland. No sign of a rider! This was serious, for there surely would be violence here promptly.

"Who the hell air yu?" shouted Wallen, hoarsely.

"Wal, I know this hombre," said Wallen's partner. "It's Texas Shipman."

"That means nothin' to me."

"Then yu do the talkin', pard," returned his companion, in cool hard voice that told Brite much. This lieutenant was the more dangerous man.

"I shore don't need yu, Ross Hite, to do my talkin'," snorted Wallen.

Ross Hite! Brite responded to that name well known to trail drivers. Hite had run the gamut of all Texas occupations known to the range.

"Wal, *talk* then, damn yu, an' make it short," shot out Texas. "What yu want?"

"We're drivin' our stock on ahaid," replied Wallen, bluntly. "Yu travel too slow, an' they're crowdin' us. . . . I want this rider, Reddie Bayne. He come to me in a deal I made with Jones at Braseda."

"Ahuh. Does Bayne owe yu his services?"

"He shore does."

"What yu say, Reddie?"

Reddie leaped forward. "He's a damn liar, Texas," shrilled Reddie, passionately. "I've run off from three ranches to get away from him."

"Shet up or it'll be the wuss for yu," replied Wallen, stridently.

"Slow there, Wallen," rang out Texas. "This heah is a free country. The day of slaves, white or black, is over."

"Reddie, tell *why* Wallen wants yu," spoke up Brite, cunningly. His Texan blood was not proof against this evasion. Besides, out on a far ridge top he descried a dark rider coming fast. Pan Handle!

"Oh—Tex," burst out Reddie, poignantly, "he's after me because—'cause I'm—a—I'm not what yu—think."

Texas stiffened slightly, but never turned the breadth of a

hair from the rider he was facing. Wallen's face turned a dirty gray.

"What air yu—Reddie?" queried Texas, low and cool.

"I—I'm a—girl, Texas. . . . An' thet's why," replied Reddie, huskily.

"*Look oot!*" shouted Ross Hite, piercingly.

Wallen clapped his hand to his hip. Texas appeared to blur in Brite's strained sight. A gun belched red, and with the loud crack Wallen jerked up with terrible sudden rigidity. His dark face changed from hideous rage to an awful ghastliness, and he pitched from the saddle to fall with sodden crash. His horse lunged away. The other horse reared and snorted.

"Haid aboot or I'll bore yu!" yelled Texas, his gun outstretched. "Brite, back me up with yore rifle. Reddie, line oot heah!"

Brite had scarcely needed the ringing order, for his rifle was leveled before Texas had finished. Likewise Reddie leaped forward, fearless and menacing.

All the riders except Ross Hite had wheeled abruptly. Several were walking their horses away. Hite showed no fear in his lean sallow face as he peered from Texas to the prostrate Wallen, and then back across the camp. Brite heard the thud of flying hoofs, and farther back the violent cries of riding cowboys.

"Brite, do yu want us to pack Wallen away?" queried Hite.

"No, thanks, we'll 'tend to him," retorted Brite, sarcastically.

Just then a horse plunged by the chuck-wagon and, being pulled up short, slid to a halt, scattering dust and gravel everywhere. Pan Handle Smith leaped off in their midst, a gun magically appearing in each hand. It was then Brite's tension relaxed.

"What's the deal?" asked Smith, quietly.

Ross Hite stared hard at Smith and then laughed harshly.

"Wal, Brite, yu air a trail driver thet goes heeled. Texas Shipman an' now Pan Handle Smith!"

"Rustle oot of heah!" ordered Texas.

"Men, this was Wallen's deal, not mine," returned Hite, and turning his horse he drove his companions ahead of him, quickly breaking into a gallop. Soon they passed round the corner of timber whence they had come.

Only then did Texas Joe move. He gave a quick glance at the dead Wallen and then wheeled with pale face and glittering eyes.

"Heah yu, Reddie Bayne," he called, and in two long strides he confronted Reddie. "Did yu say yu was a girl?"

"Yes, Texas Joe—I—I am," replied Reddie, and took off her sombrero to prove it. Her face was ashen and her eyes darkly dilated with receding terror. Texas fastened his left hand in her blouse and drew her up on her toes, close under his piercing gaze. His tawny hair stood up like the mane of a lion. But his cold fury was waning. Bewilderment hung close upon his passion.

"Yu—yu . . . all the time—yu've been a—a girl?" he broke out, hoarsely.

"Yes, Texas, all the time," she whispered, sagging in his iron grasp. "I—I didn't mean to fool yu. I told the boss. . . . I—I wanted to tell you, but he wouldn't let me. . . . I—I'm sorry."

CHAPTER 5   Texas Joe appeared to shrink. He released Reddie so suddenly that she sagged and almost sank down, her hand at the neck of her blouse.

"Ootrag-eous of yu!" panted Texas as his pallid face grew red. "Makin' oot yu was a boy—before us all! . . . An' lettin' me spank yu—an'—"

"Let yu!" flashed Reddie, her face flaming worse than his. "Why, yu darn big brute, I couldn't help myself!"

"An' all thet camp cussin' of ours—an' dirty talk before a girl! . . . My Gawd! Yu done a turrible thing, Miss Reddie Bayne!"

"I reckon, but it was these damn hombres like *him*—the

drove me to it," declared Reddie, passionately, pointing a shaking finger at the ghastly, quiet Wallen.

With that Texas Joe seemed to realize the tragic side of what had happened. Wheeling abruptly away from the girl, he sheathed his gun and bent a grim, strange look upon the dead man.

"Search him, some of yu," he said, sharp and cold. "Drag him oot an' throw him in thet wash. . . . Come a-rustlin' now, all of yu. Let's get oot of this."

"Where yu goin', Tex?" called Brite, as the driver strode away.

"Take my hawse," cried Reddie, after him.

But Texas Joe paid no heed to either. Soon he passed out of sight in the low brush. Then the strain among those around the camp fire relaxed. Reddie sat down as if her legs had grown weak.

"I've seen men shot before—but *never* for *me*," she whispered. "I feel like a—a murderer."

"Nonsense, Reddie," spoke up Brite, brusquely. "I'd have bored Wallen myself if Texas hadn't. . . . Pan Handle, did yu see thet one of Wallen's ootfit forked a hawse of mine?"

"No, boss, I didn't. Fact is I had eyes only for Ross Hite."

"Wal, it's true. When I bought thet bunch of stock I happened to take notice of a little bay mustang with a white face. I don't mistake hawses I've once looked over. Wallen's ootfit stampeded some of our *remuda* this mawnin'."

"Boss, I don't know Wallen, but he shore was ridin' in bad company," said Pan Handle.

"Ahuh. Yu know this Ross Hite?" rejoined Brite.

"Wal, rather. He was a cattle-buyer at Abilene. But he got into shady deals an' found Abilene too hot for him. Surprises me, though, to find him stampedin' a few hawses. I reckon thet was just by the way. Or else he's goin' to work somethin' big on this Chisholm Trail."

"Humph! Mebbe Hite is at the haid of this new game," declared the boss, seriously. "Cattle-drivers sometimes lose half their stock from stampeders. I've heahed of one whole herd bein' stole."

"Texas Joe ought to have done for Hite same as Wallen. Hite will give us trouble on the way up," said Smith, darkly.

Meanwhile Ackerman, with Whittaker and San Sabe, had dragged the dead Wallen out of camp. They returned presently, packing gun and belt, spurs, a huge silver watch, and a heavy, fat wallet.

"Boss, I opened this," said Ackerman, handing over the wallet. "He shore was heeled."

Brite found the greasy wallet stuffed full of greenbacks.

"Say, he must have robbed a bank," declared the boss, in amaze. "Boys, hundreds of dollars heah. What'll we do with it?"

"What yu think?" queried Deuce Ackerman, sarcastically. "Yu want me to ride after Wallen's ootfit an' give thet money to his pards?"

"No. I was only figgerin' . . . I'll keep this an' divide it among yu boys at the end of the drive. It'll be a big bonus."

The drivers gave vent to great appreciation of this decision. Brite stowed the money away in his saddlebag, and put the other articles of Wallen's in the chuck-wagon.

"Boys, did yu look where Texas Joe hit thet Wallen?" asked Pan Handle Smith, curiously.

"Shore. Right in the middle of Wallen's left vest pocket. Bullet went through his tobacco-pouch."

"Pretty daid-center shot for such a quick throw," went on Smith, ponderingly. "Thet Texas Joe must be there on the draw."

Brite was familiar with this peculiar interest of the gunman in regard to the proficiency of others. He replied that the cattleman who had recommended Shipman had made significant mention of the fact.

"Hurry an' eat, boys," went on Brite. "We want to be on the prod."

All but Reddie Bayne answered to that suggestion with alacrity. Reddie sat with her face in her hands, her red-gold curls exposed. She made a pretty and a pathetic little figure, which Brite observed was not lost upon the shy cowboys.

Deuce Ackerman looked at her several times, and finally conquered his evident embarrassment.

"Come on, Reddie. Don't take it so hard," he said, gallantly. "Shore if *we* can stand it, yu can. We know yu're a girl now an' if yu can only overlook our—our—"

Deuce broke off there, manifestly unable to find words to express his shame for their talk and behavior before a girl. Reddie answered to that instantly, arising to come to the wagon, a blush dyeing her pale cheek.

"Thank yu, Deuce," she replied, bravely conquering her confusion. "But none of yu boys need feel bad aboot it. . . . Texas was the only one who hurt my feelin's. . . . I'm shore glad not to be ridin' under false colors no more."

Whittaker gave her a smile. "I doan' mind tellin' yu thet I knowed aboot yu all the time," he drawled.

"Wha-at?" faltered Reddie, in alarm.

"Reddie, he's a durned liar," spoke up Deuce, forcibly. "Whit, yu cain't come none of thet on her. Can he, Sabe?"

But San Sabe was not vouchsafing for anyone, or else he was tongue-tied. Moze rolled his great ox eyes at Reddie.

"Yo done fool us all, Miss Reddie, an' dat's no mistake," he said, wagging his head. "An' so youse a gall Wal, Ise doag-goned glad to have a lady in de ootfit."

"Air we all supposed to go on callin' yu Reddie?" queried Pan Handle, dryly, as he fixed his keen eyes upon her.

"Why—of course."

Soon they had finished their hasty breakfast, and saddling up, were off for the day's drive. As Brite rode down to head the wash, he saw where the boys had tumbled Wallen. They had not taken the trouble even to crumble some of the soft bank of earth over upon him. Perhaps they thought that Wallen's gang would return, and Brite himself concluded that was likely. This was the first tragic happening on any drive Brite had made. It augured ill for this one. But he could not expect always to have phenomenal luck. Many a story of trail drivers had been harrowing. Brite fortified himself anew. And this morning there was a subtle change to the thrill and zest of trail driving. He looked out over the vast rose-and-purple expanse with hard eyes, quickening to more than the beauty of nature.

The herd was well pointed and moving perceptibly some miles ahead. Reddie and Pan Handle were off to the eastward with the *remuda*, catching up. Brite rode to the highest knoll available and then took his morning survey. The air was clear. Far to the south, perhaps twenty miles, a low black line penciled the gray expanse. Buffalo or cattle, Brite could not decide which. He hoped they were buffalo. Forward the purple range billowed, and to the west skeleton shadows of hills pierced the haze. Deer and rabbits and coyotes appeared to be numerous this morning.

Finally Brite set off at a trot after the riders, who had caught up with the herd. One of them had been leading a saddled but riderless horse, undoubtedly meant for Texas Joe, who was on foot. Not for hours did Brite get a glimpse of his foreman, and by that time he was astride again.

The slow miles passed to the rear, and the westering sun had sunk low and dusky red before Shipman halted for the night. This day's drive would total fifteen miles, a long journey for grazing cattle. Water had been crossed about mid-afternoon, which was well for the stock, because this was a dry camp. Grass was luxuriant, and buffalo chips abundant. Moze halted his chuck-wagon in the lee of an outcrop of rock, which was the only obstruction on the level land. Brite finished his own chores and then packed in chips for the camp fire. Not until a dusky haze had mantled the range did he stop gazing back to the southward.

Texas Joe did not ride in until after the night shift had gone on guard. He was silent and taciturn, aloof as Brite had seen other men who had lately snuffed out human life. Texas ate alone, kneeling beside the fire. More than once Brite caught him kneeling there, cup in hand, motionless, his thoughts far from the moment. Presently he slipped away in the darkness and Brite saw him no more. Rolly Little, Ben Chandler, and Roy Hallett betrayed their knowledge of the marvelous fact that the Brite outfit had a young girl in it now, and not only a very pretty one, but also romantic and appealing. They were a changed trio. Excited, gay, decidedly on their good behavior, they amused Brite. Not once did Brite hear them mention the killing of Wallen. That seemed far past. Rolly was the only one of the trio who had the courage to speak directly to Reddie. Ben took his attention out in covert glances, while Roy talked loudly, almost boastfully, a singular transformation in this boy.

The most noticeable change, however, and a pleasing one, appeared to be in Reddie Bayne. She seemed natural for the first time, and no longer slunk in and out of camp hurriedly, with her old sombrero pulled down over her eyes. In fact, she did not have it on at all, and only one glance at her pretty head was needed to ascertain that she had brushed her golden curls. Where had she done that, Brite wondered? After supper she helped Moze at his tasks, apparently not heeding the noisy trio around the fire, although a sharp observer might have detected that she heard every word. More than once she flashed a furtive glance off in the direction in which Texas Joe had disappeared. Next she tipped her bedroll off the wagon, and was about to shoulder it when the three cowboys piled over each other to get it. Rolly was the quickest.

"Whar yu want it unrolled, Re . . . Miss Reddie?" he asked.

"Thanks. But give it to me," returned Reddie, bluntly. "Say, I've been totin' this roll every night, haven't I? Why not tonight?"

"Wal, yu see, Miss Reddie, yu—we—it ain't jest the same now."

"Oh, ain't it? What ain't?"

"Yu know. The situation heah. . . . We boys have talked it over. Ridin' *remuda* is enough for yu. No more packin' saddles, bedrolls, firewood, water, an' sich chores. We'll do all thet for yu."

"Yu're awfully good, Rolly. But please wait till I drop, will yu?"

Whereupon she lifted the roll of canvas and carried it over significantly close to where Brite had unrolled his. When she had finished a like task for herself she came over to sit beside Brite.

"I'm still sick to my stomach," she confided. "An' I have thet queer heavy feelin' up heah." She put her hands to her breast, high up, and pressed them there.

"I savvy, Reddie. All thet this mawnin'. . . . Wal, it sort of faded for me. So much to think aboot!"

"Gee! I've thought 'til my pore haid aches," declared Reddie. "Mr. Brite, these cowboys air funny now. Have yu noticed it—since I been found oot?"

"Reckon I have. Shore it's funny," replied Brite. "It's unusual to have a girl on a trail drive. Shore it's goin' to be somethin' beside funny, Reddie."

"I'm afraid so. What do *yu* think?"

"Wal, yu're an awful pretty girl, an' thet's goin' to make complications."

"Oh dear! . . . I reckoned so. But, Mr. Brite, they're *nice* boys. I—I like them. I'm not afraid. I'll be able to sleep. This is the nicest ootfit of men I ever rode with."

"Wal, thet's a compliment to all of us, Reddie. Thank yu for it. I'll bet the boys would like to heah thet. I'll tell them."

"Oh, I cain't get this mawnin' off my chest," she whispered. "Wasn't he terrible?"

"Who? Wallen?"

"Wallen! No, he was just low down. . . . I mean Texas Joe. . . . Wasn't he fierce? I could have dropped in my tracks when he shot Wallen. . . . Just as quick as thet! Just the moment I confessed I was a girl—an'—Wallen was after me. . . . Oh! He *killed* him! I prayed for some rider to do thet very thing. But when it was done I was sick. My blood curdled. . . . Yet even thet wasn't as bad as when Texas grabbed me by the throat an' nearly jerked me oot of my boots. . . . 'All the time yu was a girl—*all* the time,' he barked at me. I'll never forget thet."

"Aw, yes, yu will, Reddie," replied Brite, soothingly. "Tex took the sap oot of me, too. Gawd! how quick he bored thet skunk! Why even Pan Handle remarked aboot it. . . . Just forget it, Reddie. We've lots more comin', I reckon, this trip."

"But, Mr. Brite," she faltered. "I—I got the idee Texas Joe thought Wallen had—thet I was a—a hussy."

"Reddie! I'm shore he's thought nothin' of the kind," replied Brite, hastily.

"Oh, yes he did. He looked at me so! I could have sunk in my boots. . . . Mr. Brite, I—I just couldn't go on with yore ootfit if he thought I was a bad girl."

"Tex was only shocked. Same as me—an' all of us. It doesn't happen every day, Reddie—a pretty kid of a girl droppin' in on us oot of the sky. Yu see, Tex had swore at yu, an' spanked yu thet time, an' otherwise put familiar hands on yu withoot the least idee yu was anythin' but a boy. He's so ashamed he cain't come aboot."

"It's very kind of yu to say thet, Mr. Brite," rejoined Reddie. "I wish I could believe yu. But I cain't. An' I cain't ask him—dammit!"

"Ask him what?"

"If he thinks I'm bad."

"Wal, I reckon Tex would be hurt to find oot yu believed he could so insult yu in his mind. But ask him. Thet'll settle it."

"But I cain't, Mr. Brite. I cain't be mad at him—no matter what he believed me. 'Cause he killed a man for my sake! 'Cause he saved me from wuss'n hell—an' from spillin' my own blood."

"Reddie, yu're all upset," replied Brite, moved at the convulsed pale face and the dark eyes. "Yu go to bed. In the mawnin' yu'll feel better."

"Sleep! What's to keep thet man Hite from sneakin' in heah with his ootfit, knifin' yu all, an' makin' off with me?"

The startling query acquainted Brite with the fact that there was not very much to oppose such a catastrophe. Too many drivers were required on guard. That left the camp force weak.

"Reddie, thet's sort of far fetched," said Brite.

"It's been done over Braseda way. I heahed aboot it."

"I'm a light sleeper, Reddie. No Comanches, even, could surprise me."

Reddie shook her curly head as if she were unconvinced.

"It's tough enough to be a girl in town," she said. "Oot heah on the trail it's hell."

"No one but Wallen's ootfit knows. An' shore they won't come bracin' us again. Go to bed, Reddie, an' sleep."

Brite lay awake, thinking. This waif of the ranges had disrupted a certain tenor of the trail drivers' life. Having her with them was a drawback, a risk. But Brite could not entertain any idea of not keeping her. The fact that Reddie was a strong, skillful, enduring rider, as good a horse wrangler as any boy, did not alter the case. She was a girl, and growing more every minute a decidedly attractive girl. Impossible was it to keep the cowboys from realizing that alluring fact in a way characteristic of Texan youths in particular, and all youths in general. They would fall in love with her. They would quarrel over her. Nevertheless, suppose they did! Brite would not surrender to dismay. He refused to admit that youth, beauty, romance, might detract from the efficiency of a group of trail drivers. On the other hand, they would rise to the occasion. That free, wild, spirit to do and dare would burn more fiercely and make them all the more invincible. No, Reddie Bayne was not a liability to this enterprise, but an asset. Brite satisfied himself on that score, and when that conclusion had been reached he realized that the orphan girl had found a place in his heart which had ever been empty.

The events of the day had not been conducive to undisturbed sleep. Brite was awake on and off until the guard changed at midnight. Reddie Bayne was also awakened.

"Boss," she said, "I'm goin' to have a look at my *remuda*."

"Come along. I'll go with yu."

Ackerman brought in the relief horses and reported that all was quiet, with the herd bedded down. The moon in its last quarter was low on the horizon. Sheet lightning flaring behind dark, stringy clouds in the west told of heat and storm.

As they rode out together Texas Joe swept by on a lope and hailed them gruffly. "Hang close together, yu!"

Brite heard Reddie mutter something under her breath. How she watched that dark rider across the moonlit plain!

They found the horses resting, with only a few grazing. The grass was knee high. Out beyond, a great, black square defaced the silvery prairie, and this was the herd of long-horns. San Sabe's voice doled out a cowboy refrain. The other guards were silent. Brite and Reddie rode around the herd twice, and finally edging the horses into a closer unit, they turned campward. Reddie appeared prone to silence. Several times Brite tried conversation, which elicited only monosyllables from the youngster. They went to bed, and Brite slept until sunrise.

That day turned out uneventful. Shipman drove at least twelve miles. Brite observed that his foreman often faced the south to gaze long and steadily. But nothing happened and the night also proved quiet. Another day saw a lessening of anxiety. Ross Hite had not passed them in daylight, that was a certainty. A mild thunderstorm overtook the drivers on the following day, and the wet, shiny horns of the cattle and the fresh, dank odor of thirsty earth were pleasant.

Coon Creek and Buffalo Wallow, Hackberry Flat, The Meadows, and night after night at unnamed camps took the drivers well on into June. Buffalo began to show in straggly lines on the rise of prairie to the west. A few unfriendly riders passed at a distance. Brite began to think that good luck attended his trail again, and forgot the days and camps.

Meanwhile, except for the aloof Texas Joe and Pan Handle, the outfit had grown into a happy family. Reddie Bayne had been a good influence so far. Rivalry for her favor, for who should wait upon her in any conceivable way that she would permit, lacked not friendly spirit, for all its keenness. Smiles grew frequent upon her pretty face. She improved visibly under such pleasant contact. And Brite came to the day when he decided he would adopt her as a daughter, if one of these cowboys did not win her for a wife. Still, Brite, sharp watch and guardianship as he kept over her, found no serious courting. No one of them ever had a chance to get her alone. It just happened that way, or else Reddie was clever enough to bring it about.

Nevertheless, where Texas Joe was concerned there appeared to be smoldering fire. He watched Reddie from afar with telltale eyes. And Reddie, when she imagined she was unobserved, let her dreamy gaze stray in Joe's direction. As foreman he had the responsibility of the herd, and day and night that was his passion. All the same he followed imperceptibly in the footsteps of his riders. Seldom did Joe address Reddie; never did he give her another order. Sometimes he would tell Brite to have her do this or that with the *remuda*. In camp he avoided her when that was possible. He seemed a weary, melancholy rider, pondering to himself.

Brite saw how this aloofness worked upon Reddie. She had come into her own, and his indifference piqued her. Reddie never lost a chance to fret and fume to Brite about his foreman. Pride and vanity had come with the championship of the cowboys. Despite her ragged male attire, she no longer could have been taken for other than a girl. Some kind of a climax was imminent. Brite had his choice of a suitor for Reddie, but he liked all his boys. They had warmed to her influence. Perhaps if she had shown any preference then there might have been jealousy. But so far they were all her brothers and she was happy, except at such times when Texas Joe projected his forceful personality and disturbing presence upon the scene.

One early evening camp at Blanco River all the drivers but three were in, and Texas Joe was among the former. It had been an easy day until the crossing of the wide stream, where some blunders, particularly with the *remuda*, had ruffled the foreman. He gave Ackerman one of his roundabout orders for Reddie. They were through supper and Joe about ready to take the night guard out. Suddenly Reddie flashed a resentful face in Joe's direction.

"Deuce, I cain't heah yu," she said, quite piercingly. "If Mister Shipman has any orders for me, let him tell them to *me*."

Ackerman was not slow in translating this into his own words, for the benefit of Joe and all. But it really had not been necessary.

"I'll give orders any way I like, Miss Bayne," said Texas.

"Shore. But if yu got anythin' for *me* to do yu'll say so, an' not through somebody else."

"Wal, I'll fire yu when we get to Fort Worth," rejoined Joe, coolly.

"Fire me!" cried Reddie, astounded and furious.

"Yu heahed me, miss."

"Then yu'll fire the whole damn ootfit," declared Reddie, hotly. "The idee! When I've not done a single thing wrong. . . . Tell him, boys. Deuce, Roy, Whit, Rolly—tell him."

There were nonchalant and amiable remarks tending to the veracity of Reddie's declaration.

"My Gawd! what a lousy ootfit!" ejaculated Joe, in disgust. "Less Holden—my pard—air yu in cahoots with her?"

"Shore, Tex," replied Lester, with a laugh. "We jest couldn't drive cattle withoot Reddie."

"Yu too!" burst out Texas, deeply chagrined and amazed.

"Say, what kind of a foreman air yu—givin' orders to yore hawse-wrangler through a third person?" flashed Reddie, scornfully. "I'm on this ootfit. I'm gettin' wages. Yu cain't ignore me."

"Cain't I?" queried Texas, in helpless rage. It was evident that he could not. More than evident was it that something inexplicable and infuriating was at work upon him.

"No, yu cain't—not no more," continued Reddie, carried beyond reserve. "Not withoot insultin' me, Texas Jack Shipman."

"Stop callin' me Texas Jack," shouted the driver.

"I'll call yu wuss'n thet pronto. An' I'll say right now of all the conceited, stuck-up cowboys I ever seen yu're the damnedest. Yu're too proud to speak to poor white trash like me. So yu order me aboot through the boss or one of the boys, or even Moze. An' I'm callin' for a show down, Tex Shipman."

"Boss, do I have to stand heah an' take all this?" appealed Joe, turning shamefacedly to Brite.

"Wal, Tex, I don't reckon yu have to, but I'd take it if I was yu an' get it over," advised Brite, conciliatingly.

Thus championed by her employer, Reddie gave way utterly to whatever complicated emotions were driving her. Like a cat she sprang close to Texas and glared up at him, her eyes blazing, her breast heaving.

"Yu can tell me right heah an' now, in front of the ootfit, why yu treat me like dirt under yore feet," demanded she, huskily.

"Wrong again, Miss Bayne," drawled Texas. "Yu flatter yoreself. I jest didn't think aboot yu atall."

This seemed to be a monstrous lie to all except the pale-faced girl to whom it was directed.

"Tex Shipman, yu killed a man to save me, but it wasn't for *me* particularly? Yu'd done thet for any girl, good or—o bad?"

"Why, shore I would."

"An' yu had yore doubts aboot me then, didn't yu, cowboy?"

"Wal, I reckon so. An' I—still got—them," rejoined Texas haltingly. He had doubts about himself, too, and altogether the situation must have been galling to him.

"Yu bet yu have!" flashed Reddie, scarlet of face. "Come oot with them then—if yu're not yellow! . . . First—yu think I— I'm bad, don't yu?"

"Wal, if yu're keen aboot thet, I don't think yu're so—s damn good!"

"Oh-h!" cried the girl, poignantly. Then she gave him stinging slap with her right hand and another with her left.

"Heah! Yu got me wrong!" yelled Texas, suddenly horrified at the way she took his scathing reply; and he backed awa from her flaming assault. But it was too late. Reddie was to violently outraged to comprehend what seemed clear to Brite and no doubt all the gaping listeners.

"I ought to kill yu for thet," whispered Reddie. "An' would, by Gawd! but for Mr. Brite! . . . Oh, I've knowed a along yu thought I was a hussy. . . . Thet Wallen had . . Damn yu, Tex Shipman. Yu don't know a decent girl when y meet one! Yu gotta be told. An' I'm tellin' yu. . . . Wallen wa a dirty skunk. An' he wasn't the only one who hounded m oot of a job. All because I wanted to be decent. . . . An' I a decent—an' as good as yore own sister, Tex Shipman—or an other boy's sister! . . . To think I—I have to *tell yu!*—I ought to do thet—with a gun—or a hawsewhip."

Suddenly she broke down and began to sob. "Now—yu can go to hell—Tex Shipman—with yore orders—an' with what—yu think aboot me! Yu're dirt—under—*my* feet!"

CHAPTER 6

REDDIE PLUNGED away into the gathering dusk as if she meant to leave that camp forever. Brite decided he would not let her go far, but before following her he took note of the group at the camp fire. Texas Joe stared after Reddie. The boys began to upbraid him in no friendly terms, when Pan Handle silenced them with a gesture.

"Tex, this is liable to split our ootfit," he said, putting a hand on the cowboy's shoulder. "It won't do. We all know yu didn't think Reddie's no good. But *she* doesn't know. Square thet pronto."

Brite hastened after Reddie, and coming up with her just out of the camp-fire light he detained her with a gentle hand.

"Lass, yu mustn't go runnin' off."

"Oh, I—I could run right—into the river," she cried, miserable. "I—I was so—so happy."

"Wal, it'll all come right," returned the cattleman, and put a kindly arm around her and led her to a seat on a near-by rock. Reddie was not proof against sympathy and she sank on his shoulder.

"Tell me yu don't—believe it," she begged.

"Believe what, lass?"

"What Texas thinks—aboot me?"

"Wal, I should smile not. None of the boys do. An' I reckon Tex himself . . . Heah he comes, Reddie."

She stiffened in his arms and appeared to hold her breath. Texas strode up to them, bareheaded in the dusk. Only his eyes could be seen and they gleamed darkly.

"Reddie Bayne, yu listen to me," he began, sternly. "If yu wasn't such a darned little spitfire yu'd never disgraced me before the ootfit. I —"

"Disgraced *yu?*" she interrupted.

"Yes, me. . . . I swear to Gawd I had no idee atall thet yu wasn't as honest an'—an' good as any girl. I meant yu was a queer, contrary, temperish, spiteful little devil. But only thet. Sabe? . . . An' I'm sorry I upset yu an' I want to apologize."

"Yu're aboot six days too late, Texas Jack," she burst out, defiantly. "An—an' yu can go to hell, anyhow."

He gave her a slow, strange glance as she lay with her head on Brite's shoulder.

"Wal, I'll have company, for thet's where this ootfit is haided," he replied, coldly, and stalked away.

Reddie raised to peer over Brite's shoulder after the cowboy. She was not aware how she clung to Brite. But he felt the strong, little hands on his vest. Slowly then she dropped back, head and breast against him, where she all but collapsed.

"There! . . . I've—done—it—now," she whispered, as if to herself. "I should have—acted the—the lady. . . . But I—I hate him so."

Brite formed his own conclusion about how she hated Texas Joe. It also came to him, and stronger than formerly, how he had come to feel toward Reddie. This was the time to tell it.

"Lass, I reckon folks oot on the Chisholm Trail can have feelin's the same as when they're home safe an' sound. Mebbe stronger an' deeper an' better feelin's. Anyway, I'm goin' to ask yu somethin' particular. I'm alone in the world. No near kin. An' I'd like to have yu for a daughter. How aboot it?"

"Oh, it'd be my dream come true," she cried, ecstatically. "Oh, if only I'm worthy!"

"Let me be the judge of thet," he replied, happily. "I have a ranch ootside Santone. An' yu can make it yore home. All I ask is thet yu care a little for me."

"I love yu now, Mr. Brite," she whispered, generously, and hugged him. "Oh, it's too good to be true."

"Wal, then, do yu accept me as yore adopted dad?"

"I cain't thank God enough," she murmured.

"It's settled an' I reckon I'm doin' some thankin' on my own hook."

"Yu air so good an' kind. . . . Oh, this ootfit is different. . . . I wonder what *he* will say when he finds oot."

"Who?"

"Thet cowboy."

"Aw, he'll have me to reckon with now. But, Reddie, we'll keep it secret till we get to Dodge."

Brite was unrolling his bed when he felt something fine and cold touch his cheek. Rain! He had been so preoccupied that he had not observed any change in weather conditions. The stars had grayed over. All the north appeared gloomy and black. Storms were the bane of the trail drivers. Texas was noted for storms, from the *del norte* of the Mexicans to the Pan Handle cyclone.

"Reddie, it's goin' to rain," he called. "Fetch yore bed over under the wagon."

But Reddie was in the land of dreams. Brite took his long slicker and, stepping across to where Reddie lay, spread it over her bed. Brite experienced a new sensation—a warm wave of joy at realization of his new responsibility. Hearing voices, he went over to the wagon. The boys were moving their beds under it. The wind had quickened, blowing a fine, chilly mist in Brite's face.

"Wal, boss, our luck has changed," spoke up Texas, grimly. "We've shore been too damn lucky. Now it's comin'.'"

"What's comin', yu gloomy geezer?"

"A norther, first off. I don't know what after thet."

"It's a late spring. We could have a norther even this late," replied Brite, ponderingly.

"Moze, where'n hell air yu?" called Joe.

"I wuz under de wagon, Mars Joe, till I got rolled oot," answered Moze.

"Wal, yu roll oot farther an' pack all the dry wood yu got in the caboose."

"Yes, suh. Ise done on de way."

"Where's yore ax? I'll split some more wood. Boss, we might as wal use thet extra tarp for a wind an' rain break. Moze has one over the wagon. Lawd! I do hate the wet an' cold. . . . Hadn't yu better wake Reddie an' call her oot heah?"

"I spread my slicker over her," replied Brite, pleased with the solicitude in Shipman's voice. "She'll be all right unless it pours."

Texas went off, muttering to himself. Soon the ring of the ax attested to his occupation. Moze was having his troubles putting wood in the canvas that had been stretched under the wagon for such purpose. The cowboys were in his way.

"Moze, let 'em sleep," suggested Brite. "We'll put up the extra tarp. Yu can lay the wood under thet till mawnin'. . . . Heah. Tie one end of the tarp to the hoops of the wagon an' peg down the other."

"Reckon dat'll save dis black chile's life."

Texas came up staggering under a load of wood which he deposited very considerately without making a noise.

"Boss," he said, "if thet wind comes stronger with rain we'll have a driftin' herd. An' I'd shore hate to have them drift south. Bad for us."

"It's kind of northwest, Tex," replied Brite, holding his hand up.

"Jest as bad, 'cept a norther lasts three days. Mebbe it's nothin' much. We'll know in a couple of hours. Which I'm gonna use sleepin'."

They rolled in their blankets in the shelter of the stretched tarpaulin. Texas dropped off into slumber by the magic of youth. Soon Moze snored like a sawmill. Brite did not feel sleepy. The warmth of his blankets told him just how cold the air had grown. He lay there resting and listening. The wind moaned steadily, weirdly, and whipped in chilly gusts under the wagon, flopped the canvas, and swept away mournfully. Coyotes barked about the camp. Somewhere out there in the black, windy void the great herd would be stirring uneasily in their beds. The old mossy-horns would be bawling. And the guards would be singing to them. What a singular and tremendous movement this was—the driving of cattle herds north! Lying there, Brite seemed to have a vision of what magnitude this business would attain, how it would save Texas and pave the way for an empire. No doubt old Jesse Chisholm had seen that vision first of all the pioneers. These cowboys who were driving up the Trail by hundreds— or those of them who survived the hardships and perils— would see the day their prosperous ranches owed all to this heroic beginning.

These pondering thoughts might have merged into dreams, for all Brite knew, but they were disrupted sooner or later by the thud of plunging hoofs and a ringing voice.

"All oot. Herd driftin'."

When Brite sat up, Texas Joe was on his knees, rolling his bed.

"What time, Deuce?" he called.

"After midnight. Cain't see my watch. Colder'n hell!"

"Rainin' much?"

"Not yet. Mixed with sleet."

"Sleet in June! Wal, I forgot aboot it bein' Texas."

"Tex, we'll need lanterns. Cain't see yore hand before yore face."

"Moze, air yu awake?"

"Yas, suh, I reckon I is."

"Air the lanterns filled? An' where'll I find them?"

"All ready, boss. Settin' inside the front wheels where I keeps them every night."

Brite got his heavy coat which had served as a pillow, and while putting it on he advised the drivers to don their warmest.

"Reddie Bayne!" yelled Texas.

No answer! Joe yelled again, with unnecessary peevishness, Brite thought. Still no sound came from Reddie.

"Must be daid. Never knowed Reddie to be hard to wake."

"I heah hawses," spoke up Deuce.

Soon Brite followed the others out from under the shelter into the yellow light of the lanterns. Brite was about to go over to awaken Reddie when a pounding of hoofs preceded a dark, ragged bunch of horses coming into camp.

"Heah she is! Dog-gone!" Deuce Ackerman called.

In the windy gloom Brite espied Reddie on foot, leading half a dozen horses by halters. The long slicker glistened wet in the lantern-light.

"Where'd yu get them hawses?" queried Texas.

"I had them tied oot heah."

"Ahuh. So yu can see in the dark, same as a cat?"

"Yes, sir," replied Reddie, meekly.

"Wal, I shore hate to admit it, but yu beat holler any hawse-wrangler I ever seen," concluded Texas, gruffly.

"Thanks, Jack," returned Reddie, sweetly.

They bridled and saddled the horses. Texas mounted, and calling for one of the lanterns, he headed away from the wind.

"Deuce, yu fetch the other lantern," he called. "Moze, hang right heah till we come back. Have a fire an' hot drinks, for we'll shore need 'em."

Brite and the others followed, soon to catch up with Texas. The horses were unwilling to go and rubbed close together. Texas lifted his lantern.

"Thet's Reddie's black, ain't it?" he queried, sharply.

"Yes, I'm heah," replied Reddie.

"Wal, yu go back to camp. This won't be no job for little girls."

"Jack, yu go where it's hot. I can stand the cold."

"Stop callin' me Jack," he retorted, testily. "Or I—I'll box yore ears. An' I tell yu to stay in camp."

"But, Texas, I'd be afraid in camp withoot yu-all," she returned, seriously.

"Wal, come to think of thet, I reckon yu're right. . . . Deuce, where'n hell air we haidin'?"

"Darned if I know. I shore had a time findin' camp. Took me half an hour."

"How far oot was the herd?"

"Coupla miles, I reckon."

"Spread oot to the right, Deuce. An' go till yu can just see my light. Rest of yu hang in between. . . . Hell, but it's nasty!"

A stiff wind was blowing at their backs. It carried fine rain and sleet, that could be distinctly heard by the impact and the rustling in the grass. The darkness appeared inky black. And Texas' lantern shone fitfully upon weird spectral figures of horses and riders. When they had covered a distance of two or three miles Texas and Deuce began to yell to locate the guards with the herd. No answering yells rewarded them. They went a couple of miles farther, and then the line, with Texas at one end and Deuce at the other, began to sweep in a circle. The situation grew serious. If the herd took to drifting badly, the few guards could not hold them, and they might stampede, or at least travel many miles. Mossy-horns were as limber and enduring as horses when they wanted to go.

"Hold on, fellars," ordered Texas, at last. "I heahed somethin'. Mebbe it was only a coyote. But I'll pile off an' get away so I can heah shore."

Leaping off, he stalked apart from the horses, his light swinging to and fro in his hand. Then he pealed out a stentorian yell. Brite listened, but could hear nothing. After a short silence Texas called: "Yep, I was right. I got an answer."

He hurried back to his horse, and mounting, led somewhat to the left. "Reckon I cain't keep thet direction long. But we'll stop an' yell till we locate them."

By this method Texas Joe found the other guards and the herd at last. But the guards were on the far side of the herd, which was drifting with the wind. Texas called for Brite and Reddie to follow him, and for the others to follow Deuce, who would circle the herd from his end. Time and time again Texas' light fell upon stragglers of the herd, evidently far behind the main body.

"Wal, the drags air good for somethin'," said Texas. "An' thet in a storm."

Answering yells became frequent and louder. Soon Texas led his followers round in front of the herd, where they encountered Pan Handle and Rolly Little.

"How aboot yu, Pan?" shouted Texas.

"They're driftin', Tex, but not bad," came the reply.

"Where are the other boys?"

"Sometimes near, sometimes far. Now I can heah them an' again I cain't."

"Oh, ho, ho! Oh, ho, hell!" sang out Texas. "Line up all. Take yore medicine, boss. Yu will buy cattle at twelve bits a haid. Reddie, heah is where we make a man oot of yu."

The drivers faced the wind and the oncoming herd. A bawling mass of cattle showed a square front to Texas' lantern. They were not ugly and probably could have been wholly halted but for the crowding from behind. Back a hundred yards, the light and the yells and singing of the drivers had little effect. So there was no hope of stopping them. The best that could be done was to retard their advance, to prevent a possible stampede, and give way before them.

Fortunately they had bunched closely, which fact became manifest when Deuce's welcome light showed up half a mile distant. Between these two lights ranged all the other drivers, shouting and singing. They had to rely absolutely on the sight of their horses, for only near the lights could they see anything. They could hear, however, and often located the front line that way. At intervals Deuce would ride across the front with his light and Texas would pass him going the other way. Thus they kept some semblance to a straight line.

It was slow, tedious, discouraging work, not without considerable risk, and bringing weariness and pain. The wind blew harder and colder; the sleet cut like tiny blades. Brite had always been susceptible to cold. The hour came when his heavy gloves and coat appeared to afford no protection to the storm. He could scarcely endure to face the sleet, yet he had to do it or be run over by cattle. Necessarily the action of his horse had to be slow, seldom more than a walk, and this was not conducive to active blood circulation. Reddie Bayne stayed with him, so near that they could locate each other without yelling. When Texas or Deuce passed with the lanterns they established their positions again.

"Hang on, drivers," Texas shouted, cheerily. "It ain't gettin' no wuss an' we shore air lucky."

Brite knew that if the storm increased he and no doubt others of the drivers, certainly Bender and Reddie, would find themselves in desperate straits. The cold, tooth-edged wind grew harder to bear, but evidently it did not increase in volume. Monotonously Brite beat his gloved hands, and his one ear and then the other under the collar of his coat.

"Cheer up, Reddie; the mawnin's aboot to bust," yelled Ackerman, the last time he rode by.

"It shore better come soon or I'll bust," replied Reddie.

Brite peered with tear-dimmed eyes away from the herd. The blackness had grown faintly gray in that direction. He watched it, turning often. How slowly it lightened! The hour dragged with hateful slowness. But almost imperceptibly the dawn came, until all the black void changed to gray, and the gray to pale, obscured stretches of prairie and the dark wall of twisted horns and heads and legs. Soon Brite could distinguish Reddie on her horse, and then the other riders, one by one. The lanterns were extinguished, and the drivers, aided by light enough to see, made far better success of their job. They could ride at a trot, and an occasional lope, from one pressing point to another. Horses as well as riders benefited by this brisker exercise.

Slowly the front line yielded. The mossy-horns would stop and try to graze a bit, only to be pushed on again by the surging from behind.

Brite was sure that but for the sleet turning to rain and the wind lessening a bit the herd would have had to be abandoned until the riders could thaw out and get fresh horses.

Daylight came broadly at last, revealing a dreary range land, and a dragging herd under a low-sailing bank of clouds, and bowed and sodden riders, stuck in their wet saddles. To turn the herd back became imperative. A day lost might mean loss of hundreds, even thousands, of cattle. Texas drove the weary riders to incredible exertions, concentrated at one end; and by hard riding, shooting to take the place of voices gone, he turned that end and the rest followed, like sheep follow a leader. Cattle and drivers then faced the north. The reluctant herd could not be driven faster than a plodding walk. Heads down, weary and hungry, the mossy-horns covered ground like snails. The horses, except Reddie Bayne's black, were spent, and would be useless the remainder of that drive.

Sometime during the afternoon Brite recognized landmarks near camp. He saw the *remuda* apparently intact and none the worse for the storm. Texas Joe and Ackerman left the herd bunched on a square of rich grass, and cutting out some horses they drove them into camp.

Brite was not the last by two to ride in. Pan Handle, haggard and drawn, came after him, and finally Bender, who sagged in his saddle. He had to be lifted off his horse. Brite was not so badly frozen, but he did not recall when he had been in such a plight.

"Wal, boss, yu rode in," said Texas, his voice low and hoarse. He stood steaming before a hot fire. Moze was dealing out hot drinks. Brite wondered what would have been the outcome if no fire or reviving whisky had been available.

Reddie Bayne was the only one not wet to the skin. The long slicker had saved her, and though she looked peaked and wan, she had evidently finished better than some of them.

"Coffee—not whisky," she whispered, huskily, as she smelled the cup Moze forced upon her.

"Reddie, yu're shore there," remarked Deuce, admiringly.

"Where?"

"I should have said heah. Shore was plumb worried aboot yu."

"Wal, I gotta hunch she's a man, after all," growled Texas, at which sally Reddie joined in the laugh on her.

"Boys, the herd's shiftin' a little south," remarked Texas, anxiously. "But I reckon we can hang them heah. Sabe, yu come with me. Deuce, send oot two men in an hour, an' we'll come back for grub. After thet regular guard, an' we'll bed down heah tonight."

"Wonder if any herd's gained on us today?" asked Brite, speaking with difficulty.

"Reckon all the drivers back lost as much as us, boss. . . . On second thought, dose Bender up good an' put him to bed." As another afterthought Texas halted as he passed Reddie beside the fire and queried, "Say, kid, yu want any orders from me?"

"Kid! Who air yu addressin', Mister Jack?" retorted Reddie. He fixed piercing hawk eyes upon her ruddy face. "Don't call me Jack no more."

"All right—Jack."

"I hate thet name. It reminds me of a girl who used to call me by it. She was 'most as uppish as yu, Reddie Bayne."

"I just cain't remember to say Joe—thet is, if I *would* get so familiar."

"Aw, indeed. So familiar? Yu call the rest of this ootfit by their given names. I even heahed yu call the boss Daddy."

"So I did . . . but I'd no idee I was heahed," replied Reddie, blushing.

"Wal, if yu cain't be so awful familiar as to call me Joe or Tex, yu can call me Mister Shipman," returned Texas, sarcastically.

"Ump-umm! I like Jack best," said Reddie, with a roguish look in her eye. Still she did not look at Texas.

"Listen. Thet settles yu," he flashed, with something of the ringing note in which he had addressed Wallen. "I cain't spank yu any more, much as yu deserve it. I ain't hankerin' for any more lead. But yu'll shore call me Jack somethin' or other before this drive ends."

"Somethin' or other! What?" exclaimed Reddie, very curiously.

"Wal, it might be Jack darlin'," replied Texas, and wheeled away.

The boys howled merrily. Reddie for once looked squelched. It was not the heat of the fire that added the crimson to her face. Brite caught a glimpse of her eyes before she lowered them, and they had a look of startled surprise. But her disheveled head did not long stay drooping; it bobbed up with a toss of curls, the action of a spirited girl strange to see in one wearing rough and muddy male attire.

"Never on this heah green earth!"

The night was long and uncomfortable, both in camp and out on guard. But the morning brought slowly clearing weather, and by the time the herd was pointed there was promise of sunshine. Wet grass and frequent pools of water made an easy day for the stock, a fact Shipman took advantage of with a long drive until dark. No droll repartee around the camp fire that night!

Two more uneventful drives brought the outfit to Austin, the first settlement on the Trail. Brite halted to see a rancher who lived three miles or less out of town, and got disturbing news about conditions to the north. The usual run of disasters multiplied! But particularly the Colorado River, which ran by Austin, was flooded to its banks, and there would be a necessity of waiting to use the customary ford or go up the river and swim the herd. When Brite passed this information on to Texas Joe he received a reply to his liking: "Wal, we shore won't hang aboot thet burg."

Austin, like other settlements along the Chisholm Trail, was subject to fluctuations of populace, and sometimes it was just as well for a driver not to be sociable. In the second place, cowboys usually looked upon red liquor at such places, always a deterring and uncertain factor.

Texas gave the place a wide berth, and aimed to strike the river five miles west, where Brite's rancher informant claimed there was a good gradual slope to point the herd across. Brite rode into Austin alone. He ate supper at a lodging-house where he had stopped before, and then went down street to call at Miller's store. In the darkness, where so few lights flickered here and there, it was difficult to tell whether Austin was full of men or not. It appeared quiet and lonely enough. Miller, a gaunt Missourian, greeted Brite cordially, as became him toward a customer.

"Been lookin' for you," he said. "How close are the herds behind?"

"Wal, there's one a day or so," replied Brite. "In a week they'll be comin' like buffalo."

"So Ross Hite reckoned."

"Hite. Is he heah?" asked Brite, casually.

"Yes. He rode in a few days back," returned Miller. "Had a bunch of mustangs he's been sellin' around."

"How many in Hite's ootfit?"

"Can't say. Only couple of men, strangers to me, with him when he came in here. Didn't he pass you on the way up?"

"There was some outfit went by. Aboot seven or eight, I reckon. Somebody said it was Wallen's."

"Wallen? Don't know him. Well, the more outfits comin' the better I like it. And I ain't curious or particular. Ha! Ha!"

Brite left orders for a pack of supplies, tobacco for the riders and sundries for Moze, and while these were being filled he strolled out to enter Snell's saloon. It was a big barnlike place full of yellow light, blue smoke, odor of rum, and noise. He had been in Snell's on each drive north, and all the other times together had not totaled the number of inmates present on this occasion. Gambling games were in progress, and at one of the rude tables sat Ross Hite with other gamesters, all obsessed in their play. Brite gazed sharply to see if he recognized any of the other faces. But the light was poor and many faces were in shadow. He had not a doubt, however, that all of Wallen's outfit were there. Cowboys, as Brite knew them, were conspicuous for their absence. The majority consisted of rugged, matured men; the minority, Mexicans and a few Negroes. Brite gravitated to a corner where he was in shadow and could watch all of the gamblers and one corner of the bar. He was just curious and thought he might happen on some chance talk. Ranchers, as a rule, did not spend their evenings in gambling-halls. Nevertheless, Brite thought he knew the inveterate cattlemen well enough to identify a few present. He had been there scarcely longer than a half-hour when he was chagrined to see Roy Hallett and Ben Chandler jostling to get room at the bar.

Possibly Shipman had let them off, but the probabilities were that they had ridden in without permission and expected to ride back without discovery. That was the cowboy of it.

Chandler was red-faced and manifestly jocose, but Hallett looked more than usually somber. Drink, instead of changing him, augmented his peculiar characteristics. But he was not drunk. He had to drag Chandler away from the bar. That worthy was out to make the most of this opportunity. Hallett, however, evidently had other designs. At least he did not show the usual disposition of a cowboy free to indulge. Brite concluded that Hallett had something on his mind. They sat down at an empty table, where Hallett began a low and earnest talk with his partner. It was not pleasing for Ben to listen. More than once he essayed good-humoredly to get up, but could not escape. Then he showed indications of sullenness. Hallett was plainly trying to persuade him into something. It might have been more drinking, or gambling, or staying in town all night, but somehow Brite leaned to neither of these. Presently Ben spoke out quite clearly: "I'm —— if I'm gonna go through with it!"

There was that in his hard look, his angry tone, which warned Brite to interrupt this colloquy. Only on the very moment he saw Ross Hite give Hallett a meaning glance, dominant and bold, though unobtrusive. Brite jerked up, transfixed and thrilling. What was this?

Two of the gamblers left their chairs, at a significant word from Hite, and approached the bar. Whereupon the leader called to Hallett: "Want to sit in for a spell? Two-bit limit."

"Don't care if I do," replied Hallett. "Come on, Ben, le's skin 'em."

"I'm rustlin' back to camp," declared Ben, rising.

Hallett seized him, and pushing a fierce red face close to Ben's, he hissed something inaudible but that was none the less forceful to Brite for that. Chandler reacted with like fierceness, which led, after a short tussle, to free himself, to a lunge and a swing. He knocked Hallett flat, and then crouched, his hand on his gun. But his caution appeared needless. Hallett was not senseless, though he recovered slowly. Chandler glared from him to the gaping Hite, then, wheeling, he hurried out of the saloon. Hite spoke in a low tone to one of his associates, a thick-necked, heavy-visaged man, who arose and hurried out after Chandler.

Hallett got up and joined Hite at the gaming-table, with his hand to his face. He glowered malignantly at the door, as if he expected Chandler to come back. Hite sat shuffling the cards and talked low to Hallett. They had conversed before. Hite dealt cards all around, as if a game were in progress. But the watchful Brite saw that this was only a blind. It ended presently with Hite and Hallett going to the bar, where they drank and left the saloon.

Brite was in a quandary. Some deviltry was stirring. He wanted to hurry out and warn Chandler that he was being followed. On the other hand, he did not care to risk encountering Hite and Hallett. Uncertainty chained him for a few moments, then, realizing that he must get out of the place he pulled his sombrero down and made a break for it. The street appeared dark and empty. The few lights accentuated the blackness. Upon walking down toward the store to call for his purchases, he caught a glimpse of Hite and Hallett crossing the flare from the open doorway. Brite slunk into the shadow off the road. The two men went by, talking low. The listener could not distinguish their words; nevertheless, their tone was subtle, calculating.

When they had re-entered the saloon Brite went on to the hitching-rail to find his horse. He did not feel safe until he was astride in the middle of the road, headed for the upriver trail. He kept keen lookout for Chandler, to no avail. Once he thought he heard the beat of hoofs. Soon he had gained the open range out under the starlight. He had much to ponder over on the way to camp.

CHAPTER 7

THE ROAD out of Austin ended at the river, from which point a trail ran along the bank to the west. The old Colorado was in flood and that hour a magnificent sight, broadly gleaming under the stars, and rolling on in a low, sullen roar. Brite had not yet in his several drives encountered such a flood as this. The herd would have to be put across, if that was humanly possible. The trail drivers' habit was to take any risk rather than have several herds bunch together. More cattle were lost in that kind of a mix-up than in even the big stampedes. There had been instances, however, where stampedes had spelled loss of the whole herds.

Brite had no hope of coming up with Ben Chandler. If that cowboy had gotten to his horse he would be far on the way to camp by this time. Brite had an uneasy conviction that Chandler would be late if he got there at all. And as for Hallett, the chances were that if he showed up in camp it would be at dawn. Brite was keen to impart his information to Shipman and get his angle on it. At the very least Hallett was capable of extreme disloyalty. On the face of it his action looked suspicious.

Brite rode on, slowly over uneven places, at a trot on the long stretches. At the end of an hour or so he began to attend to the lay of the land. Camp ought to be somewhere within a mile. He had no idea where it would be, but the herd could scarcely be missed. And so it proved. He located the cattle by the bawling of cows. They were out of sight back in the gray gloom some distance from the river. A little further on Brite's roving gaze caught the flicker of a camp fire. He rode toward that and soon reached it, to recognize the chuck-wagon.

No one was astir. He sighted several sleepers lying dark and quiet near the wagon. On second thought he decided not to wake any of them. If he was asleep when the guard changed, it would be time enough in the morning. Brite unsaddled and let his horse go. Then finding his bed, he crawled into it and went to sleep.

Brite awoke with a start. It seemed he had not lain there more than a moment. Daylight had come. He heard the ring of an ax. But that hardly had awakened him. Rolling over to face camp, he sat up.

Hallett sat astride his horse, his sullen countenance betraying recent signs of dissipation. Pan Handle and Deuce Ackerman stood by the fire, facing the others. Then Brite espied Texas Joe glaring at the rider. Evidently words had already been exchanged.

"An' where the hell have yu been?" queried Joe.

"Rode to town last night. Didn't mean to stay all night, but I did," replied Hallett, coolly.

"Yu didn't ask me if yu could get off."

"Nope. I just went."

"Ahuh. So I see. Wal, it'll aboot cost yu yore job," drawled Texas.

"Shipman, I don't take much store in this job nohow."

Ackerman made a passionate gesture and stepped forward. "Roy, what's got into yu lately?" he demanded.

"Nothin' 'cept a little rye. I'm fed up on this job, Deuce. Too many steers an' too few drivers."

"Why'n hell didn't yu *say* so? I'm responsible for yu. I picked yu oot for this drive."

"Wal, yu ain't responsible for me no more," replied Hallett, rudely.

"By thunder! I had a hunch yu'd—"

"Shet up, Deuce," interposed Texas, curtly. "I don't hold yu responsible for Hallett. An' I'll do the talkin'."

"Aw, talk an' be damned. Yu're pretty windy, Shipman," returned Hallett, sarcastically, as he lighted a cigarette.

"Shore. An' I may blow on yu if yu keep slingin' yore gab so free. Looks like yu want to quit this job."

"I'd just as leave."

"Wal, yu're off. An' now I'll tell yu somethin'. It's a dirty mean deal yu're givin' Mr. Brite. We're short of hands. An' yore deal has a queer look."

"Has it? Yu ought to know Texas is the place for queer deals."

"Yes, an' for yellow cowhands, I'm ashamed to say," rejoined Shipman, his gaze fixed in piercing intensity upon the rider.

Hallett responded to that significantly. Brite's sharp eyes followed the rider's sweeping survey of Texas Joe. The latter had just rolled out of his blankets. He had one boot on and the other in his hand; he had not buckled on his gun-belt. Hallett slid off his horse to step clear. His face was lowering and his eyes shone like dull coals.

"There's more'n one yellow cowhand in this ootfit," declared Hallett. "An' I'm gonna tell yu what'll make yu take water. It was Ben Chandler who got me to go in town last night. He had some queer deal on. But I didn't know thet then. I went just for fun. An' I stayed to keep Ben from double-crossin' this ootfit. An' I couldn't do it."

"Ahuh," ejaculated Texas, unconvinced, but certainly checked.

Brite meanwhile had pulled on his boots, and now he arose, meaning to interject a few pertinent words into this argument. But he did not get very far. Ben Chandler stalked into their midst, wearing a bloody scarf round his head.

"Tex, he's a —— liar!" he announced.

"Where yu come from?" queried Texas, astounded.

"My bed's over there in the bushes, Tex. I just crawled oot an' happened to heah this confab."

"Wal, by gum! yu aboot got heah in time."

Hallett's appearance and demeanor underwent a drastic change. He first showed complete astonishment and incredulity. These gave way to deeper emotions, sudden anger and fear and hate.

"So *yu* turned up, hey?" he queried, scornfully. "I'll bet yu don't remember yu was drunk last night?"

"Not me, Hallett."

"Huh. I reckon yu'll say yu wasn't in a fight, either."

"I wasn't. Somebody bounced lead off my haid, all right. I rode oot to camp, as yu see, an' now, by Gawd! I'm gonna come clean with what I done an' what I know."

"Shipman, this cowhand was so drunk last night thet he cain't remember shootin' up Snell's place."

"So yu say, Hallett. But Ben has called yu a —— liar. If I know Texans thet calls for a show down."

Brite stepped out from behind the group.

"Tex, I was in Snell's last night. I saw Hallett an' Chandler there. Ben was not drunk."

During the moment of silence that ensued Hallett's face turned a pale, livid hue. He crouched a little, as if about to spring, and with a hand at each hip he slowly edged toward his horse. His mask was off. His motive was to escape. But he looked venomous.

"Shipman, yu squawk again an' I'll bore yu," he rasped, his eyes deadly.

Texas swallowed hard, but he kept a cool silence.

"Bah, yu wouldn't bore nobody," shouted Ben Chandler, passionately. "Yu're a bluff an' a liar. Yu cain't lay this on to me, Hallett."

"Shet up, yu —— fool!" rejoined the rider, backing toward his horse.

"Ben, don't say any more," advised Brite, recognizing what seemed so plain to Shipman.

"But, Mr. Brite, I'm ashamed of what I've done," protested Ben, his face flaming. "An' I want to confess it an' call this lyin' four-flush cowhand to his face before yu all."

"*Wait!*" came in cold, sharp exclamation from Pan Handle Smith.

"Lend me a gun, somebody," hurriedly broke out Chandler.

"Don't nobody move," ordered Hallett, darkly. Evidently he thought he had the situation in hand.

"Hallett, I'm gonna give yu away right heah," shouted Chandler, stridently. "I don't stand for yore dirty deal bein' laid on me."

"Hold yore chin, Chandler," hissed Hallett.

"Hold nothin'. I'm givin' away yore deal with Ross Hite. I'm—"

"Take it then!" As Hallett rang out those words he jerked at his guns. Out they leaped and were flashing up when a heavy shot cracked from behind Brite. Smoke and fire burned his cheek. Hallett's intense action ceased as if he had been struck by lightning. His left eye and temple appeared blotted out in blood. He sank down as if his legs had telescoped under him, his face rooting in the dust, his hands sliding forward, lax and nerveless, to release the guns.

"Boss, I cain't stand around an' see yore good boys bored," Smith's cool, vibrant drawl broke the strained silence.

"So help me—Gawd!" burst out Ackerman, excitedly. "He got it. I was leery aboot him."

"Pan Handle, I'd forgotten yu were aboot," declared Brite, in excited relief. "Thet was wal done. . . . I saw Hallett with Ross Hite last night."

"Ben, come clean with yore story," ordered Texas Joe. "Yu damn near got yore everlastin' then."

"Texas, yu were in line, too. I saw thet in his eye," said Smith, dryly.

"Hah! Mebbe *I* didn't see it," replied Texas, huskily. "Pan, thet's one I owe yu. . . . An' if I ever get caught ag'in withoot my gun!"

"Come on, Ben, get it off yore chest," interposed Brite. Chandler sagged on a pack and dropped his head into his hands.

"Boss, there ain't much to tell," he replied, in a low voice. "Hallett got around me. Persuaded me to go in with him on a deal with Hite. One night back on the Trail, Hite got hold of Hallett when he was standin' guard. Offered him five hundred to leave a breach in the line so Hite an' his ootfit could cut oot a big bunch of stock. . . . First, I—I agreed. I shore was yellow. But it rode me day an' night—thet low-down deal. . . . An' when it come to the scratch I—I weakened. I couldn't go through with it. . . . Thet's all, sir."

"My Gawd, Ben! . . . To think yu'd double-cross us like thet!" exclaimed Deuce Ackerman, wringing his hands. "I never knowed Hallett very good. But *yu*, Ben—why, we've rode together—slept together for years."

"It's done. I've told yu. I'm makin' no excuses—only Roy always had likker to feed me," replied Ben, miserably.

"Ben, in thet case I forgive yu," spoke up Brite, feelingly. "An' I hope to heaven yu never fall down thet way again."

"Thanks, Mr. Brite. I promise yu—I won't," returned Chandler, brokenly.

"Ben, what yu suppose Reddie Bayne will say to this?" queried Texas Joe, in ringing scorn. "She sort of cottoned to yu most of all."

"I've no idee, Tex. But I'll tell her myself."

"Heah she comes with the *remuda*," added Deuce.

"Wonder why Reddie's rustlin' in so pert with all them hawses?" inquired Texas.

"Somebody cover up thet daid man," said Ackerman.

"Not so yu'd notice it, cowboy. Let the little lady take her medicine. Wasn't she kinda sweet on Hallett?" rejoined Texas.

"Not so yu'd notice it, Tex."

No more was said directly. Reddie circled the *remuda* about a hundred yards outside of camp, and came tearing on, her big black horse swinging with his beautiful action. She made the drivers jump before she pulled him to a halt.

"Mr. Brite—Texas—Pan Handle," she panted, her eyes wide with excitement. "I've shore got news. Nichols with his herd of two thousand odd haid is right on our heels. An' followin' him close is Horton in charge of a big herd for Dave Slaughter."

"Thunderation!" ejaculated Brite, throwing up his hands.

Texas Joe used language equally expressive, but hardly for a young girl's ears. Then he pulled on his boot, a task that made him struggle.

"Both drivers sent a man over to tell us to hop the river pronto or they'd be on our heels," went on Reddie, her cheeks aglow. "Oh! Look at the river! It was dark when I went oot. . . . Mr. Brite, it cain't be possible to swim our ootfit across thet flood."

"Reddie, it may not be possible, but we must make the attempt," replied Brite.

"Ah-h!" screamed Reddie, suddenly espying the bloody-faced Hallett on the ground. "What's—happened? Isn't thet Roy?"

"I reckon 'tis, lass."

"Oh! He's daid!"

"So it would seem."

"*Who?*" flashed Reddie, plainly stirred to righteous wrath.

"Reddie, I'm the bad hombre," drawled Pan Handle.

"Yu—yu bloody gunman! Why on earth did yu shoot thet poor boy?"

Pan Handle turned away; Texas dropped his head; Brite watched, but spoke no word. Then Ben looked up.

"Why, Ben! Yu shot too?"

"Only a scratch, Reddie. Yu see it was this way," he began, and bravely outlined his part in the tragedy, scoring Hallett mercilessly, but not sparing himself.

"Ben Chandler!" she cried, in shocked voice. Then as the realization dawned on her and she gazed from Texas to Brite, to the ghastly Hallett, and back with blazing eyes to Ben, the enormity of such an offense seemed to mount prodigiously.

"Yu agreed to double-cross our boss!" she burst out, in withering scorn. "To steal from the hand thet paid yu! Lawd! but thet's a low-down trick!"

"But, Reddie, give the devil his due," interrupted Texas, sharply. "Ben was easy-goin'. He cottoned to Hallett. An' his weakness was the bottle. An' after all he didn't—he couldn't go through with it."

"I don't care a damn," cried Reddie, the very embodiment of ruthlessness. "I'd never forgive him in a million years. . . . Why, the dirty sneakin' cowhand was coaxin' me for a kiss— only two nights ago!"

"Wal, in thet case, it's plumb important to know if Ben got it," drawled Texas.

"Yu bet yore life he didn't," retorted Reddie, her face on fire. "If he had, I'd jump in the river this minute."

"Reddie, I've overlooked Ben's break," interrupted Brite.

"Ahuh. Wal, all I say is yu're a lot of soft melon haids," replied Reddie, with passion. "I'll never overlook it. An' I'll never speak to him again or stand guard near him or—"

"Come an' git it while it's hot," sang Moze.

Texas Joe was studying the river. It was two hundred yards wide at that point, a swirling, muddy, swift flood, carrying logs and trees and driftwood of all descriptions. The current had to be reckoned with. If it carried the stock below a certain point there would almost certainly be a disaster. For two miles below on the opposite side the bank was steep and straight up as far as the eye could see.

"Boss, I swear I don't know aboot it," said Texas. "But we cain't turn back now. The boys have their orders an' heah comes the herd in sight."

"We'll try it, win or lose," replied Brite, grimly, stirred with the gamble.

"Hey, Reddie," yelled Texas, waving his hand. "Come on."

Reddie sent back a pealing cry and wheeled to ride behind the *remuda*. They came on in a bunch, restless and scared, though not wild. Pan Handle rode below the taking-off slope while Texas rode on the upstream side. Reddie drove her mustangs down the slope on a run. Some sheered aside below and above, only to be driven back by Pan Handle and Texas. In a moment more the leaders were pointed and with shrill snorts they plunged into the shallow river. The others followed in good order. Texas rode out with them until the water deepened perceptibly. He was yelling at the top of his voice. Pan Handle shot in front of mustangs leading out of line. Reddie, with her wild cries, drove them off the land, and when her black splashed the water high the leaders had gone off the bar and were swimming.

"WHOOPEE, KID!" yelled Texas, brandishing his sombrero. "Keep upstream yoreself an' let 'em go."

When Texas got back to the shore the rear and broad end of the *remuda* was well out, and the leaders about to hit the swift current.

"Tex, we ought to have gone with her," expostulated Pan Handle, seriously.

"Thet's a grand hawse she's forkin'," said Brite, hopefully.

Texas Joe did not voice his fears or hopes, but he fixed his hawk eyes intently on that marvelous scene of action. Brite's last count had totaled one hundred and seventy-nine mustangs in the *remuda*. The doughty little Spanish stock had no dislike for water. Whistling and rearing, the thickly-bunched body of ponies went off into deep water with the intrepid girl close behind, waving her sombrero and pealing her shrill cry to the skies. How her red-gold head shone in the sunlight! Once the black horse struck out into deeper water, Brite got rid of his fright. He could swim like a duck. Reddie kept him upstream to the left end of the bobbing line. Trees and logs floated into their midst, hampering the mustangs. Here and there one would fetch up to paw over the obstruction, slide off, go under, and come up to go on. Downriver swept those in the current, swiftly leaving those in the still water. But they kept on swimming, and they had plenty of leeway to clear the steep bank far below. Soon the whole *remuda* was in the current, and then the spectacle seemed moving and splendid to Brite. If his heart had not gone out to this orphaned girl long before she braved that flood as a part of her job and scorning help, it would have yielded to her then. The long black patch of lean heads disintegrated and lengthened and curved away downriver, a wild and beautiful sight.

A mile below where Brite and his men watched breathlessly the leaders waded out into shallow water, and the long string curved faithfully toward that point. One by one, in twos and threes, and then in bunches, the mustangs struck the bar, to bob up and heave wet shoulders out, to flounder and splash ashore. Soon the wedge-shaped line thickened as the ponies passed the swift current; and it was only a matter of a few minutes before the last horse was wading out. And Reddie Bayne bestrode him!

"Dog-gone! Thet was great," breathed Texas.

"Shore was a pretty sight," agreed Pan Handle.

"Wal, I reckon we had our fears for nothin'," added Brite.

"Boss, we ought to stop her. It's different comin' this way. Not enough room to allow for thet current," replied Pan Handle, anxiously.

"By Gawd, can yu beat thet!" exclaimed Texas, and whipping out his gun he shot twice. Then he waved his sombrero and yelled in stentorian tones: "GO BACK! GO BACK!"

Reddie heard, for she waved her hand in reply, and she kept coming on. In another moment her horse would be in over his depth, and the swift current, with big muddy waves, right ahead of her. Texas shot all the remaining charges left in his gun, and he aimed so the bullets would hit the water not a great way below Reddie. Then he roared like a giant:

"Turn aboot! Reddie, it ain't the same. . . . DAMN YU—I'M GIVIN' ORDERS!"

Reddie's high-pitched, pealing cry came sweet and wild on the wind.

"Too late, Tex. She's in now."

"Thet's a hawse, Brite. I say let her come," put in Pan Handle.

Texas Joe became as an equestrian statue in bronze. The big muddy waves curled over the neck and head of the black, and up to the shoulders of the girl. They were swept downstream with a rush. But in a hundred yards the powerful horse had left the high waves and was entering the swirling, lesser current. Brite saw the girl check him to let a log pass, and again turn him downstream to avoid a huge mass of green foliage. That horse and rider knew what they were doing. Again he breasted the current with power and worked across. But he would never make the point of bar where the *remuda* had taken off. This worried Brite. Only so few rods below where the high bank began! Already Pan Handle was riding down to head her off. The black, however, was coming faster than the watchers had figured. His lean head jerked high, his wet shoulders followed and with a lunge he was out of the depths into the shallows. He had made it with room to spare. Reddie came trotting ashore.

Here Texas got off his horse, and in the very extreme of rage or exasperation or something, he slammed his sombrero down, he stamped to and fro, he cursed like a drunken cowhand. Plain it was to Brite that his foreman had surrendered to the release of pent-up agony.

"Come back, Pan," Reddie was calling, gaily. "Shore had fun. What yu think of my hawse?"

"He's grand, but yu took a big chance, all for nothin'."

"Yu'll need me an' don't overlook thet," declared Reddie. Then as she joined Pan Handle she espied Texas going through remarkable actions. "Gee! Our Trail boss is riled aboot somethin'."

Soon Reddie rode up to rein in before Texas and Brite. She was something to gaze at. Pale with suppressed excitement, her eyes large and dark and daring, she sat awaiting sentence to fall. She was wringing wet to her neck. Her blouse no longer hid the swelling contour of her breast.

"Sorry I scared yu, gentlemen," she said, a little fearfully. "But yu need me over heah an' I had to come."

"Reddie Bayne, I yelled to yu," began Texas, sternly.

"Shore. I heahed yu."

"I ordered yu back. Did yu heah *thet?*"

"Course I did. Laws! yu'd woke the daid."

"Wal, then, yu have no respect for me as Trail boss of this drive?"

"I wouldn't of turned back for Mr. Brite himself," retorted Reddie, spiritedly. But her face had paled and her eyes were dilating.

"Yu disobeyed me again?" thundered Texas.

"Yes, I did—dammit."

"Not only thet—yu scared us oot of our wits, just to be smart. Yu're a spoiled girl. But yu cain't disorganize this ootfit no more."

"Cain't I?" echoed Reddie, weakly.

"Reddie Bayne, yu listen. Just 'cause yu've got the boss eatin' oot of yore hand—an' 'cause yu're the distractin'est pretty girl—an' 'cause I happen to be turrible in love with yu, don't make no damn bit of difference. Yu're wearin' driver's pants, yu're takin' driver's wages, yu're pullin' driver's tricks."

Texas stepped over to her horse, and flashing a lean, brown hand up, like a striking snake, he clutched the front of her blouse high up and jerked her sliding out of her saddle.

"Oh-h!" cried Reddie, in a strangled voice. "How dare . . . Let me go! Texas, wha—what air yu goin' to—"

"I cain't slug yu one as I would a man—an' I cain't spank yu no more as I once did," said Texas, deliberately. "But I'm shore gonna shake the daylights oot of yu."

Then he grasped her shoulders and began to make good his threat. Reddie offered no resistance whatever. She was as one struck dumb and helpless. Brite grasped that Texas' betrayal of his love had had more to do with this collapse than any threat of corporal punishment. She gazed up with eyes that Texas must have found hard to look into. But soon she could not see, for he shook her until she resembled an image of jelly under some tremendous, vibrating force. When from sheer exhaustion he let her go, she sank down upon the sand, still shaking.

"There—Miss Bayne," he panted.

"Where—Texas Jack?" she gasped, flippantly.

"Gawd only knows," he burst out, helplessly, and began to tear his hair.

"Heah comes the herd!" rang out the thrilling word from Pan Handle.

CHAPTER 8

THE OLD BULL Mossy-horns, huge and fierce, with his massive horns held high, led the spear-shaped mass of cattle over the brow of the long slope. Densely packed, resistless in slow advance, they rolled like a flood of uprooted stumps into sight.

"By all thet's lucky!" yelled Texas, in elation. "Pointed already! If they hit the river in a wedge like thet they'll make Moses crossin' the Red Sea only a two-bit procession."

"Orders, Texas, orders," replied Brite, uneasily. "It won't be long till they roll down on us."

"Got no orders, 'cept keep on the upriver side. For Gawd's sake don't ride in below 'em. The boys have been warned. . . . Ben, yu ride on the wagon. We'll come back an' float it across."

"I will like hell," shouted Ben, derisively, and he ran for a horse to saddle. Brite did likewise, and while he was at the task he heard Texas cursing Chandler for not obeying orders. When he was in the saddle the magnificent herd, a moving, colorful triangle of living beasts, had cleared the ridge, and the leaders were close. Drivers on each side of the wedge rode frantically forward and back, yelling, shooting, waving. But the noise they made came faintly through the din of bawls.

"Reddie," called Texas, earnestly, turning a stern, tight-lipped face and falcon eyes upon the girl, "this heah's new to yu. Yore hawse is a duck, I know, but thet won't save yu if yu get in bad. Will yu stick close to me, so I can tell yu if yu start wrong?"

"I shore will," replied Reddie, with surprising complaisance.

"Boss, yu hang to their heels," concluded Texas, curtly. "Pan, yu drop back aboot halfway. Above all, don't drift into the herd. . . . Come on, Reddie!"

Bad rivers had no terrors for old Mossy-horns. A rod ahead of his herd he ran, nimble as a calf, down the sandy slope, roaring like a buffalo. All sound was deadened in the trampling thunder of the cattle as they yielded to the grade and came on pell-mell. The ground shook under Brite. Nearly five thousand head of stock in a triangular mass sweeping like stampeding buffalo down a long hill! Certain it was that Brite's sombrero stood up on his stiff hair. No daring, no management, no good luck could ever prevent some kind of a catastrophe here.

Texas plunged his horse into the river ahead of Mossy-horns, swinging his lasso round his head and purple in the face from yelling. But Brite could not hear him. Reddie's big black lashed the muddy water into sheets as she headed him after Texas. Then the great wedge, like an avalanche, hit the shallow water with a tremendous sound. Hundreds of cows and steers had reared to ride on the haunches of those ahead, and the mass behind pushed all in a cracking, inextricable mass. But those to the front, once in the water, spread to find room. Herein lay the peril of the drivers, and the dire necessity of keeping the herd pointed as long as possible. Such a feat seemed utterly futile to Brite.

Across the backs and horns Brite espied Ben Chandler on the downstream side of the herd, close to the leaders, and oblivious or careless of danger. Bent on retrieving his fatal error, he had no fear. Soon Brite lost sight of Ben's bloody, bandaged head in the flying yellow spray. Try as he might, he could not see the reckless driver again. San Sabe and Ackerman, both on the downriver side, slowly gave ground toward the rear of the herd, intending to fall in behind as soon as the end passed. Rolly Little, Holden, and Whittaker passed Brite in order, fire-eyed and gaunt with excitement.

When next Brite cast his racing glance out ahead he was in time to see old Mossy-horns heave into deep water. He went clear under, to bob up like a duck and sail into the current. Like sheep the sharply pointed head of the herd piled in after him. Texas went off the bar far upstream, and Reddie still farther. As Brite gazed spellbound the wide rear of the herd, in crashing momentum, rolled past his position. It was time for him to join the drivers. He spurred ahead, and the mustang, excited and fiery, his blood up, would have gone anywhere. Brite had one last look out into the current, where a thousand wide-horned heads swept in a curve down the middle of the river. Then he leaped off the bank and into the water, just even with the upriver end of the herd. Thunder would not have done justice to the volume of sound. It was a strange, seething, hissing, bone-cracking roar. But that seemed to be diminishing as the cattle, hundreds after hundreds, took to the deeper water. Texas and then Reddie passed out of sight. The great herd curved abruptly. Next Ackerman disappeared round the corner, and then Holden. That left only Whittaker in sight and he was sweeping down. Behind the herd Brite espied Bender, who was nearest to him, and certainly a scared young man if Brite had ever seen one.

In a maelstrom of swishing water and twisting bodies the broad rear of the herd smashed off the bar. Magically then all sound ceased. There was left only a low, menacing swish and gurgle of current against Brite's horse. Easily he took to deep water, and Brite felt at once that he had drawn a river horse. What wonderful little animals those Spanish mustangs of Arabian blood!

The scene had immeasurably changed. No white splashes now! A mile of black horned heads, like a swarm of shining bees, sweeping down the river! The terror, the fury of the onslaught upon the flood were no longer evident. There was left only the brilliance, the action, the beauty of this crossing. Brite had never seen anything in his life to compare with it; and once he had seen a million buffalo cross the Brazos River. But they just blotted out the river. Here the wide flood held the mastery. The sun shone down on an endless curve of wet, shiny horns and heads; the sky bent its azure blue down over the yellow river; the green trees of the opposite bank beckoned and seemed to grow imperceptibly closer.

Then Brite's mustang met the swift center current of the river. Here there were smooth waves that rolled over the horse and wet Brite to his shoulders. And he saw that he was going downstream, scarcely quartering at all. The long head of the curve appeared far toward the opposite shore.

To Brite's right the three drivers were working their horses away from the herd, or so it appeared to him. Then Brite saw San Sabe point up the river. A mass of driftwood was coming down on the crest of a rise. What execrable luck to be met by a heavy swell of flood and current in the middle of the river at the most critical time! Brite reined his mustang to avoid the big onrush of driftwood. With hands and feet he pushed aside logs and branches. A whole tree, green and full-foliaged, surrounded by a thick barrage of logs, drifted right into the middle of the swimming herd. This the drivers were unable to prevent. They could only save themselves, which in the case of two of them, at least, was far from easy.

The swift-floating island of débris split the herd, turned the rear half downstream, and heralded certain disaster. Brite saw the broad lane between the two halves, one quartering away toward the north shore, the other swimming with the current. If it kept on downriver it was doomed.

Brite came near to becoming entangled in heavy brush, which he had not seen because his attention was fixed on the separated half of his herd. He owed it to the clever mustang that he was not engulfed. Thereafter he looked out for himself and his horse. All the while they were sweeping down, at the same time gaining toward the shore. Looking back, Brite was surprised to see the chuck-wagon, a dot on the horizon line, a mile back up the river. Ahead and below somewhat less of a distance, began the cutting edge of the steep bank Texas had warned all they must not pass. Standing in his stirrups, Brite made out the head of the herd now beyond the current, well toward the shore. There! A horse and rider had struck shallow water again. That must be Texas.

An eddy caught the mustang and whirled him around and around. Brite was about to slide off and ease the burden, but the horse tore out of the treacherous whirlpool and, thoroughly frightened, he redoubled his efforts. Brite's next discovery was sight of the vanguard of cattle wading out on the wide bar below. Already two of the riders were out. Grateful indeed for so much, Brite turned to see what had become of the endangered half of the herd. They were milling back toward the center of the river. This amazed Brite until he heard the boom-boom-boom of a heavy gun. Chandler, the daredevil, must be on the other side there, driving the cattle again into the current.

The milling circle of horned heads struck into the swift current, to be swept on down the river, past the wading vanguard, surely to slide by that steep corner of bank, beyond which could lie only death. Brite could stand the loss of stock. But a rider sacrificed hurt him deeply. He had never lost one until this drive. Still he clung to hope. Somewhere down around the bend, on one bank or the other, there might be a place for Chandler to climb out.

At this juncture Brite saw another rider, one of the three ahead of him, wade his horse out and go across the bar at a gallop, to mount the bank and ride swiftly along its edge, the mane and tail of the mustang flying wildly in the wind. He did not recognize either Texas' or Pan Handle's horse, so that rider must have been Ackerman, speeding to give aid to Chandler.

When Brite at last waded out on the bar there were only a few hundred head of stock behind and below him. They were wearied, but safe, as all had found footing. Three riders were waiting. Texas and Reddie had vanished. Bender, Pan Handle, and San Sabe were working out behind the cattle, and all three were facing downriver, no doubt watching the cattle that had been swept away.

Presently Brite joined the six drivers on the bar and surely encountered a disheartened group of cowboys. Pan Handle was the only one to present anything but a sad countenance.

"Mr. Brite, we had bad luck," he said. "The herd split in the middle an' the back half went downriver taking Chandler with it. Our good luck is thet more of us might have been with him."

"Hell with—the cattle!" panted Brite. "Any hope for Chandler?"

"Shore. He's a gamblin' chance to get oot somewhere. But I wouldn't give two-bits for the cattle. Ackerman is ahaid, keepin' up with them. Texas followed with Reddie."

"What'll we do?"

"Make camp heah on the bank in the grove. Plenty of grass. The stock shore won't move tonight."

"Thet chuck-wagon's to be got over. An' I wouldn't give much for it."

"Boss, thet wagon was made to float," said San Sabe. "It's got a double bottom of heavy planks. Don't worry none aboot our grub."

They rode up the sandy slope to a level bank of timber and grass, an ideal place to camp. The horses were heaving after their prolonged exertions. "Get off an' throw yore saddles, boys," said Brite, suiting action to his words. "Somebody light a fire so we can dry oot."

A little later, while Brite was standing in his shirt sleeves before a fire, Texas Joe and Reddie rode into camp.

"We cain't send good money after what's lost," he said, philosophically. "I reckon Ben is gone, an' there's only one chance in a thousand for thet bunch of cattle. We gotta look after what's left an' fetch Moze across. . . . Reddie, yore hawse ain't even tired. Wal, I never seen his beat. But yu don't weigh more'n a grasshopper. Let San Sabe have him to help me with the wagon."

"Shore. But I'd like to go," replied Reddie, eagerly.

"My Gawd! air yu still wantin' more of thet river?" queried Texas, incredulously.

"Oh, I was havin' a grand time until the herd split. . . . Poor Ben! If he's lost I'll never forgive myself. I—I was mad an' I said too much."

"Wal, yu shore said a heap," drawled Texas. "If yu'd said as much to me I'd drowned myself pronto."

"Don't—don't say it—it might be my fault," wailed Reddie, almost weeping.

"No kid. I was only foolin'. Ben was just makin' up for the wrong he did us. An' he's shore square with me."

"Oh, I hope an' pray he got oot," rejoined Reddie as she dismounted.

San Sabe removed her saddle and put his own on the black. Then he followed Texas, who was already far up the bar, making for the bend of the river, from which point they would head across. It was a somber group that stood drying out around the blazing fire. Reddie looked sick and wretched. Her gaze ever strayed down the stream, where the muddy current swept out of sight.

Texas and San Sabe gave their comrades some bad moments when even their heads disappeared in the waves, but it turned out they crossed safely. Meanwhile Moze had driven the chuck-wagon down to meet them. It was too far for Brite to see distinctly, but he knew that the riders would tie on to the wagon with their ropes and encourage and help the team. With little ado they were off and soon in the water. Great furrows splashed up as the wagon plowed in. Brite had his doubts about that venture, and when horses and wagon struck off the bar into deep water, to be swept down by the current, he expected it was but a forerunner of more misfortune. The wagon floated so high that part of the bed and all the canvas showed above the water. It sailed down like a boat and gradually neared the shore, at last to cross out of the current, into the slack water, and eventually to the bar. He had suffered qualms for nothing. Moze, however, although he was a black man, looked a little pale about the gills. The usual banter did not appear to be forthcoming from the dejected drivers, an omission Moze was quick to catch.

"Men, I reckon yo-all will hev to dry yo beds," he said, his big eyes rolling. "I packed them under de grub."

"Aw, my tobacco!" wailed Deuce.

"Niggah, I ooght to petasterize yu," added Whittaker, severely. "I had my only extra shirt in my bed."

"What is dis petasterizin'?" asked Moze, beginning to throw off the packs. "Yo-all is a glum ootfit."

"Moze, we lost half my stock an' Ben Chandler, too," replied Brite.

"Lawd Amighty! I done reckoned trubble when I seen dis ribber."

That was the end of jocularities, as well as other conversation. The hour was approaching noonday, an astounding fact to Brite. If it had been at all possible for the stock to move on for several hours more, he would have ordered it. But cattle and horses alike were spent.

The herd following Brite's would bed down that night on the south shore, and cross in the morning. It was too close for comfort. But the cattleman could not see how that might be avoided. Presently the silent drivers stirred to the advent of Deuce Ackerman riding into sight up the river bank. His posture and the gait of his horse were significant of what had happened. Deuce rode into camp, haggard of face, his garb mud from head to foot, and he all but fell out of the saddle.

"Come to the fire, Deuce. I'll throw yore leather," said Little, solicitously.

"Mr. Brite, I have to report thet Chandler was drowned," he said.

"So we all reckoned," returned Brite, resignedly.

"Stake me to a drink, if yu want to heah aboot it."

But Ackerman did not soon begin his narrative. Finally he began: "Wal, I rode along the bank an' ketched up with the cattle. An' there was thet idjit Chandler hangin' along the leads, slappin' his rope ahaid of him. He hadn't given up pointin' thet bunch of longhorns to this shore. I yelled an' yelled my lungs oot, but he never heahed me. After a while, though, he seen me. I waved him oot of the river an' he paid no attention. He kept on, the herd kept on, an' so did I. I'd run a coupla miles, I reckon, before I ketched up. An' we wasn't long travelin' another mile or so. Then I seen far ahaid on my side a wide break in the bank. Dam' if Chandler hadn't seen it, too. An' he lashed them lead cattle like a fiend from hell. He beat them farther an' farther to this side. An' I'm a son-of-a-gun if he didn't work 'em over to shore just when the current had carried 'em to this break. The water close in was shallow too. Once the leads hit bottom they come to life, an' my! how they swarmed off thet bar!"

"Yu mean to tell us Ben drove them cattle oot on dry land?" demanded Texas, incredulously.

"Dam' if he didn't! But his hawse was all in, an' on account of the cattle blockin' his way he couldn't get oot of deep water. So he was carried on downriver, past the break. I rode on for all I was worth, yellin' to Ben to hang on. By this time he was on his hawse's neck. But for the current thet little dogie would have sunk. He could hardly swim a lick. I seen where the swift water run close under the bank, an' I made for thet place. Shore enough Ben swept in close, an' I leaped off with my rope. Fust throw I hit Ben clean with my loop. But it was too small. It didn't ketch, an' he missed it. I kept runnin' an' throwin', but no good. The bank was awful steep an' crumbly. Then I broke off a section an' damn near fell in myself. Seein' thet wasn't gettin' us nowhere, I run ahaid a good ways an' waited for Ben to float by a likely place. . . . But jest as they was aboot to come within reach of my rope the game little pony sunk. Ben made a feeble effort to stay up. He seen me. He opened his mouth to call. . . . Only a gurgle! His mouth filled—an' the water come up over his bloody face. My Gawd! There he floated, a hand up, then his back, his haid onct more—an' thet was the last."

Reddie burst into tears and ran from the camp fire. Texas knelt to throw bits of wood upon the coals.

"Ross Hite or no—Ben shore paid for his fling," he muttered to himself.

"Ackerman, thet was a terrible thing," declared Brite, badly upset.

" 'Most as tough on me as Ben," said the cowboy, huskily. "I'll never forget his eyes. At the last he wanted to be saved. I seen thet. When I first come up to him he didn't care a dam'. All he wanted was to get the haid of thet string of cattle pointed to land. An' he done it. Never did I see the like of thet."

Texas rose dark and stern. "I'll get me a hawse an' ride down to locate thet bunch. How far, Deuce, aboot?"

"I don't know. Four miles, mebbe."

Shipman trudged wearily away, despite Brite's call for him to rest awhile longer. Perhaps Texas wanted to be alone, a disposition more than one of the drivers soon manifested. Reddie had evidently hidden in the green brush. Being a woman, she would take this tragedy hardest to heart, believing she had been partly to blame.

"Then, judgin' from what I've heahed at Dodge an' Abilene, we're just gettin' a taste of real trail drivin'," said Pan Handle. "It's a gamble an' the cairds air against us."

"I take the blame," spoke up Brite, feelingly. "It was my hawgishness. Half my herd would have been plenty to start with."

"We doan' know how things ever will come oot," declared Whittaker, in his quaint drawl.

Moze called them to eat, to which they answered eagerly, if not quickly. Reddie Bayne did n t c me in. And Brite decided he would let her alone awhile longer, until the drivers had gone. But even after eating they remained in camp, still damped by the misfortune, no doubt waiting for Texas to return with orders.

"He ooght to be back," complained Deuce. "Hadn't I better have a look?"

"Wal, yu'd likely miss him, Deuce."

They conjectured as to the probable movements of the separated halves of the herd, gradually gathering conviction among themselves that all was well. The hot fire dried Brite's clothes and made him drowsy. Lying down in the sand under a tree, he fell from rest to slumber. Upon awakening, Brite was chagrined to note that the sun was westering. Pan Handle, Reddie Bayne, Rolly Little, and Texas were in camp, a stone-faced quartet. The other drivers were gone.

"Ha, Tex, yu back?" queried Brite, sitting up with stiffened joints.

"Yeh, boss, I'm back," replied the cowboy, wearily.

"How far's the split half of the herd?"

"Wal, countin' the half hour I been heah, I'd say aboot ten miles to the northard."

"Wha—at?"

"Shore, an' travelin' to beat hell!"

Brite sensed more tragedy, and braced himself to continue coolly: "How come?"

"Boss, I plumb hate to tell yu," rejoined Texas, miserably. "Reddie, clap yore hands over yore ears. I gotta let go! . . . Of all the — — — luck any — ootfit ever had we've had the wust. I'm seein' red. I'm madder'n any rattler-bitten coyote yu ever seen. I gotta get pizen drunk or kill—"

"Hell! yu're not *tellin'* me anythin'," interrupted Brite, testily.

"Tell him, Pan."

"Mr. Brite, it's an unheahed-of deal an' I'm not agreed with Texas aboot its bein' so bad as he reckons," complied Pan Handle. "Texas rode oot to get a line on thet split herd an' couldn't see it nowhere. So he rode up a high ridge an' soon spotted yore cattle. They was travelin' north at a good lick in front of aboot ten drivers."

"Ross Hite!" thundered Brite, in a sudden rage, leaping up.

"So Tex reckoned. An' as was right an' proper he rode back to tell us. We been havin' a pow-wow aboot it. Tex was riled somethin' fierce. He wanted to take fresh hawses an' ride oot to shoot up thet stampedin' gang of Hite's. So did all the boys except me. I was against thet an' the more I reckon the stronger I am set."

"I agree with yu, Pan Handle," rejoined Brite, at once. "We air let down. If we chase Hite an' pick a fight, win or lose, some of us air goin' to get killed. An' we leave what's left of my herd heah to mix in with the herds comin' behind. No! Let's stick with the bird in the hand."

"By all means," agreed Pan Handle, with satisfaction. "Now if yu follow me on thet maybe yu'll see what I see. Ross Hite cain't get so far ahaid thet we cain't ride him down in a day. Let him go. Keep close on his trail aboot a day behind. He's drivin' our cattle for us. But he's the damnedest fool in this range. There's no sale for cattle short of Dodge. He'll take thet branch of the Chisholm Trail, because it's much farther to Abilene. An' the night before we expect him to ride into Dodge I'll take a fast hawse, cut off the trail, an' be there to meet him."

"Boss, it's a good idee, except Pan wants to go it alone, an' I won't stand for thet," interposed Texas.

"Meet Hite?" echoed Brite.

"Thet's what I said," concluded Pan Handle, tersely.

"Wal, Pan, on the face of it, thet's hardly fair to yu," replied Brite, ponderingly. He understood perfectly. Pan Handle Smith chose to attempt this single-handed. It was the way of the real gunman to seek the dramatic, to take advantage of the element of surprise, to subject no other to risk than himself.

"Boss, on second thought I stand by Pan," spoke up Texas. "But thet's the last way to get our cattle back. Shorer'n Gawd made little apples somethin' else will turn up. We got a dozen more rivers to cross, an' redskins to meet, an' buffalo. Buffalo by the million! This hombre Hite is no trail driver. His ootfit air a lot of hawse thieves, some of them gray-haided. They cain't drive cattle. Hite is plumb loco. He reckons he'll clean up aboot thirty thousand dollars. An' thet'll hold him to the trail an' the herd. He's got no more chanct to get thet money than a snowball has in hell!"

CHAPTER 9

THE NIGHT FELL warm, with a hint of summer in its balmy sweetness; the stars shone white through the foliage of the trees; the river gurgled and murmured along the shore, without any of the menace that it had seemed to have by day; the frogs trilled lonesome music. And all the vast range was locked in silence and slumber. Yet even then thieves and death were at work.

Brite felt all this while trying to woo sleep. But it would not come. Reddie had made her bed near him in the shadow of the heavy bushes. Presently a tall, dark form stalked between Brite and the pale starlight. Texas Joe was roaming around camp, as usual, in the dead of night, perhaps about to call change of guards. But he stealthily went around Brite to halt beside Reddie, where after a moment he knelt.

There followed a moment of silence, then Reddie murmured, drowsily: "Huh? . . . Who is it?"

"Ssssch! Not so loud. Yu'll wake the boss up. . . . It's only Tex."

"Yu again! My Gawd! man, cain't yu even let me sleep?" returned Reddie, in a disgusted whisper.

"I heahed yu cryin' an' I wanted to come then. But I waited till everybody was sunk."

"What yu want?"

"I'd like to talk to yu a bit. Never have no chance in daytime. An' since I run into Ben sittin' beside yore bed thet night I haven't had no nerve."

"I hadn't noticed thet," whispered Reddie, with faint sarcasm. "Wal, if yu *must* talk, move over a little. Yu're settin' aboot on top of me."

"Ben was turrible in love with yu, too, wasn't he?"

"Texas, I don't know aboot him bein' *too*, as yu call it, but I reckon he was. Anyway he swore it. I don't trust no cowboys."

"So I seen. Reddie, they ain't all bad. . . . Was yu sweet on Ben?"

"No, of course not."

"But yu let him kiss yu!"

"I did nothin' of the sort. Thet night yu caught him it wasn't no fault of mine. He grabbed me. At thet he never kissed my mouth."

"Aw! I reckoned different. I'm sorry."

A long silence followed. Brite had a desire to cough or roll over, or do something to acquaint the young couple that he was awake. He had also a stronger desire, however, not to do it. The river murmured on, the frogs trilled, the leaves rustled. There seemed to be something big and alive and wonderful abroad in the night.

"Wal, thet all yu wanted to say?" resumed Reddie.

"No. I always have a lot to say. An' I cain't say it," whispered Texas, sadly. "I feel awful sorry aboot Ben. He was no good, Reddie. I've knowed thet for some time. But he shore died grand."

"Don't make me cry again."

"Wal, did Ben ask yu to marry him?"

"Land's sake, no!" exclaimed Reddie, with an embarrassed little laugh.

"It's not so funny. Haven't any of this ootfit asked yu?"

"Not thet I heahed, Texas," replied Reddie, almost with a titter.

"Funny!"

"Thet's not so funny. They shore ought to have."

"Wal, I'm gonna ask yu someday."

"Texas, yu're oot of yore head!"

"Shore I reckon I am. But it's the first time—aboot a girl."

"Taffy! What do yu think I am?"

"Honest Injun, kid. Since I growed up I've been too busy ridin' range an' dodgin' gun-slingers to get moony over girls."

"Wal, I'll bet yu've mixed up with bad women, like Mr. Brite tells me Dodge is full of."

"Ump-umm, Reddie. If I ever did I was so drunk I never knowed it. But I don't believe I ever did, 'cause somebody would have told me."

"I'd like to believe yu, Texas."

"Wal, yu can. I wouldn't lie to any girl, much less yu."

"But yu lied to me when yu swore yu knowed I was a girl. All the time yu swore yu knowed."

"Reddie, I wasn't lyin'."

"Shore yu was. All yu wanted was to pretend to have the edge on the other boys. I was on to yu, Texas."

"Wal, I'll tell yu, if yu swear yu'll forgive me."

"Forgive yu! Say, cowboy, yu're talkin' strange."

"Wal, I feel strange. But I reckon I better confess."

"Texas Jack, don't confess anythin' thet'll make me hate yu."

"Yu're forgettin' aboot thet Texas Jack handle. I've warned yu. . . . Reddie, since way back on the trail I've knowed yu was a girl. Before I killed Wallen. Do yu reckon I could have shot him so quick—if I hadn't known?"

"Damn yu! I'm scared. . . . How'd yu know?"

"Reddie, yu remember thet creek bottom where we camped. Prettiest camp so far. Willows an' pecans an' blackberries an' flowers hangin' over thet clear creek. It was aboot sunset. I'd been below an' took a short cut to camp. The brush was awful thick. I heahed a floppin' aboot in the water an' I sneaked up to peep through the green."

"Yu—yu. . . . Tex Shipman!" she cried, in a low, strangled voice.

"Yes. I seen yu bathin'. . . . Only seen the—the upper part of yu. . . . Don't be so awful ashamed, Reddie. . . . Just one peep—then I fell down an' lay there as if I was shot. Then I crawled away. . . . After thet I was never the same."

"I—I should think not. . . . But why did yu ever tell me? . . . Yu're no gentleman. . . . An' I do hate yu now!"

"Wal, I cain't help thet. But I don't believe yu, Reddie. There's no sense or justice in hatin' me. For Gawd's sake, why?"

"Yu've been so mean to me."

"Mean! Say, I had to fool everybody. I had to keep yu an' all our ootfit from findin' oot I'd gone plumb, starin', stark mad aboot yu. So I picked on yu."

"Tex Shipman—thet time yu spanked me—did yu know I was a girl then?"

"So help me Gawd—I did."

"Now! I'll never look at yu again."

"But, Reddie, don't yu want a man to be honest?"

"Not—not when he knows too much."

"I had to tell yu thet before I could ask yu to marry me. An' I'm doin' thet now."

"Doin' what?" she flashed, in a full, thrilling whisper.

"Askin' yu to marry me."

"Oh, indeed! Yu think I'm a poor waif of the range? No kin, no home, no friends. Just an outcast."

"Yu come to us a pretty lonely kid, if I recollect. Reckon yu've had a tough time. I shore wonder how yu got through so good an' fine a girl."

"Yes, it is a wonder, Texas. But I did, thank Gawd. An' now I'm the happiest girl alive."

"Reddie! Has my askin' yu to—to be my wife—has thet anythin' to do with how yu feel?"

"Wal, it's a satisfaction, Tex," she replied, demurely. "Cowboy, yu don't know how high yu're aspirin'. I *was* a waif but *now* I'm an heiress!"

"What? . . . Yu're a locoed kid."

"Texas, I'm Mr. Brite's adopted daughter!" she announced, proudly.

"Aw! . . . Honest, Reddie?"

"Cross my heart. I don't know how it all come aboot. I don't care. I only know I'm happy—the first time in my whole life!"

"Dog-gone!—I'm shore glad. It's aboot the best thet could

happen to yu. The boss is a fine old Southern gentleman. A real Texan. He owns a big ranch ootside Santone. . . . Yu'll have a home. Yu'll be rich some day. Yu'll have all the hawses any girl could set her heart on. . . . An' beaus, too, Reddie!"

"Beaus? Oh, dear! How—how funny! Me, Reddie Bayne, heah sleepin' in my overalls!"

"Yep, an' them beaus mean Tex Shipman an' all his gun-totin' breed can go hang. But no one of them will ever love yu so turrible as Tex Shipman."

"Faint heart never won fair lady, Texas Jack," she taunted.

Then followed a sudden low thump, a convulsive wrestling, and the soft sound of a kiss.

"Oh! Don't—yu—yu—"

"I told yu," he whispered, passionately. "I warned yu. . . . An' now I'll get even. I swore once thet if yu didn't quit callin' me Texas Jack I'd make yu call me Jack darlin'. An' I'm shore goin' to."

"Yu air not," flashed Reddie, with heat. But she was frightened.

"I shore am."

"If yu try thet again I—I'll scream."

"I'll bet yu won't. I'll risk it, anyway."

"Texas, yu're hurtin' me, yu big brute. . . . Don't press me down so hard. . . . Yore hands. . . . Ah-h!"

"There!—Now say Jack darlin'—or I'll kiss yu again."

"I—won't—I won't—I—"

A tense interval elapsed, significant with faint straining sounds.

"Wal, I had to take two—then. . . . My Gawd! I'm ruined! . . . I never knowed what a kiss was. . . . Now yu can hold off sayin' Jack darlin' as long as yu want."

Evidently she fought fiercely for a moment, to judge by the commotion, then she gasped and gave up.

"Please, Tex. . . . This is no way to treat a girl. . . . Oh-h! . . ."

"I can do thet all night," replied Texas, his full whisper poignant and rich. "Air yu goin' to say Jack darlin'?"

"But, man, thet won't mean nothin'!" she exclaimed, wildly.

"Very wal." And he kissed her again and again. Brite heard the slight, sibilant, thrilling contacts of lips, and he was living this romance with them both.

"Oh!—yes—yes—I give—in," she found voice to say. "Let me —breathe!"

"Not till yu say it. Pronto now, unless—"

"Devil! . . . Jack—dar-lin'!"

"Thanks, Reddie. An' heah's for givin' in! . . . Next time yu'll ask *me*."

Evidently he released her and sat up, breathing hard.

"I'm sorry to offend yu. Yet I'm glad, too," he said, no longer in a whisper. " 'Cause yu're oot of a pore trail driver's reach now, Miss Reddie Bayne Brite. Yu been kissed an' yu called me darlin'. Thet'll have to do me all my life."

He stood up. His tall, dark form crossed the pale starlight glow under the trees.

"But I didn't mean it—Texas Jack!" she ended, in a whisper that was not comprehensible to Brite. Manifestly it was no more comprehensible to Texas, and vastly provocative, for he rushed away like the wind into the darkness.

After he had gone, Reddie sighed and sighed, and rolled restlessly in her bed, and murmured to herself. Then she quieted down. Brite knew when she dropped to sleep again. The moan of the river and lament of the coyotes and the song of insects once again became unbroken. He lay there amused and stirred at the eternal feminine that had so easily cropped out in Reddie Bayne. She might be a waif, used to male attire for years, and accustomed to the uncouth and rough life of the range, but she had a woman's heart, a woman's subtlety and secretiveness. Brite could not tell now whether she was in love with Shipman or not. He was sure of one thing, however, and that was that she would make Texas the most wretched cowboy on all the plains before she capitulated.

At last Brite slept. Call to breakfast awakened him. San Sabe, Whit, and Less Holden were sitting cross-legged on the ground, eating. Reddie was gone and her bed had been rolled, and was now leaning on the hub of the front wagon-wheel. The morning was fine, but the cowboys appeared oblivious to that. While Brite ate, Reddie rode in bareback, driving some fresh mounts.

"Boys, where's the trail from heah?" queried Brite, remembering the drive had crossed the river above the town.

"Deuce said aboot four below," replied Holden. "Fact is, it come across where Ben haided the cattle. An', Mr. Brite, it's shore interestin' to know Deuce forgot to tell us aboot the boat."

"Boat?" echoed the boss.

"Yes. He seen a boat across the river, on the town side. An' he an' Tex reckon whoever stole our cattle came over in thet boat an' swum their hawses."

Brite felt an eagerness to be on the move again. He had resigned himself to a loss of half his herd; nevertheless the deal rankled in him, and no doubt would grow into a bitter defeat. It was one thing to decide upon a wise and reasonable course after being robbed, and an entirely different one to follow it. These cowboys would obey orders, but they would never accept such a loss. Texas Joe and Pan Handle were the wrong men to rob.

By sunup the drivers were on the trail again, with the cattle stepping along around two miles an hour. Moze had caught up and had stopped to let his horses graze.

That day passed without any of the drivers catching a glimpse of the half of the herd which had been driven on ahead.

"Wal, if I know cow tracks, thet ootfit lost instead of gained on us last night," said Texas. "They cain't drive a herd. Funny thing, boys. Yu know we have aboot all the mean old mossyhorns in thet back half. An' Ross Hite had the bad luck to get them. Pan's got the deal straight. The d—— stampeder will do our work for us an' get shot full of holes for his pains."

Camp had lost its jollity. A different spirit prevailed. These drivers reacted visibly to betrayal by two of their number, to the death of the traitor, to the ordeal of the flood, and Chandler's fate. Loss of half their herd had made them grim and stern. Excepting Texas Joe, who had changed most overnight, they all lent a hand to Reddie wherever possible, but the fun, the sentiment, the approach to love-making, had vanished. Texas had scarcely ever a word for Reddie, or anybody else. Instinctively they all began to save themselves, as if what had happened was little compared with what was to come.

But Round Top and Brushy Creek camps, and Cornhill, Noland Creek, Loon River, Bosque River, were reached and passed with only minor mishaps. Once from a swell of the vast prairie, which had taken them all day to surmount, San Sabe pointed out the stolen half of Brite's herd, only a long day ahead. They knew for a certainty now that Ross Hite was driving those cattle. At Belton, a little ranch settlement on Noland Creek, Hite had left behind enough to identify him.

Rains had been few and far between, but enough to keep the creeks fresh and the waterholes from drying up. Much anticipation attended their arrival at the great Brazos River. Here Brite expected another flood and strenuous crossing, but was agreeably disappointed. The Brazos had been up recently, but now offered no obstacle. They camped on the north shore, where a fine creek came in, and struck again, for the first time in days, an abundance of game. Turkeys and deer were so tame they scarcely moved out of the way of horse or man. The young turkeys were now the size of a hen chicken, and made a most toothsome dish.

Brite calculated that at this rate of travel they would drive the distance in ninety days. A third of that time had passed, and more. But he had lost track of the date. Four more days brought them halfway to Fort Worth from the Brazos; and it was noticeable that the drivers began to respond to the absence of the evil that had dogged their trail.

Fort Worth at last! It might have been a metropolis for the importance it held for the drivers. But there were only a few buildings, a store and saloon, and not many inhabitants. Texas Joe bedded down the herd outside of town, wholly unaware that the other half of Brite's cattle were not far away this night. That news was brought to camp by San Sabe, who was the only one of the four boys sober enough to tell anything straight. That was some time before midnight. In the morning

Texas Joe hauled these recalcitrants out for what Brite anticipated would be dire punishment.

"Fellars, yu laid down on me last night," said Texas, soberly, with not a trace of rancor. "Yu got drunk. If yu hadn't an' had rustled back heah pronto with this news aboot our cattle—why, we'd all sneaked over while Hite's ootfit was in town, an' drove 'em back. I found oot this mawnin' thet Hite drove away early in the evenin'. He got wind of us."

All the cowboys, one of whom was Less Holden, showed shame and consternation at their delinquency.

"Wal, it's too late now for this chance," went on Texas. "But I'm askin' yu to let this be the last till we get to Dodge. There we can get awful drunk. I shore wanted some drinks. I'd like to forget, same as yu. When we cross Red River, then we'll have hell. Them infernal lightnin' storms thet play hob with cattle. An' the buffalo. We'll shore meet up with them. So, even if we miss the Comanches, we'll shore have hell enough."

"Tex, we won't take another drink till the drive's over," announced Ackerman. "I promise yu. I'll cowhide any fellar who tries to break thet."

"Fine, Deuce. I couldn't ask no more," replied Texas, satisfied.

Before the drivers broke camp that morning a company of soldiers passed, and a sergeant halted for a chat with Brite. Disturbing information was elicited from this soldier. The detachment was under Lieutenant Coleman of the Fourth Cavalry, and was on the way to Fort Richardson, where a massacre of settlers had been perpetrated by Comanches not long before. Comanches and Kiowas were on the warpath again and raiding all the wide territory between the Brazos and Red Rivers. Buffalo herds were to be encountered frequently south of the Red, and north of it, according to Coleman, were packed almost solid clear to the Canadian River. Beef- and hide-hunters, rustlers and horse thieves, were also following the buffalo.

"Lieutenant Coleman advises you stay at the fort for a

while," concluded the sergeant. "There's only one herd ahead of yours. An' that outfit wouldn't listen to reason."

"Ross Hite's ootfit?"

"Didn't get the name. Tall sandy-complexioned Texan with deep slopin' lines in his face an' narrow eyes."

"Thet's Hite," confirmed Pan Handle.

"He'll run plump into everything this range can dig up. You'd better hold up for a spell."

"Impossible, Sergeant," replied Brite. "There air two big herds right behind us. One an' two days. An' then six days or so more there's no end of them. Two hundred thousand haid of stock will pass heah this summer."

"My word! Is it possible? Well, a good many of them will never get to Kansas. . . . Good-by and good luck."

"Same to yu," called Texas, and then turned to his outfit with fire in his eyes. "Yu all heahed, so there's nothin' to say. We'll go through shootin'. Boss, I reckon we better load up with all the grub an' ammunition we can pack. No store till we get to Doan's, an' they're always oot of everythin'."

Brite's outfit of drivers went on, prepared for the worst. And again they had days of uneventful driving. At Bolivar, a buffalo camp, the Chisholm Trail split, the right fork heading straight north to Abilene, and the left cutting sharply to the northwest. The Abilene branch was the longer and safer; the Dodge branch the shorter, harder, and more hazardous, but it ended in the most profitable market for cattle and horses.

"Brite, do yu reckon yu can find oot which fork Hite took? A coupla drinks will do it. Shore this ootfit heah might be just as bad as Hite's. All the rustlers an' hawse thieves call themselves hide-hunters."

"Yu go, Tex. I'll lend yu my flask," replied the boss.

"All right. Come with me, Pan Handle," replied Texas.

"Let me go, too," spoke up Reddie.

"What! Why yu want to go?"

"I'd like to see somebody. I'm tired of all yu cross men."

"Ahuh. Yu want to meet some new men? Wal, it's nix

on thet. The Brite ootfit wants to hang on to yu, seein' we done it so far."

The afternoon was not far spent and camp had been selected on a stream that ran on into Bolivar, some little distance east. There was a beautiful big swale for the stock to graze on without strict guarding. It was the second best site so far on the drive. The stream was lined with trees that hid the camp from the little settlement. Brite proposed to Reddie that they go fishing. This brought smiles to the girl's discontented face. Whereupon Brite procured fishing lines and hooks from his bag, and cutting poles, proceeded to rig them while Moze was instructed to get grubs, worms, or grasshoppers for bait.

Then followed a happy and a successful hour for Brite. Reddie was a novice, but wildly enthusiastic and excruciatingly funny. The climax of this little adventure came when Reddie hooked a heavy catfish which not only could she not hold, but that was surely pulling her down the bank on the stout line and pole. She was thoroughbred enough not to let go, but she yelled lustily for help. It was one of Brite's rules never to aid a fisherman; in this instance, however, he broke it and helped Reddie hold the big fish until it became exhausted. They landed it, and adding it to their already respectable string, hurried back to camp in triumph. Moze was delighted. "I sho's glad of dis. Yu-all beat the niggahs fishin'. Mebbe a change from dat meat will be good."

Before supper was ready Texas Joe and Pan Handle returned, to Brite's great relief.

"Wal, boss, Hite took the Dodge trail yestiddy aboot noonday," said Texas, cheerfully. "He's ahaid of us right smart, but accordin' to them buff hunters he'll be stuck in no time."

"Wal, thet's good news, I guess," replied Brite, dubiously. "What yu mean—stuck?"

"Wal, if nothin' else stops Hite, the buffalo shore will."

"Then they'll stop us, too."

"We don't give a damn so long's we get our cattle back. Thet Hite deal shore went against the grain for me."

"A rest wouldn't hurt us none," rejoined Brite.

"Reckon this'll be the last peaceful rest in camp we'll get," drawled Texas. Then he espied Moze cleaning the fish. "Dog-gone! Where'd yu get them?"

"Miss Reddie an' the boss snaked dem oot of de crick dere."

"Did yu ketch any?" Texas asked Reddie.

"Shore. I got three—an' thet big one."

"No! Yu never pulled thet oot."

"I had to have help. Took us both. Gee! it was fun. Thet darn catfish nearly pulled me in. I yelled an' yelled for Mr. Brite. But he only laughed an' never came till I was shore slidin' in."

"Ahuh. Yu like to fish?"

"Like it? I *love* it. Nobody ever took me before. Oh, I've missed so much. But I'll learn or die."

Texas Joe nodded his head gloomily over what seemed a fatalistic, inevitable fact.

"Who ever heahed of a girl lovin' to fish? Dog-gone yu. Reddie Bayne, yu're just the natural undoin' of Tex Shipman. Of all things I love in this turrible Texas it's to set in the shade along the bank of a creek an' fish, an' listen to the birds an' all, an' watch the minnows, an'—an'—"

"Gosh! Mr. Brite, our Texas Jack is a poet," burst out Reddie, gleefully.

There were indications, for a moment, of a cessation of hostilities between Reddie and Texas. They looked at each other with absorbing eyes.

"Tex, I thought yu'd stopped her Texas Jackin' yu," drawled Brite, with a sly glance at Reddie. She blushed for the first time in many days.

"Reckoned I had. Wal, I'll have to see aboot it," replied Texas, leaving no doubt in Reddie's mind what he meant. Wherefore the truce was ended.

Toward the close of their supper two strangers approached in the dusk. Texas greeted them, thereby relieving Brite's concern. The visitors proved to be hide-hunters stationed at Bolivar.

"We been lookin' over yore herd," announced the taller of the two, undoubtedly a Texan. "An' we want to inform yu thet Hite's cattle wore two of yore brands."

"No news to us. But yore tellin' us makes a difference. Much obliged. It happened this way," rejoined Texas, and related the circumstances of the fording of the Colorado and loss of half the herd.

"Then yu needn't be told no more aboot Ross Hite?" queried the hide-hunter, in a dry tone.

"Nope. Nary no more."

"Wal, thet's good. Now heah's what Pete an' me come over to propose. We want to move our ootfit up somewheres between the Little Wichita an' the Red, whar we heah thar's a million buffs. An' we'd like to go with yu thet fer."

Texas turned to interrogate his boss with a keen look.

"Men, thet depends upon Shipman," returned Brite. "We shore could use more hands, if it comes to a mess of any kind."

"Wal, I'd like to have yu, first rate," said Texas, frankly. "But we don't know yu. How can we tell yu ain't in with Hite or have some deal of yore own?"

"Hellno, yu cain't tell," laughed the hunter. "But yu've got guns."

"Shore, an' yu might spike 'em. . . . Tell yu what I'll do, fellars." Texas proceeded leisurely to replenish the fire, so that it blazed up brightly in the gathering dusk. Standing in its glare the two visitors showed to advantage.

"Reddie, come heah," called Texas. The girl was not slow in complying. She had moved away into the shadow.

"What yu want?" she replied, slowly coming forth.

"Reddie, these two men want to throw in with us, far as the Little Wichita. If yu was Trail boss of this ootfit what would yu say?"

"Geel give me somethin' easy," retorted Reddie, but she came readily closer, sensing an importance in the event. And certainly no two strangers ever received any sharper, shrewder survey than they got then.

"Howdy, lady. Do yu know Texans when yu see them?" queried one, quizzically.

The shorter of the two removed his sombrero to bow with all Southern politeness. The act exposed a ruddy, genial face.

"Evenin', miss. If it's left to yu I'm shore we'll pass," he said, frankly.

"Texas, I've seen a heap of bad hombres, but never none thet I couldn't size up pronto. Guess it got on my mind. If I was foreman I'd be glad to have these men."

"Wal, thet was my idee," drawled Texas. "I only wanted to see what yu'd say."

"What yu got in yore ootfit?" asked Brite.

"Two wagons an' eight hawses, some hides an' grub. An' a box of needle-gun ammunition."

"Thet last may come in handy. . . . But I understood from my foreman thet there was six in yore ootfit."

"Thet's correct. But Pete an' me want to pull leather away from them, an' not answer any questions, either."

"All right. You're welcome. Be heah at daybreak. . . . An' say, what's yore handles?"

"Wal, my pard goes by the name of Smilin' Pete. An' mine's Hash Williams. Much obliged for lettin' us throw in with yu. Good night. See yu in the mawnin'."

When they left, considerable speculation was indulged in by some of the drivers. Pan Handle settled the argument by claiming he would not be afraid to sleep without his guns that night. The guard changed early, leaving Brite, Reddie, and Texas in camp, the very first time that combination had been effected.

For once Texas stayed in camp beside the fire, and appeared more than amenable. He and Brite discussed the proximity of Hite's outfit and the certainty that a clash would intervene before they reached the Canadian. However, when the conversation drifted to the late Indian depredations Reddie vigorously rebelled.

"Cain't yu talk aboot somethin' else?" she demanded. "I always had a horror of bein' scalped."

"Wal, kid, yore red curls would shore take the eye of a

Comanche buck," drawled Texas. "But yu'd never be scalped. Yu'd be taken captive to be made a squaw."

"I'd be a daid squaw, then," said Reddie, shuddering.

"Wal, to change the subject, Brite, we'll shore have a party when we get to Dodge."

"I'm in for it. What kind of a party, Tex?"

"Darn if I know. But it wants to come off quick before yu pay us hands. 'Cause then we'll soon be mighty drunk."

"Why do yu have to drink?" queried Reddie, in unconcealed disgust.

"Dog-gone! I often wondered aboot thet. I don't hanker much for likker. But after a long spell oot on the prairie, 'specially one of these turrible trail drives, I reckon it's a relief to bust oot."

"If yu had a woman, would yu go get stinkin' drunk?" queried Reddie.

"A—a woman!" blustered Texas, taken aback. "Reddie Bayne, I told yu I never mixed up with thet sort of woman, drunk or sober."

"I didn't mean a painted dance-hall woman, like Mr. Brite told me aboot. . . . I mean a—a nice woman."

"Ahuh. For instance?" went on Texas, curiously, as he poked the red coals with a stick.

"Wal, for instance—one like me."

"Lawd's sake! . . . I shore couldn't imagine such a wonderful girl as yu carin' aboot me."

"Cain't yu answer a civil question just for sake of argument?"

"Wal, yes. If I had a nice wife yu can bet yore sweet life I'd not disgust her by gettin' stinkin' drunk."

A silence ensued. Brite smoked contentedly. He felt that these two were scarcely aware of his presence. Some fatal leaven was at work on them. Sooner or later they would rush into each other's arms, which probability had Brite's heartfelt approval. Still, he had an idea that since Reddie had refused once to accept Texas, if she ever wanted him, she would have to take the bit in her teeth.

"Thanks, Tex," replied Reddie, finally. "I sort of had a hunch yu'd be thet sort."

Texas betrayed that he realized he had been paid a high tribute from this waif of the ranges. But all he said was: "Dog-gone! Did Reddie Bayne say somethin' good aboot me?"

"Tex, it's only three hours till we go on guard," spoke up Brite.

"Yu're talkin'. I'm gonna turn in right now an' heah." Whereupon Texas unrolled his bed close to the fire, threw the blankets over him so that his spurred boots stuck out, and was asleep almost as soon as he stretched out.

Reddie gazed at him a long time, then she shook her curly head and said: "No hope. . . . Dad, yu can make my bed an' roll me in it, if yu want to."

"Wal, I'll do the first, shore an' certain," replied Brite, with alacrity. And he proceeded to pack their bed-rolls in under the trees close to camp.

"Not so far away, Dad," objected Reddie. "I may be wearin' men's pants an' packin' a gun, but I'm growin' all queer an' loose inside. I'm gettin' scared."

"So am I, dear," admitted Brite. "I've got some funny feelin's myself."

"We're darn lucky to have Texas an' Pan Handle with us," replied Reddie, and rolling her bed so close to Brite that she could reach out to touch him, she bade him good night.

Next morning, two hours after the start, a dust-devil, whirling down into the herd, stampeded them. Fortunately, it was toward the north. The drivers had nothing much to do save ride alongside and keep the herd bunched. They ran ten miles or more, in a rolling cloud of dust and thunder before they slowed up. It was the first stampede for Brite that trip, and was unfavorable in that it gave the herd a predisposition to stampede again.

Texas drove on until the chuck-wagon and the two hide-hunters caught up, which was late in the day.

That night at the camp fire the trail drivers compared

notes. San Sabe had seen smoke columns rising above the western hills; Ackerman and Little reported buffalo in the distance; Brite thought he noted an uneasy disposition on the part of all game encountered; Reddie had sighted a bunch of wild horses; Pan Handle averred he had spotted a camp far down a wooded creek bottom.

Texas apparently had nothing to impart, until Reddie tartly said: "Wal, Hawkeye, what're yu haid of this ootfit for, if yu cain't see?"

"I wasn't goin' to tell. I shore hate to do it. . . . I seen two bunches of redskins today."

"No!" they chorused, starting up.

"Shore did. Both times when I was way up front, an' had first crack at the hill tops. Country gettin' rough off to the west. We're nearin' the Wichita Mountains. I shore had to peel my eyes, but I seen two bunches of Injuns, aboot two miles apart. They come oot on the hill tops. Might have been only one bunch. They was watchin' us, yu bet, an' got back oot of sight pronto."

"*Comanches!*" cried Reddie, aghast.

"I don't know, kid. But what's the difference? Comanches, Kiowas, Apaches, Cheyennes, Arapahoes, it's all the same."

"No, Tex. I'll take all the last on to pass up the Comanches."

"Men, it's nothin' to be seen by Indians," spoke up Pan Handle, coolly. "From now on we'll probably see redskins every day. We'll get visits from them, an' like as not we'll get a brush with some bunch before we're through."

Smiling Pete and Hash Williams had listened quietly, as became late additions to the outfit. Whatever apprehensions Brite may have entertained toward them were rapidly dissipating. When they were asked, however, they readily added further reason for speculation. Both had seen Indian riders so near at hand that they recognized them as Comanches.

"Reckon yu've seen some Indian-fightin'?" queried Brite.

"Wal, I reckon. But not so much this spring an' summer as last. Our camp was only raided onct this trip out."

Later council developed the fact that these hunters were a valuable addition to Brite's outfit. They advised that the *remuda* be kept close to camp and strongly guarded. Comanches were fond of making raids on the horses of the trail drivers. Seldom did they bother with cattle, except to kill a steer for meat when it suited them.

A couple of hours' sleep for each driver was all he got that night. The herd was pointed at dawn. This day the range land grew wilder and rougher, making travel slow. Buffalo showed in every swale and hollow; wolves and coyotes trotted the ridge tops too numerous to count. Their presence in any force attested to the proximity of the buffalo herd. That night these prairie beasts made the welkin ring with their mourns and yelps. The coyotes boldly ventured right into camp, and sometimes sat on their haunches, circling the camp fire, and yelped until driven away. But the night passed without any other untoward event.

CHAPTER 10

EVERY DAY'S TRAVEL was fraught with increasing suspense. Tracks of Indian ponies, old camp fires in the creek bottoms, smoke signals from the hill tops, and lean wild mustangs with half-naked riders vanishing like specters in the distance—these kept the Brite contingent vigilant and worried all the way to the Little Wichita.

Ordinarily it was a small river, easily forded by stock. But now it was a raging torrent, impassable until the freshet had gone by. That might take a day or longer. A short consultation resulted in a decision to find a protected swale or valley where grass would hold the cattle and timber would afford cover for the trail drivers in case of attack.

The drivers of the herd ahead of them, presumably the one stolen by Ross Hite, could not have crossed, and no doubt had gone up the river with the same idea Texas Joe had decided upon. Buffalo were everywhere, though only in scattered bunches in the river bottom and along the grassy slopes. Up on the range it was probably black with them.

Texas sent San Sabe down the river to reconnoiter and he proceeded up the stream for a like purpose, leaving the rest of the drivers to tend to the stock.

The hour was about midday, hot and humid down in the protected valley. The stock rested after days of hard travel. All the drivers had to do was sit their horses and keep sharp lookout. Most of the attention was directed to the low brushy rims of the slopes. Texas had driven off the trail half a mile to halt in the likeliest place, which was good for the cattle, but not so good for the drivers, as they could be reached by rifle-shot from the hills. The three wagons were hauled into the thickest clump of trees. It looked like a deadlock until the river went down. Smiling Pete and Hash Williams, the hide-hunters, climbed under cover of the brush to scout from the hill tops. The trail drivers held their rifles across their saddles. Brite had two, the lighter of which he lent to Reddie. Armed to the teeth, alert and determined, the drivers awaited events.

Reddie called to Brite that she heard a horse running. Brite made signs to the closest rider and then listened intently. Indeed, Reddie's youthful ears had been right. Soon Brite caught a rhythmic beat of swift hoofs on a hard trail. It came from down river and therefore must be San Sabe. Also Brite heard shouts from the slope. These proved to come from the hide-hunters. Pan Handle and Ackerman evidently heard, for they rode around to join more of the drivers. Then in a bunch they galloped to a point outside the grove where Brite and Reddie were stationed.

"It's San Sabe," shrilled Reddie, pointing. "Look at him ride!"

"Injuns after him, I'll bet," added Brite. "We want to be huntin' cover."

Soon they were surrounded by Pan Handle and the others. San Sabe reached them only a moment later.

"Injuns!" he shouted, hoarsely, and he reined in. "But

they ain't after me. They didn't see me. Haven't yu heahed the shootin'?"

No one in Brite's company had heard shots. "Wal, it's down around thet bend, farther than I reckoned. . . . I was goin' along when I heahed yellin' an' then guns. So I hid my hawse in the brush an' sneaked on foot. Come to a place where hawses had just rid up the bank oot of the river. Sand all wet. They was Injun ponies. I follered the tracks till I seen them in an open spot. Heahed more shots an' wild yells. The timber got pretty thick. Takin' to the hillside, I sneaked along under cover till I seen what the deal was. Some settlers had made camp in a shady place, no doubt waitin' to cross the river. I seen three wagons, anyhow, an' some men behind them shootin' from under. An' I seen Injun arrows flashin' like swallows, an' I heahed them hit the wagons. Then I sneaked back to my hawse an' come ararin'."

"Brite, we'll have to go to their assistance," replied Pan Handle, grimly.

"Shore we will. Heah comes the hunters. Let's get their angle on what's best to do while we're waitin' for Tex."

The hunters came running under the trees, and reaching the drivers, they confirmed San Sabe's story in a few blunt words. Whereupon Brite repeated briefly what San Sabe had told them.

"How many redskin ponies?" queried Hash Williams, in business-like tones.

"No more'n twenty—probably less."

"How far?"

"Half mile aboot below the bend."

"Pile off, cowboy, an' draw us a map heah in the sand."

San Sabe hopped off with alacrity, and kneeling he picked up a stick and began to trace lines. In a twinkling all the drivers were off, bending over to peer down with intense interest. Brite heard a horse coming down the trail.

"Must be Tex comin' back."

"Heah's the bend in the river," San Sabe was saying. "Injun hawses' trail aboot heah, aboot half a mile below. Anyway to make shore there's a big daid tree all bleached white. We can risk ridin' thet far. . . . Heah's the open spot where the redskins took to the woods. Thet's aboot even with a big crag like an eagle's haid on the rim. The wagons air not more'n a quarter below thet. On the level ground in a nice grove of trees with heavy timbered slope on three sides. The reddies air in thet cover, low down."

"Boys, halter a couple of hawses for Pete an' me. Don't take time to saddle."

"What's all the confab aboot?" queried a cool voice. Texas Joe had come up behind them to dismount, holding his bridle in one hand, rifle in the other. San Sabe gave him the facts in few words. Then Hash Williams spoke up: "Shipman, I'm takin' it yu'll go pronto to the rescue?"

"Hellyes! Have yu any plan? Yu're used to redskins."

"We'll split, soon as we leave the hawses. Come on. We might get there too late."

San Sabe led off down the trail at a canter, followed by the drivers, except Texas, who waited a moment for the hunters to mount bareback. One mustang threatened to buck, but a sharp blow from Texas changed its mind. Soon the trio overtook the others, and then San Sabe spurred his horse into a run. Brite did not forget Reddie in the excitement. She was pale, but given over to the thrill of the adventure rather than to the peril. Brite would not have considered leaving her behind with Moze. The cavalcade rounded the river bend, stringing out, with Brite and Bender in the rear. San Sabe soon halted, and leaping off led into the timber on the right of the trail. Brite and Bender came up just as Reddie was following Texas on foot into the woods. They tied their horses in the thick brush at the foot of the slope. Heavy booms of buffalo guns, and the strange, wild, staccato yells of Indians soon sounded close.

"Comanches," said Williams, grimly.

Presently San Sabe parted the bushes. "Heah's their ponies."

"Less'n twenty. Wal, they're our meat, boys," replied Hash Williams as his dark eyes surveyed the restless, ragged mustangs, the river bottom beyond, the densely wooded slope, and lastly the rugged rim, with its prominent crag standing up like a sentinel. The place was small and restricted. To Brite the slope appeared to curve below into a bluff sheer over the river.

"Shipman, keep Pete heah with yu, an' choose five men to go with me," said Williams, swiftly.

"What's yore idee?" flashed Texas, his hawk eyes roving all around, then back to the hunter.

"If I can git above these red devils they're our meat," replied Williams. "Most of them will have only bows an' arrers. They'll crawl under the brush an' be low along the slope. . . . Strikes me there ain't enough shootin'. Hope we're not too late. . . . When we locate them an' let go, it's a shore bet they'll run for their hawses. Yu'll be hid heah."

"Ahuh. Thet suits me. I see where we can crawl within fifty feet of them Injun mustangs an' be wal hid. . . . All right. Yu take San Sabe, Ackerman, Whittaker, an' Little."

"Boys, throw off spurs an' chaps, an' follow me quiet."

In another moment the five men had disappeared and only soft steps and rustling could be heard. Texas peered keenly all around the glade where the mustangs had been left.

"Come on, an' don't make no noise," he whispered, and slipped away under the brush. Holden followed, then Smiling Pete, then Bender and Pan Handle, after which went Brite with Reddie at his heels. Shrill yells occasionally and an answered boom of a needle gun augmented the excitement. Texas led to a little higher ground, at the foot of the slope, and on the edge of the glade, where broken rock and thick brush afforded ideal cover.

"Heah we air," whispered Texas, to his panting followers. "Couldn't be better. We'll shore raise hell with them redskins. Spread along this ledge an' get where yu can see all in front. When yu see them wait till we give the word. Thet's all. Keep mighty still."

In the rustling silence that ensued Brite took care to choose a place where it was hardly possible for Reddie to be hit. He stationed her between him and Texas, behind a long, low rock over which the hackberry bushes bent. Pan Handle knelt beyond Texas with a gun in each hand. He was the only one of the party without a rifle. Bender, showing evidence of great perturbation, was being held back by Smiling Pete. Holden crawled to an even more advantageous position.

"All set. Now let 'em come," whispered Texas. "I shore hope to Gawd the other fellars get there in time. Not enough shootin' to suit me."

"It ain't begun yet or it's aboot over," replied Pan Handle. "But we couldn't do no more. Tex, heah's Reddie to think of."

"Dog-gone if I didn't forget our Reddie. . . . Hey, kid, air yu all right?"

"Me? Shore I am," replied Reddie.

"Scared?"

"I reckon. Feel queer. But yu can bet I'll be heah when it comes off."

"Think yu can do as yu're told once in yore life?"

"Yes. I'll obey."

"Good. . . . Now everybody lay low an' listen."

Brite had been in several Indian skirmishes, but never when the life of a woman had to be taken into consideration. He had to persuade himself of the fact that little peril threatened Reddie Bayne. Perhaps there were women folk with these settlers, and surely terrible danger faced them.

The Indian mustangs were haltered to the saplings at the edge of the glade. What a ragged, wild-eyed bunch! They had nothing but halters. These they strained against at every rifle-shot. And more than a few of them faced the covert where the drivers lay in ambush. They had caught a scent of the whites. Heads were pointed, ears high, nostrils quivering.

"Fellars, I smell smoke, an' not burned powder, either," said Texas Joe, presently, in a low voice. "Pete, what yu make of thet?"

"Camp fire, mebbe."

Suddenly the noonday silence broke to the boom of guns. Fast shooting, growing long drawn out, then desultory. Brite saw Texas shake his head. Next came a series of blood-curdling yells, the hideous war-cry of the Comanches. Brite had been told about this—one of the famed facts of the frontier—but he had never heard a Comanche yell till now.

"By Gawd! They've charged thet wagon train," ejaculated Pete, hoarsely. "Williams mustn't hev located them."

"He can do it now," replied Texas.

Reddie lay flat, except that she held head and shoulders up, resting on her elbows. The stock of her rifle lay between them. She was quite white now and her eyes were big, dark, staring.

"Looks bad for them, Reddie," whispered Brite.

"Yu mean our men?"

"No. For whoever's corralled there."

"Oh-h! What awful yells!"

"No more shots from them needle guns!" said Pete. "Reckon we've come only at the fag end of thet massacre. Another tally for these Comanches! But our turn'll come. Williams an' his men will be on thet bunch pronto."

All at once the whoops and piercing yells were drowned in a crash of firearms.

"Ho! Ho! Listen to thet! . . . Gawd! I hope they were in time! . . . Now, men, lay low an' watch. It'll be short now. The Comanches will be comin' in a jiffy, draggin' their wounded. They won't stop to pick up their daid—not in the face of thet blast."

The shooting ceased as suddenly as it had commenced. Hoarse yells of white men took the place of the Comanche war-cry. Cracklings of dead snags came faintly to Brite's ears.

"Oh—Dad!—I heah 'em—runnin'," whispered Reddie.

"Men, they're comin'," said the hunter, low and hard. "Wait now—mind yu—wait till they get out in the open!"

Swift oncoming footfalls, rustlings of the brush, snapping of twigs, all affirmed Reddie and the hunter. Brite cocked his rifle and whispered to Reddie: "Aim deliberate, Reddie. Yu want to count heah."

"I'm—gonna—kill one!" panted the girl, her eyes wild,

as she cocked her rifle and raised to one knee while she thrust the barrel over the rock.

"Reddie, after yu paste one be shore to duck," advised Texas, who must have had eyes in the back of his head. "Pan, look! I see 'em comin' hell-bent."

"Shore. An' some way far back in the woods. They're draggin' cripples. Don't shoot, men, till they're all oot.'"

Brite gripped his rifle and attended to the far side of the glade and the shadowy forms under the trees. The foremost ones flitted from tree to tree, hiding, peering back. Lean, bronze devils—how wild they seemed! Four or five flashed into plain sight, then disappeared again. Swift footfalls, soft as those of a panther, sounded quite a little closer to the ambushers. Brite espied a naked savage stepping forward, his dark face turned over his shoulder, his long, black hair flying with his swift movements. Reddie's gasp proved that she saw him, too. Then farther down the edge of the woods other Indians emerged into the sunlight. Two carried rifles, most of them had bows, but Brite saw no arrows. They made for the mustangs, peering back, making signs to others coming, uttering low, guttural calls. In a moment more, when several bucks had mounted their ponies, four or five couples emerged from the woods, dragging and supporting wounded comrades.

A warrior let out a screeching cry. No doubt he had seen or heard something of the ambushers. Next instant Reddie had fired at the nearest Comanche, halfway across the glade, facing back from the direction he had come. He let out a mortal yell of agony and stumbled backward, step after step, his dark face like a ghastly mask of death, until he fell. Simultaneously then with fierce shouts the ambushers began to fire. The shots blended in a roar. Brite downed the Comanche he aimed at, then strove to pick out among the falling, leaping, plunging Indians another to shoot at. Out of the tail of his eye he saw Pan Handle flip one gun out, aim and shoot, and then the other, alternately. He was swift yet deliberate. No doubt every bullet he sent found its mark. The wounded and terrorized mustangs tore away their halters, and scattered in every direction. The firing thinned out, then ceased, after which there followed a dreadful silence.

"Reckon thet's aboot all," drawled Texas Joe, with a little cold laugh. "Load up quick. All down an' 'most daid."

"Thet first buck who yelled got away," replied Pete. "I missed him. But I didn't see no more. We shore dropped them pronto. I know I only bored one. Yu must have some daid shots in this outfit."

"One I know of, anyway."

"Let's charge 'em, men, an' baste the cripples," said the hunter, and he plunged up to burst out of the brush. Texas and Pan Handle followed, as evidently had Holden and Bender. Brite laid a restraining hand upon the agitated girl, who appeared about to rush after the others.

"Yu stay heah, lass," he said. "It's all over so far as we're concerned. An' there'll be a mess oot there."

"Oh-h!" cried Reddie, breathing hard. She pushed the rifle before her and sank face down on the stone, beginning to shake like a leaf in the wind.

"Reddie, yu shore conducted yoreself in a way to make me proud," said Brite, patting her shoulder. "Don't give way now."

"Listen! Oh, that's terrible."

The drivers were cracking the skulls of the crippled Comanches, accompanying every whack from a rifle butt with a demon-like yell. Brite did not look in that direction. He heard halloes from the vicinity of the wagons and also answers from Texas' men.

"Come, Reddie, let's get oot in the open," suggested Brite, dragging at her. "But we won't go near thet shambles."

She picked up her rifle and followed him out into the glade. A curtain of smoke was drifting away. It disclosed the first victim of the ambush—the Comanche who had backed away from the grove, to fall at Reddie's shot.

Texas Joe stalked back toward them, bareheaded, his hair disheveled, and halted beside the prostrate Comanche.

"Boss, yu didn't plug this buck," he asserted.

"Shore I did."

"Yu're a liar. Thet gun yu had is a needle gun. It was Reddie who done it. . . . Dog-gone! Right plumb through his middle!" He came up to them, hard-faced and tremendously forceful, his slits of amber eyes upon Reddie.

"Wal, yu opened the bawl pronto," he said.

"Texas, I—I couldn't wait. I had to shoot thet Indian," she faltered.

"Wal, Miss Bayne, allow me to congratulate yu on bein' a real shore-enough Texas pioneer's daughter."

"I—I feel like a murderer. But I'm not sorry. How cruel they looked—like lean, bloody wolves."

"Boss, if I go to ranchin' soon, I'd like a wife after Reddie's breed," concluded Texas, with a little satire in his flattery.

"Tex, heah comes Williams an' our boys," shouted someone.

The hunter could be seen approaching hurriedly, yet warily, with several men at his heels.

"Hash, only one got away," called Smiling Pete. "We done 'em up quick an' brown."

"Good! But we was too late. —— our souls!" boomed the hunter, stridently. "Come along heah back with us."

Texas Joe and the others rushed after Williams, who had turned to follow the drivers with him. Brite and Reddie fell behind. The strip of woodland grew more open until it let sunshine into a little park where a camp had been established. Three wagons had been lined up to enclose a triangular space. The wheels had been barricaded in places with packs and beds. Indian arrows stuck out with ominous significance. In the foreground lay a white man on his face. An arrow head protruded from his back. His scalp had been half torn off.

"Pete, we slipped up as fast as we could," Williams was explaining. "But too late. I reckon we was in only at the finish."

Brite bade Reddie remain back while he followed the hunters. He had seen gruesome sights before, yet it was a shock to renew such experiences. Williams dragged two dead men from under the wagons, and then a third who was still alive. Evidently he had been shot, for no arrow showed in him. They tore open his shirt and found a bad wound high up, just about missing the lung. The bullet had gone clear through.

"Reckon this fellar will live," said Williams, practically. "One of yu tie a scarf tight over this hole an' under his arm. . . . Search everywhar, fellars. This has been a pretty long scrap. Yu see the blood has dried on thet man."

"I know I seen a girl just as we bust loose on 'em," said Ackerman, sweaty and grimy, his face working. "There was two redskins chasin' her. I crippled one. Seen him go down an' crawl. Then the other grabbed him into the brush."

"Heah's a daid woman," called Texas Joe, from the back of the third wagon. His comrades hurried to confirm this statement. Brite shuddered to see a woman, half stripped, hanging scalpless and gory half out of the wagon.

"Thet's not the girl I seen," shouted Ackerman. "I swear it, men. She was runnin'. She had light hair. She wore a plaid skirt."

"Wal, spread oot, some of yu, an' search," ordered Texas Joe.

"Three daid men, one daid woman, this heah man thet's still alive," Hash Williams was counting. "Thet's five. An' the girl yore cowboy swears he seen—thet makes six. There may be more. 'Cause when we cut loose on the red devils it'd be natural for any one alive to run, if he was able."

Deuce Ackerman went rushing around in a frenzy, calling aloud: "Come oot, girl, wherever yu air. Yu're saved."

But neither the wagons, nor the brush, nor the clumps of trees rewarded their hasty search. Deuce strode to the river bank, which was not far away, and thickly covered by willows. Here he called again. Suddenly he gave a wild shout and leaped off the bank out of sight. Texas Joe and other drivers ran in that direction. Before they could reach the bank Deuce appeared, half supporting a light-haired girl. They all ran then to meet Deuce, and Reddie flew after them.

"There, little lady, don't be scared," Ackerman was saying

as he halted with the girl. "We're friends. We've killed the Indians. Yu're all right."

He helped her to a log, where she sank down, and her head fell against his shoulder. She appeared to be about sixteen years old. Wide horror-stricken blue eyes gazed at the men. Freckles shone on her deathly white face.

"Lass, air yu hurted?" queried Williams, anxiously.

"I don't—know. . . . I guess—not," she answered, faintly.

"How many in yore party?"

"Six," she whispered.

"There's one man alive. He has a black beard. Reckon he'll live."

"My father! Oh, thank God!"

"What's yore name?"

"Ann Hardy. My father is—John Hardy. We were on our way to Fort Sill—to join a wagon train there. . . . The Indians had attacked us—for days—then left us. . . . We had to stop—on account of the high water. . . . They came back today."

"Is the woman yore mother?"

"No, sir."

"Wal, that's all now," concluded Williams. "Men, we better not lose any time gettin' this girl an' her father up to our camp. Some of yu rustle now. Take the girl. I'll stay with Pete, an', say, three more of yu. We'll do what we can for Hardy an' fetch him along. Then if all's well we can come back heah, bury the daid, an' look over this ootfit."

"I'll put her on my hawse," said Ackerman. "Come, Miss Hardy. . . . Lean on me."

"You saved my life," she replied, and fixed strained eyes upon him. "I was just—about to jump into the river."

"All's wal thet ends wal," rejoined Deuce, with a nervous little laugh. "Yu an' yore dad air lucky, I'll tell yu. . . . Come. We have a girl in our ootfit. Heah she is. . . . Reddie Bayne."

"Oh, yu pore dear!" cried Reddie, putting her arm around the girl. "But yu're safe now with us. This is Brite's ootfit. An' there's some hard fighters an' gunmen in it. Texas Jack an' Pan Handle Smith an' Deuce Ackerman heah. All bad hombres, lady, but shore good to have around when stampeders an' redskins come."

Deuce and Reddie led the girl up the trail, followed by Brite, Texas Joe, and the other drivers who were not going to stay with Williams. The trail ran between the river and the spot where the Comanches had met their doom. Texas and Holden forged ahead to get the horses. Deuce put the girl up on his saddle and mounted behind her. In a few minutes after that they reached a familiar grove of trees. But Brite did not recognize it.

"Wal, I'll be ——!" vociferated Texas Joe, suddenly halting. To curse so formidably under the circumstances could mean only disaster.

"What ails yu, Tex?"

"Look aboot yu, boss. Heah's camp an' our chuck-wagon. But where's Moze—an' where's our hawses an' cattle?"

"*Gone!*" screamed Reddie.

CHAPTER *11*

BRITE SCRATCHED his stubby chin. His two thousand odd cattle, less than half the original number he started with, had disappeared as if by magic.

"Wal, I'm not surprised," snorted Texas. "Boss, when I rode back from upriver awhile ago, San Sabe had just come in hollerin' Injuns. So I had no time to tell yu thet Ross Hite's ootfit was up there with the other half of yore herd."

"Damnation!" swore Brite. "Did they have the nerve to steal the rest of them? Right under our eyes!"

"Mebbe not. Long-horns air queer brutes. They might have just sloped off an' then again they might have stampeded. Shore they didn't come downriver."

"Where's Moze?"

"Heah, yu Alabama coon!" yelled Texas.

"I'se heah, boss," came from the thick clump of trees, high up among the branches. "Heah I is."

Presently they heard his feet thud on the soft turf and soon he appeared, shuffling toward them at a great rate.

"Moze, what's become of our cattle?" demanded Brite.

"I dunno, suh. Jest after yu-all left I seen some riders comin' down de ribber. An' dis chile perambulated up de tree. Pretty soon I heahed them close, an' I seen dat long lean Hite man. I sho did. They dess rode behind de cattle an' chased dem at a run up de ribber. An' dey missed our hawses."

"Ahuh. Now, boss, we have no more trouble atall," drawled Texas. "Pile off an' soon as the rest of our ootfit gets heah we'll put our haids together."

"Moze, we've got a visitor, Miss Hardy," announced Ackerman, as he leaped off to help the girl down. "All her ootfit except her dad got killed by the Comanches."

"Yu may as wal start a fire, Moze," added Texas. "We're stuck heah for I don't know how long. Heat water, get oot some clean bandages. We'll have a cripple heah pronto."

"Lawd, but dis Chissum Trail is waxin' hot," exploded Moze, showing the whites of his eyes.

Deuce unrolled a bed for the Hardy girl, and he and Reddie made her comfortable in the shade. Brite had the same thought he divined was passing in Reddie's mind—that the Uvalde cowboy had been shot through the heart by something vastly different from a bullet.

The girl was more than pretty, now that the ghastliness was fading from her face and the horror from her eyes. She was about medium height, slender, but strong and well-rounded of form. Reddie sat beside her and held her hand while Deuce made a show of serious attention.

"Shut yore eyes an' don't think," advised Reddie. "Let our men folks do thet."

Brite's survey of Texas, Pan Handle, and the others convinced him that never had they cudgeled their brains so fiercely. Moreover, they were silent. Brite paced to and fro, under the trees, doing his own thinking. It was inconceivable that Ross Hite should ultimately succeed in this second outrage. The fight that had been deferred must now be hastened. A grave risk for the two girls! Brite was in a quandary whether to permit it or not. But he reasoned that men of the stamp of Texas Joe and Pan Handle could not be held back any longer. The two hide-hunters had materially added to the strength of the outfit. Hite, now encumbered by all the cattle, was in a tight hole.

"Wal, they must have been drunk," declared Texas, suddenly.

"Who?" queried one of the drivers.

"Hite's ootfit. Onless they got a lot more hands then they had when Wallen braced us, they're just committin' suicide."

"Tex, would it do for me to scout up the river? On foot, of course, an' keepin' to cover?" asked San Sabe.

"Wal no. Thet idee come to me. But it's no good. We're shore Hite drove the cattle an' they cain't be far. He cain't cross the river anyway neah heah."

"So far so good. What're we gonna do?"

"Dam' if I know, San," replied Texas, gloomily. "We're saddled with two girls now, an' a crippled man, besides. Mebbe thet Hash Williams will have an idee. He 'pears to be an old-timer."

Texas walked out a few rods to look down the river. "They're comin'," he announced, with satisfaction. "Now we'll soon see where we air."

While still some distance from camp, Williams, evidently missing the cattle, came on at a gallop.

"Whar's our long-horns?" he roared.

"Hite drove them off while we was fightin' the Comanches," replied Texas.

"Whole hawg or none, huh? I'd a-reckoned he'd be smarter than to do thet."

"Williams, is it better or wuss for us?"

"Two times better, easy," declared the hunter. "I jest wonder what led to thet trick. Sort of stumps me."

"What'll we do?"

"Wal, we'll talk it over," returned Williams, dismounting. "But sight unseen I'd say let Hite go with the cattle. Foller him across the Red, anyway. He cain't dodge us. He cain't sell the stock. He cain't make a deal with the Injuns, for he couldn't get nothin' from them. An' they won't drive cattle."

Presently the approaching horsemen reached camp, two of them supporting the wounded settler, Hardy. He was conscious, but unable to sit up. They lifted him off the horse and carried him to a place beside his daughter.

"Oh, Daddy, say yu're not bad hurt," she cried.

"I'm all—right—Ann, so they tell me," he replied, weakly.

"Dig up some whisky an' fix him a bed," ordered Texas.

"Brite, what'll we do aboot them wagons? I reckon we ought to take one of them an' a load of supplies. We seen two hawses, anyway. We could haul Hardy an' his girl as far as Doan's store. What yu say?"

"I say yes, of course. Send two men back to fetch one wagon an' a load. We can cross this river with wagons as soon as the cattle can."

"Thet'll be tomorrer. River's goin' down fast. An' we'll camp right heah tonight. Thet'll give us time to bury them poor folks."

"Williams, don't yu reckon Hite will ambush the trail, thinkin' we'll be fools enough to chase him?" asked Texas.

"He'll do thet, shore. We ain't goin' to chase him. Mister Hite stole our herd too quick. We'll let him look oot for them an' we'll look oot for ourselves."

"Would yu advise me to scout up the river?"

"No, I wouldn't. But yu might send thet little chap, Sabe," replied Williams. "Heah, cowboy, yu climb the hill, keepin' oot of sight all the time. Work along the rim an' see if yu can locate thet ootfit. . . . An' come to think of it, Shipman, let's hold off on sendin' anyone down after thet wagon ontil Sabe gets back with his report."

Pan Handle sat apart, cleaning his guns. They glinted in the sunlight like polished steel. The gunman appeared absorbed in his task. His brow was corded and dark, the line of his cheek tight and gray. Brite calculated for a certainty that Smith had done away with half the bunch of Comanches. He gathered solace from that and pondered on the doubtful future of one Ross Hite.

Reddie and Ackerman were trying to induce Ann to drink something. Texas sat idle, his narrow eyes upon Reddie. Moze was busy about the fire. Williams and Smiling Pete were dressing Hardy's wound. The other drivers were resting and whispering together. San Sabe had vanished in the brush on the slope, where he made no more noise than a bird.

Brite sought a seat himself. The exertion and excitement had tired him out. He pondered upon the day and gave thanks to God for having been spared the catastrophe which had befallen Hardy's outfit. What a common thing such massacres had come to be! Wagon trains without scouts or Indian hunters or a large force for defense fell easy prey to these marauding bands of savages. He thought of rumors he had heard at Fort Dodge last trip. Santana, a chief of Kiowas, and a merciless fiend, had been reported to be in league with a band of white desperadoes whose specialty was to seek and waylay small caravans, and massacre every man, woman, and child, steal horses and supplies, and make away with the wagons so that not a single vestige of the caravan was ever discovered or heard of again.

Such terrible things seemed no longer incredible. Hundreds of wagon trains crossed the plains; thousands of trail drivers rode up the vast stretches of Texas. And if a few were lost the tragedy scarcely came home to the many. But Brite saw it now. If he got out of this drive with his life, and this dear child he had adopted, he would let well enough alone. Yet how peaceful, even pastoral, that valley scene! The river glided on yellow as corn; the summer breeze waved the grass and willows; flowers bloomed along the banks and birds sang; the sky spread a blue canopy overhead, accentuated by white cloud-sails. Across the river, on the high bluff, a huge buffalo bull came out to stand gazing, silhouetted black against the sky, magnificently wild in aspect, and symbolic of that nature dominant for the hour.

Hours passed. Still San Sabe did not return. Toward sunset

Williams deemed it advisable to get Hardy's wagon, horses, personal effects, and supplies up to Brite's camp before night. To this end he went himself, taking two men.

San Sabe hailed them from the bluff just as Moze called the outfit to supper. His call evidently was only to assure them of his safety, a fact Brite gave audible thanks for. He could not afford to lose any more drivers. In due time San Sabe burst out of the brush to approach the expectant group. His garb attested to rough work in this brush and his dark face was caked with sweat and dust.

"Had to haid a lot of canyons," he explained. "Thet accounts for me takin' so long. . . . Hite is drivin' the cattle, all one big herd again, up the river. He—"

"How far's he got?" interrupted Texas.

"Aboot five miles from heah."

"Did yu get near enough to count his outfit?"

"Shore. Seven drivers with the herd. An' one with their hawses. They're shy of saddle hawses. I counted six pack animals."

"Travelin' light. No chuck-wagon. San, don't yu reckon they'll bed down thet herd pronto?"

"Lawd only knows. What does Hite care aboot cattle? He'll lose ten per cent withoot accidents."

"He'll lose more'n thet," replied Texas, thoughtfully. "Boss, what yu say to havin' the ootfit somewhere close when Hite drives that herd into the river?"

"I say I'd like it," returned Brite, emphatically.

"Wal, we all would. We'll plan to move pronto. But not go against Williams' advice, if he says not."

"Tex, I've got confidence in thet buffalo-hunter, too."

"We all have. He's a real Texan. I'm ashamed I didn't see thet right off. But Texas Joe ain't himself these days. . . . Finish yore supper, boys, an' girls, too. Gee! We got another beauty in the ootfit."

Ann heard this from her seat under the tree, where Reddie was persuading her to eat, and she blushed prettily.

"Don't pay no attention to these trail drivers, Ann," said Reddie, quite seriously and loud enough for all to hear. "Thet is, when they're talkin' sweet. They're shore a fine fightin' bunch thet yu feel safe with. But don't let any of them get around yu."

"Aw, Reddie, thet's not kind of yu," expostulated Deuce, quite offended.

"Wal, Ann, to be honest, Deuce Ackerman—he's the boy who saved yore life—he's the best of a bad ootfit. But thet soft-voiced Whittaker with his sheep's eyes—look oot for him. An' the handsome one—he's never to be trusted."

"But there appears to be several handsome ones," replied Ann, with a hint of roguishness that showed she would be dangerous under happy circumstances.

This reply fetched the first hearty laugh for many long hours. They were young and easily stirred to pleasure. Brite laughed with them. Watching Reddie, he discerned that she had more up her sleeve.

"Shore, Ann. Our boys air all nice-lookin', an' some of them air what yu could call handsome. But I meant particular thet tall one, with the wide shoulders an' small hips—thet tawny-haided, amber-eyed devil who limps when he walks."

A shout greeted this elaborate description of Texas Joe. He did not participate in it. Blushing like a girl, he rose to doff his sombrero and make a low bow.

"Thanks, Miss Bayne. Thet's shore the first time this whole trip yu done me justice." Then with another bow, this time to Ann, he added: "Miss Hardy, there's folks who could tell yu thet the lead bullet in my laig was received in the interest of a young lady 'most as pretty as yu. An' the hombre who shot it there got mine in his haid."

Ann looked mightily impressed and embarrassed; Reddie dropped her eyes, defeated; while the riders grew silent. Texas had taken offense. Brite eased the situation by ordering Moze to hurry at his tasks and pack up ready to start at a moment's notice.

"Fetch in the team, somebody. An' round up the *remuda*. Tex, I reckon Williams will think of packin' the new wagon so Hardy can ride comfortable. An' the girl can ride on the front seat. Who'll volunteer to drive thet wagon?"

"I will," flashed Deuce Ackerman, before the other boys could get in their vociferations.

Here Texas Joe interposed, cool and authoritative, his sombrero pulled well down. Perhaps only Brite saw the mischievousness in his eyes.

"Deuce, if yu don't mind, I'll drive thet wagon. Yu see we haven't any herd to point."

"But, Tex, yu cain't drive a team," burst out Deuce, almost in a wail.

"I cain't?"

"Yu told me so. Wal, I've drove teams all my life, since I was thet high. Besides, I'm not so—so darn well, an' I'm saddle sore, an' off my feed—an'—"

"My Gawd! Deuce, yu need a doctor!" ejaculated Texas, solicitously. "I hadn't seen how seedy yu look till now. Shore yu can drive the Hardy wagon."

This effected a remarkable transformation in Deuce. He grew radiant. The boys gazed at him in slow-dawning realization at his perfidy.

"Miss Ann, air yu able to ride hawseback?" asked Texas.

"Oh yes—I can ride anything," she replied earnestly. "Really, Mister Texas, I'm not hurt or sick. I'm getting over my scare."

"Wal, thet's fine. Then yu can ride hawseback with me. I have just the pony for yu. A pinto thet come from Uvalde. He's Arabian if I ever seen one."

Deuce's face fell. He was wholly unconscious of the sincerity and depth of his emotions. Brite detected another reaction to this innocent fun Texas was having. Reddie betrayed signs of the green-eyed monster.

"An Arabian? Oh, I shall love to ride him," Ann replied, with enthusiasm. "But I'd rather go on the wagon to be close to Daddy."

"Yu win, lady," retorted Texas, with dry humor. Manifestly the fair sex was beyond him. Brite made certain that the girl had spoken the simple, natural truth. But that Texas cowboy had a suspicion that Ann wanted to ride beside her rescuer.

After that all hands became busy, except the new members

of the outfit. Ann rested with closed eyes. Her father lay still, as he had been advised, suffering patiently. Brite thought that the settler had a good chance to recover. The bullet had missed his lung. Blood poisoning was the only complication to fear. That very often set in from a dirty slug of lead, tearing through the flesh. Evidently Williams was no poor hand at dressing gun-shot wounds, and the medicine Brite had packed for just such a contingency was a sure preventive if applied in time.

Just about sundown the cowboys rode in from downriver, leading two saddle horses, and following them came a wagon with Williams and Smiling Pete on the seat.

Texas Joe lost no time acquainting the hunters with his eagerness to start at once up the river, so that they could be on hand when Hite drove the herd across the river.

"Texas, great minds run the same," boomed Williams. "I had thet idee myself. What did San Sabe report?"

When this information had been briefly imparted he said: "Good! Send Sabe an' another rider up the trail pronto. An' we'll foller as soon as we can start."

Pan Handle, Texas Joe, and Smiling Pete rode at the head of that caravan. Reddie Bayne and Brite drove the *remuda* next. Ackerman, at the reins of the Hardy wagon, with Ann on the seat beside him, came next. Whittaker was prevailed upon by vast argument and some anger to handle the third wagon. Moze followed with his chuck-wagon, and Hash Williams, accompanied by Less Holden and Bender, brought up the rear.

The wagon-drivers had orders to keep close together on the tail of the *remuda*. If there had ever been a road up this river-bottom, the herd had plowed it out. The ground was sandy and therefore made hard pulling for the horses. It was so dark that the drivers had difficulty in keeping to the most level ground.

After an hour's travel Brite noted a brightening of the sky and paling of the stars. The moon had risen. But it was behind the high bluff to their left and for the time being did not materially help their progress. Presently the rim of the opposite bluff turned silver, and this shiny line slowly worked downward. The time came when the far shore grew bright and then the river shone like silver. Eventually the blackness under the cliff yielded to the rising moon, until all was clear and blanched.

Better progress was made then. The valley narrowed until there appeared to be scarcely a quarter mile of land between the river and the bluff. It was brushy, too, and often dotted by clumps of trees. These did not offer any obstacle to Brite's caravan, but they would certainly slow down the herd of cattle.

The hours passed. It was comfortable travel for the trail men, except for the menace that gradually grew with their progress toward an inevitable climax. Suspense always wore upon Brite. Texas Joe, no doubt, chafed under it. Probably Pan Handle and the hunters were the only ones in the outfit who were not affected one way or another.

Some time long after midnight Texas rode back to halt the *remuda,* and then the wagons as they came up.

"We heahed cows bawlin' ahaid," he said. "An' I reckon we're just aboot too close for comfort now. What yu say, Williams?"

"Wal, let's haul up heah while some of yu sneak ahaid on foot. I'll go along. Texas, it ain't so long till mawnin'. An' we shore want to be around when Hite's ootfit drives the herd across."

"Hash, we *want* the cattle to get over," replied Texas, forcibly. "Thet'll save us work. An' we oughtn't begin hostilities until the rear end is halfway across."

"Ahuh. Ha! Ha! Kinda hot for the drivers at the tail, huh?"

"Miss Ann, how yu ridin'?" queried Texas as he passed the Hardy wagon.

"All right, but I'll be glad to lie down," she replied.

"Deuce, have yu made a bed for her in the wagon?"

"Not yet. But I have a roll of blankets handy. I'll take care of her," returned Deuce, too casually. He was obsessed with his importance.

"Wal, so long. Some of yu boys stand guard, so the girl an' the boss can sleep."

Reddie bunched the *remuda* on the best available space, fortunately large and grassy enough to hold it, and then unrolled her bed as usual next to Brite's.

"Yu awake, Dad?"

"Yes, lass. Anythin' troublin' yu?"

"Lawd, yes. But I only wanted to ask if yu don't think there'll be hell to pay before long?"

"Reddie, I don't see how we can avoid it," replied Brite, gloomily. "Some of our ponies gone, all our cattle gone. Two riders daid! An' not even to the Red River yet. It's between the Red an' the Canadian thet the trail drivers ketch hell."

"Oh, it'd just be my luck!" she exclaimed, disheartened, as she kicked off her boots.

"What'd be?"

"To get stole by stampeders or scalped by redskins or drowned, or lose *yu*, just when I've begun to be happy."

"Wal, Reddie, don't give up. Hang on like a Texan. Remember the Alamo!"

"Dog-gone it, Mr. Brite, them Texans shore never gave up. They hung on till they was all daid."

"I meant their spirit, honey. Now yu go to sleep."

Brite was pulled out by Texas Joe in the gray of dawn. "Boss, I just rode back with the news. Hite is crossin' the herd," he whispered. "If yu don't want to miss the fun, come on. Don't wake Reddie. We're leavin' five men heah. An' we'll be back before sunup."

"Don't wake Reddie!" spoke up that young person, derisively. "Fine chance yu have of keepin' me from seein' the fun, Texas Jack."

"Say, yu must want to be kissed some more," drawled Texas, coolly.

"Shore do. But not by the same gentleman—I mean hombre —who kissed me last."

"Gosh! Who was thet lucky hombre?" laughed Texas, and went his way.

Brite had been swift to comply with his foreman's suggestion, and had only to snatch up his rifle. Texas waited in the gray gloom with Pan Handle, San Sabe, and Williams. Reddie joined them there, rifle in hand.

"Listen," whispered Texas. "Foller me an' keep still. Do what I do. The idee is to break up Hite's ootfit before it gets across the river. Most of his drivers, yu know, will be behind the herd. When they get all in the river then we gotta do some tall shootin'. Thet's all."

He set off up the trail at a swift stride. The others followed in single file. San Sabe brought up the rear. Texas did not stop until he got around a bend in the river. He listened. The bawl of cattle arose on the still, warm air. Brite calculated that they could scarcely be more than a mile—two at the most—from the crossing Hite had chosen.

The valley had widened. On the opposite side of the river the rim of the bluff sloped down to a distant break. Soon Texas led off the trail into the woods. Here going was impeded by brush until they emerged upon the sandy bank of the river. It was wide here and shallow, flowing on with a gurgle and murmur. Judging by the wet sand and weeds, the water had dropped several feet during the night. By this time broad daylight had come, but not under a clear sky as usual. Hazy clouds presaged rain.

Texas hurried along, keeping in the lee of willows, halting to listen every hundred paces or so. At length he turned a corner to stop with a low: "Hist! . . . Look!"

Half a mile beyond, the wide river space presented a wonderful spectacle. It appeared to be blotted out by a great mass of moving cattle that extended across, and out on the opposite bank, and up under the trees. The herd had not been pointed by expert trail drivers. Brite did not see a rider. They would be, of course, on the upstream side, if the water was swift and deep. All the cattle were wading, which insured a safe, though slow, crossing.

"Wal, pards, this heah is shore low-down, Comanche work

we're goin' to do, but Hite's ootfit ain't worth us riskin' a scratch. Careful now. Watch me an' not the river. It'll come off soon enough."

He took to the willows, and glided through them, scarcely moving a leaf. Brite could see the water and hear its soft flow, but had no clear view. Meanwhile the intermittent bawling of cattle grew closer. Texas led on slower and slower. In places the willows became almost impenetrable, whereupon he had to worm a way through, but he always worked toward the river and not inshore.

Yells of the drivers halted Texas. He sank down on one knee and beckoned his followers to come close. They stooped and crawled to surround him.

"Reckon a—hundred yards—more will fetch us," he panted low. "Get yore breath. A winded man cain't shoot. Wait heah."

He crawled out to the sandbar, where he could just be made out through the willows. Soon he came back.

"In aboot five minutes—the brawl will open," he whispered. The beads of sweat dropped off his dark stern face. "They're quartering across current. Thet'll fetch the men in range, if we can—work up a little—farther."

He arose to a stooping posture and glided on, this time without any apparent caution, probably because he had ascertained that they could not be detected. Brite kept close to Reddie's heels, marveling the more at her all the time. Every few steps she would turn her head, like an alert bird, to see if he was close to her. At such moments she smiled. Her eyes were dark and daring, and only the pearly hue of her cheek indicated that her blood had receded. Faint whistling pants issued from her lips.

The cattle were now close. They made a stamping, splashing roar, above which neither the bawls of cows nor yells of drivers could be heard. Brite could smell the herd, and through interstices in the foliage he could see moving red and white.

Texas' steps grew shorter and slower, until they ceased. He knelt, and all followed suit. His eyes acquainted his comrades with the issue close at hand, and if that was not sufficient, the way he tapped his rifle and pointed surely spoke volumes. Then he listened intently to the clattering, splashing roar. It appeared to pass by their covert, working out.

"We gotta rustle," he whispered, fiercely. "We didn't get far enough up an' they're quarterin' away from us. Spread oot an' crawl to the edge."

Before Brite, who encountered a tangle of willows, could reach the open the thundering boom of needle guns dinned in his ears. He rushed ahead, split the willows with his rifle, and peered out. Reddie slipped in a few feet to his right.

The wide rear of the herd was a full hundred yards out. Half a dozen riders were beating and spurring their horses in a mad haste to escape. Brite saw horses down and one man pitching in and out of the water.

"Aim low an' shoot, Reddie," he called, harshly, yielding to the fight lust of the moment. Then he tried to cover the rider of a plunging horse, and fired. In vain! Guns were banging on each side of him, until his ears appeared about to crack. The last rider, whose horse was crippled, threw up his arms and lunged out of his saddle into the water. He did not come up.

Puffs of white smoke from the retreating drivers told of a return fire. Bullets began to splatter on the water and sand, and to whistle by into the willows. But the danger for Brite's men appeared negligible, owing to the fact that the thieves were shooting with small arms from plunging horses. Only a chance bullet could find its mark. The swift water came up to the flanks of the horses, hindering progress on foot. It was not deep enough for them to swim. Nevertheless, the riders drew nearer the shore in a hail of bullets. This pursuing fusillade ceased almost as suddenly as it had begun, because Brite's men had exhausted all the loads in both rifles and revolvers.

The yelling, frantic robbers reached the land, five of them, where they joined one who had crossed ahead of them, and they surrounded him like a pack of wolves, no doubt cursing him for this attack. They pointed to three horses down, and one man floating, face up.

Texas, having reloaded his buffalo gun, took a long shot at them by way of farewell. The big bullet splashed water and sand in their faces, making them beat a hasty retreat into the willows.

"Wal, dog-gone!" ejaculated Texas, pleased as a child. "It turned oot better'n I hoped when we got heah. What yu say, Hash?"

"Not so good as I was hankerin' for. But not bad, either," replied Williams. "Thar's three hawses down, an' yu bet I didn't see no fellar wade ashore."

"There's a crippled man in thet bunch," averred Texas. "I hit him myself."

"Mr. Brite, we'll be drivin' yore herd again before we cross the Red," said the hunter. "We'll have these robbers buffaloed from now on. They'll have to leave the herd or croak, thet's all. Reckon thet tall fellar on the bay hawse was Hite, reckonin' from the way they ranted at him."

"Load up, everybody. We mustn't forget we're now in Comanche country," advised Texas. "Boss, who's the young fellar with burnt powder on his nose?"

"This heah? Oh, this is Red Bayne," replied Brite, eager for some fun now the tension was removed. "Did yore rifle kick?"

"Did it? Wuss than a mule. I forgot to hold the darn thing tight," rejoined Reddie, in rueful disgust.

"Let's rustle back to camp, eat, an' get goin' 'cross this river," said Texas. "It'll shore be little sleep or rest Ross Hite will get from now on."

CHAPTER **12** IF IT were needed, Texas' coup inspired the drivers who had not shared it. Deuce Ackerman let out one long wild whoop.

"Hip hip, thet's great! Look what we missed, Rolly. But some of us had to stay behind. . . . Tex, we'll get goin' yet an' then Gawd help 'em!"

In an hour they were on the move, and soon after that halted at the crossing where Hite's men had been routed. The three dead horses had floated downstream some distance to lodge in shallower water. Williams had sent a scout back in the trail, another up on the bluff, and a third ahead. They met the outfit at the ford, to report nothing in sight but buffalo.

"How aboot us bein' ambushed?" queried Texas.

"Wal, strikes me Hite would pick oot a better place than thet over there," replied Williams. "Mr. Brite, suppose yu hand up yore glass to young Ackerman, so he can have a look. . . . Stand up on the seat, son."

After a long survey Ackerman shook his head decisively. "Nope. I can see all under the trees an' right through thet thin skift of brush."

"Wal, just to make shore, some of us'll ride over ahaid," said Texas. "Come, San, an' yu Bender, an' Less. . . . Look sharp, an' if yu see puffs of smoke wheel an' ride for dear life."

These riders crossed in good order, proving the validity of Ackerman's judgment. Reddie crossed next with the *remuda*, and then Moze made it without going over his wagon wheels.

The Hardy vehicle had to have help, stalling a little beyond the middle.

"Rustle before she mires down," yelled Texas, who had ridden out. "Come, Miss Ann. I'll pack yu ashore. Yu'll get all wet there."

Ackerman's face was a study while Ann Hardy readily leaned out to be taken in Texas Joe's arms and carried ashore. Then the riders, hitching on with their ropes, aided the team to pull the wagon out. Williams drove the third wagon across without mishap. But the fourth and last stuck in the mud, about halfway over.

This accident held up the caravan. It was the largest wagon, half full of buffalo hides, and it sank deeper in the mire after every effort to dislodge it. The drivers broke their ropes. Then they got off in water up to their waists and performed all manner of strenuous labor, to no avail.

Finally, Williams waded in and, unhitching the team, drove them ashore.

"Wagon's no good, anyhow, an' never mind the hides. Thar's ten million of 'em loose oot heah."

They went on with two teams hitched to the Hardy wagon, which held the heaviest load. And soon they were up out of the bottom land upon the vast heave of the range. The cattle herd had been driven almost due east. Williams said that had been done to strike the Chisholm Trail. Before long this proved to be a correct surmise.

The day was sultry and brooded storm. Bands of buffalo grazed on all sides, attended by droves of wolves and coyotes and flocks of birds. By noon Ackerman, who still retained Brite's glass, reported the herd in sight ahead less than ten miles. All afternoon the caravan gained, which fact probably was known to the Hite outfit. At sunset Hite halted the herd on the open range, where not a tree or a bush could be picked up with the glass. A little swale well watered and wooded appealed to Texas Joe, who turned off here and selected a camp site. Scarcely half a dozen miles separated the two outfits.

The sun set in a red flare and dusk trooped up from the

west, sultry and ominous. Dull rumbles of thunder heralded an approaching storm, and flashes of sheet lightning flared along the dark horizon. The silence, the absence of even a slightest movement of air, the brooding wait of nature, were not propitious to the caravan caught out upon the open range. Brite told the girls how the electric storms prevalent in that latitude of Texas were the bane of the trail drivers, actually more dreaded than redskins or buffalo.

"But why?" asked Ann Hardy, wonderingly.

"Wal, they're just naturally fearful in the first place, an' they drive hawses an' cattle crazy. Fred Bell, a trail driver I know, said he got caught once in a storm near the Canadian an' had thirty-seven haid of cattle an' one driver struck daid by lightnin'."

Reddie was no less shocked than Ann and vowed she would surely pray that they miss such a storm as that.

"I been in a coupla electric storms," spoke up Texas, who had paused in his walk to listen. "Been in hundreds of plain lightnin'-an'-thunder storms. Only two of these darn floods of electricity thet cover the earth an' everythin' on it. I've seen balls of fire on the tops of all the cows' horns. I've seen fire run along a hawse's mane, an' heahed it too. Yes, sir, bad storms air hell for cowhands."

Later, when the girls had walked away, Texas spoke low and seriously to Brite.

"Boss, any kind of a storm tonight, if it'll only flash lightnin' enough, will shore suit me an' Pan Handle."

"Tex! What's in yore mind?" queried Brite, hastily.

"We're gonna get back our herd tonight."

"Yu an' Pan? Alone?"

"Shore alone. Thet's the way to do it. Pan wanted to tackle it by hisself, an' so did I. But we compromised by joinin' forces. We're goin' together."

"Shipman, I—I don't know thet I'll permit it," rejoined Brite, gravely.

"Shore yu will. I'd hate to disobey yu, Mr. Brite. But I'm Trail boss. An' as for Pan Handle, hell! Thet fellar cain't be bossed."

"What's yore idee, Tex? I hope to heaven it ain't crazy. Yu an' Pan air grown men. An' yu shore know yore responsibility heah. Two young girls to protect now, an' a crippled man."

"Wal, the idee strikes yu wuss than it really is," went on Texas. "Pan an' me plan to strike the herd in the thickest of the thunder an' lightnin'. When we do I'll circle it one way an' he'll circle the other. If the cattle stampede, as is likely, we'll ride along an' wait till they begin to mill or stop. Now Hite's ootfit will be havin' their hands full. They'll be separatin', naturally, tryin' to keep the herd bunched an' stopped. An' in a flash of lightnin', when any one of them seen us, he wouldn't know us from Adam. Savvy, boss?"

"I cain't say thet I do," replied Brite, puzzled.

"Wal, yu're gettin' thick-haided in yore old age. Kinda gettin' dotty adoptin' this pretty kid, huh?"

"Tex, don't rile me. Shore I'm dotty, aboot her, anyway. But I don't get yore hunch. Now, for instance, when yu an' Pan circle thet herd, goin' in opposite directions, when yu meet how'n hell will yu know each other? Shootin' by lightnin' flash had ought to be as quick as lightnin', I'd say. How'n hell would yu keep from shootin' each other?"

"Wal, thet's got me stumped, I'll admit. Let's put our haids together after supper. Mebbe one of us will hit on just the idee. If we think up somethin' shore—wal, it's all day with Hite an' his ootfit."

Moze rolled out his familiar clarion blast.

"Gosh! this's fine, all heah together, first time," exclaimed Ackerman, whose spirits ran high. He had just seated Ann on a pack beside him.

"Wal, it may be the last, so make the most of it," drawled Texas, his dark, piercing eyes upon Reddie. Brite saw her catch her breath. Then silence fell.

Dusk deepened into night, still close, humid, threatening, with the rumbles sounding closer and more frequent. In the western sky all the stars disappeared. The moon was not yet up.

"Chuck on some firewood an' gather aboot me heah," said

Texas, after the meal ended. "It's shore gonna storm pronto. An' me an' Pan have a job on."

"What?" bluntly jerked out Holden.

"Thought yu was kinda glum," added San Sabe.

"Reddie, yu're in on this," called Texas. "An' Ann, too, if she likes. Shore no one ever seen an idee come oot of a pretty girl's haid. But I'm sorta desperate tonight."

In the bright light of the replenished fire they all surrounded their foreman, curious and expectant.

"Wal, heah's at yu. Me an' Pan air ridin' oot to round up Hite. Soon as the storm's aboot to break we'll ride up on the herd an' the guards. I've got them located. We plan to circle the herd in different directions, an' we want to know ab-so-loot-lee when we meet each other. How we goin' to do thet?"

"Yu mean recognize each other by lightnin' flashes?" queried Less.

"Shore."

"It cain't be did."

"Aw, yes it can. A lightnin' flash lasts a second—sometimes a good deal longer. How much time do I need to see to throw a gun—or not?"

"Oh-ho! Thet's the idee!"

"Lemme go along."

"No, it's a two man job. . . . Use yore gray matter now, pards."

"It'll be rainin', most likely, an' the herd will be driftin', mebbe movin' fast. An' of course Hite's ootfit will be surroundin' it, all separated. It's a grand idee, Tex, if yu don't plug each other."

"Wal, let's see," put in another driver. "When yu separate yu'll know for shore yu cain't meet very soon. It'll take most a quarter or mebbe half an hour to trot around a big herd, guidin' by lightnin' flashes."

"Boys," drawled Pan Handle, in amusement, "yore minds work slow. What we want to know is what to wear thet can be seen quick. Somethin' shore to identify each other. Remember we'll both be holdin' cocked guns."

One by one the male contingent came forward with suggestions, each of which was summarily dismissed.

"If it storms, the wind will blow, shore?" interposed Reddie.

"Breeze blowin' already. There'll be a stiff wind with the rain," replied Texas.

"Tie somethin' white aboot yore sombreros an' leave the ends long so they'll flap in the wind."

"White?" responded Pan Handle, sharply.

"Dog-gone!" added Texas.

"Men, thet is a splendid idee," interposed Brite, earnestly. "Somethin' white streakin' oot! It couldn't be beat."

"Where'll we get this heah somethin' white?" asked Texas. "In this dirty ootfit it'd be huntin' a needle in a haystack."

"Ann has a clean white towel," replied Reddie.

"Yes, I have," said the girl, eagerly. "I'll get it."

When the article was produced and placed in Texas' hands he began to tear it into strips. "Wal, Reddie, yu've saved my life. I shore want this Pan Handle galoot to make quick an' shore thet I'm Tex Shipman. . . . Heah, we'll knot two strips together, an' then tie the double piece round our hats. . . . Come, Reddie, take it."

She complied, and when he bent his head she clumsily wound the long streamer around the crown of his sombrero. The firelight showed her face white as the towel.

"What yu shakin' for?" demanded Texas. "Anyone would get the halloocination yu reckoned I was gonna be killed an' yu felt bad."

"I would feel—very bad—Tex," she faltered.

"Wal, thet makes up for a lot. . . . Tie it tighter, so the wind cain't blow it off. . . . There. I reckon that'll do. How aboot yu, Pan?"

"I'm decorated, too."

"Wal, I could 'most see thet in the dark. . . . Now, fellars, listen. Like as not we won't come back tonight, onless our plan fails. If it works we'll be with the herd, yu bet. So yu rout Moze oot early, grab some grub, an' ride oot soon as it's light. The wagons can foller on the road. Yu'll find us somewhere."

In utter silence, then, the two men mounted their horses,

that had been kept haltered close by, and rode away into the sulphurous, melancholy night.

"Thet's a new wrinkle on Hash Williams," ejaculated that worthy. "What them gun-throwers cain't think of would beat hell!"

His caustic remark broke the tensity of the moment. Reddie had stood like a statue, her face in shadow, gazing into the blackness where Texas Joe had vanished. Brite did not need this time to see her eyes; her form, instinct with speechless protest, betrayed her.

The wind swept in from the range with a moan, blowing a stream of red sparks aloft. Thunder boomed. And a flare of lightning showed inky black clouds swooping down from the west.

"We better think aboot keepin' ourselves an' beds dry," advised Brite. "Deuce, see thet Ann an' her father will be protected. Moze, get oot our tarp. Come, Reddie, we'll bunk under the chuck-wagon an' say we like it."

"Dad, I wonder if my *remuda* will hang in a storm?" inquired Reddie, undecided what to do.

"Wal, thet bunch of dogies can go hang if they want."

"Reddie, I'll have a look at 'em before the storm busts," said San Sabe.

"Yu'll have to rustle, then."

"Thet's only wind. It ain't rainin' yet."

By the time Moze, Brite, and Reddie had tied and stoned the ends of the tarpaulin so that it could not blow away, the rain was coming in big scattered drops. Brite felt them cool and fresh upon his face. He and Reddie rushed for their shelter, and had made it fast when the pitch blackness blazed into an intense blue-white brilliance which lighted camp, wagons, horses, and all the vicinity into a supernatural silvery clearness. A thunderbolt followed that seemed to rend the earth.

The succeeding blackness appeared an intensified medium impenetrable and pitchy. Then the thunder reverberated away in terrific concussions.

"Where air yu, Dad?" shouted Reddie.

"I'm right heah," Brite replied. "Listen to the roar of thet rain comin'."

"Gosh! I better say my prayers pronto, or the good Lawd'll never heah me," cried Reddie.

"Lass, it might be a good idee," replied Brite. "Let's don't unroll our beds till this storm is over."

Reddie answered something to that, but in the pressing fury of the deluge he could not distinguish what it was. With a rippling onslaught upon their canvas shield, rain and wind enveloped the wagon. Then the pitch black split to a weird white light that quivered all around them, showing the torrent of rain, the flooded land, the horses bunched, heads down, together. Thunder burst like disrupted mountains. Again the black mantle fell. But before that reverberation rolled away another zigzag rope of lightning divided the dense cloud, letting loose an all-embracing supernatural glow, silver-green, that lent unreality to everything. White flash after white flash followed until for moments there appeared scarcely a dark interval between, and the tremendous boom and peal of thunder was continuous.

Reddie sat huddled under the wagon, covered with the long slicker. Brite could see her pale face and dark eyes in the lightning flare. Fear shone there, but it did not seem to be for herself. Reddie was gazing out over the blaze-swept range with the terrible consciousness of what was taking place out there.

That, too, obsessed Brite's mind. He reclined on his elbow close beside Reddie and not far from Moze, who had also sought shelter under the wagon. Reddie appeared to be fairly shielded from the deluge that beat in everywhere. But Brite needed the old canvas with which he covered himself. The other drivers had huddled under the other wagons, and could be seen, a dark mass, inside the wheels.

Brite was not at all fond of Texas storms, even of the ordinary kind. He had a wholesome fear of the real electric storm, which this one did not appear to be. At this time, however, he scarcely thought of the fact that lightning struck camps frequently.

His thoughts dwelt on the unparalleled action of Texas Joe and Pan Handle, riding forth in that storm to mete dire justice to the stampeders. It must have been an original idea —stalking Hite's outfit in face of the furious rain and deafening thunder and scintillating flashes. For sheer iron nerve it had no equal in Brite's memory of cold, hard deeds. These men would be drenched to the skin by now, blinded by piercing rain and lightning, almost blown from their saddles, in imminent peril of being run down by a stampeding herd, and lastly of being shot by the men they had set out to kill.

By the strange green light Brite calculated whether or not he could shoot accurately under such conditions. The flashes lasted long enough for a swift eye and hand. All the same he would not have cared to match wits and faculties with hunted desperadoes on a night like this.

It took an hour or longer for the heavy center of the storm to pass, after which rain and wind, and an occasional flare, diminished in volume. Perceptibly the storm boomed and roared and flashed away. Whatever had been fated to happen out there was over. Brite had no doubt of its deadly outcome. Still, that might be over-confidence in his gunmen. He had nothing sure to go by. Ross Hite was a crafty desperado, and for all Brite knew he might be the equal of Texas Joe. But not of Pan Handle Smith! Pan Handle could only be compared to the great Texas killers of that decade.

Reddie had rolled in her blankets and was asleep, as Brite dimly made out by the receding flares. He sought his own bed, weary, strangely calm, somehow fixed in his sense of victory.

It was still dark when noise aroused him from slumber. A grayness, however, betrayed the east and was the harbinger of day. He reached over to give Reddie a shake, but the dark object he had taken for her was her bed. Moze was out, too, splitting wood. Brite hurried out to lend a hand.

Gruff voices sounded toward the other wagons. Dark forms of men strode to and fro against that gray light. "Pete, we got to grease the wagon," Williams called gruffly. Reddie's clean, high-pitched call came floating in. She had the *remuda* moving. One by one the cowboys appeared at the brightening camp fire, cold, cramped, wet, silent, and morose. Ackerman was not present, wherefore Brite concluded that he had gone with Reddie to round up the *remuda*. This surmise proved correct. When the mustangs got in, there followed the sharp whistle of wet ropes, the stamp of little hoofs, the grind of hard heels, and an occasional low growl or curse from a cowhand. That task done, the riders flocked around Moze to snatch at something to eat.

The dawn lightened. Ackerman called at the Hardy wagon: "Miss Ann, air yu awake?"

"I should smile I am," came the reply.

"How air yu?"

"All right, I reckon, Mr. Deuce, but pretty wet."

"How's yore father?"

"Son, I'm still alive an' kickin'," replied Hardy, for himself.

"Good! . . . Miss Ann, better come oot an' dry yoreself, an' have a hot drink. We'll be on the move pronto."

Hash Williams stamped up to the fire, spreading his huge hands.

"Cleared off fine. Gonna be best kind of a day for travel."

"Do yu reckon we'll travel?" inquired Brite.

"I'll bet we do," replied the hunter, gruffly.

"Williams, what's yore idee aboot startin'?" queried Ackerman, sharply.

"Pronto. Yu drive Hardy same as yestiddy. Pete will drive our wagon. I'll go with the boys. Let's see, thet'd be six of us. Suppose yu keep one rider back with yu."

"All right. Rolly, yu're stuck heah with us."

In a moment more the five were mounted on restive mustangs, a formidable quintet in the pale morning light.

"Take the trail an' keep comin' till yu ketch us. We'll shore bear yu all in mind."

They were off swiftly, and close together, a sight that betrayed to Brite the uncertainty of their errand and the mood in which it was undertaken.

"Mawnin', Ann," greeted Reddie to the settler girl as she

appeared, disheveled and wet, but bright-eyed and cheerful. "Did yu heah the storm?"

"Good morning. Oh, wasn't it terrible? . . . An' to think of those two who rode out. I could not sleep."

"It wasn't a very comfortable night, Miss Ann," said Brite. "Come to the fire. . . . Moze, rustle our breakfast. We must not lose any time."

They were on the trail at daylight, when the range had just awakened, and all the distant landmarks were shrouded in mist. But the sky was clear, the east reddening, the air fresh and cool.

Rolly Little took the lead to scout the way; the wagons followed close together, and the *remuda* brought up the rear, with Brite and Reddie driving it. All horses were fresh. They trotted over the hard ground and splashed through the little pools. Meanwhile the red in the east deepened to rose, and then the rose burst into glorious sunrise, before which the shadows and mists, the mysteries of distance and obscurity of draw and swale dissolved and vanished.

Five miles out Rolly Little rode off the trail and appeared to search. When the *remuda* came even with this point, Brite swerved off to have a look. He found where Ross Hite had camped. Packs and saddles, utensils left beside a sodden bed of ashes, attested to the hasty departure of the stampeders. A long yell pierced Brite's ear, startling him. Little, some distance ahead, was waving. But his action seemed the result of excitement rather than alarm. Brite, curious and thrilled, galloped to join him; before he got there, however, Little pointed to an object on the ground and rode on.

Brite soon gazed down upon a dead man, flat on his back, arms spread, gun on the ground, a telling spectacle, emphatic of the law of that range. Brite rode an imaginary circle then, soon to come upon another of Hite's outfit, still and horrible, half his face shot away and his open shirt bloody. Farther on in the lengthy curve Brite espied a dead horse and two dead men, lying in a group. Brite did not go close, and he sheered off that circle and made for the *remuda*.

Reddie gave him a flashing, fearful glance.

"Boy, would yu believe it? Four of Hite's ootfit lyin' along the trail, in a circle. I only rode the half."

Reddie swallowed hard and had no answer. They rode on, eyes now glued ahead to the wavering, deceiving prairie. Buffalo showed in spots, dark patches on the green, off the trail. The purple hills beckoned, and beyond them the Wichita Mountains loomed dimly in the clear air. To the right the range sloped away to merge into sky. And what seemed hours of watchful suspense passed while the wheels rolled, the horses trotted, the drivers urged the lagging *remuda* on.

"Look ahaid!" called Reddie, shrilly.

Smiling Pete stood on top of his wagon, waving his hat. His energetic actions could be assigned to either joy or alarm.

"Reddie! . . . Pete sees our boys with the herd—or else a bunch of Comanches. Which?"

"I cain't say, Dad, but I'm prayin' hard," she cried.

CHAPTER *13* FROM the summit of an endless slope Brite and Reddie espied far ahead that which elicited shouts of joy. Miles down in the green valley an immense wedge-shaped patch of color crawled over the prairie. It was the great herd together once more, sharp end pointed north, and the wide rear spread far to the east and west.

"Thet cowboy!" cried Reddie, in awesome wonder. She did not need to say any more.

Brite found silence his best tribute. The wagons and *remuda* quickened to a downhill grade. Soon the freshness of morning gave way to the heat of noonday, and when they reached the rolling floor of the valley, to encounter reflection from the dragging sand, horses and riders alike suffered severely.

Beyond that arid spot a gradual slope waved on toward the horizon where dim hills showed. Grass became abundant again, and toward late afternoon the herd appeared to be halted at the head of a swale where a fringe of willow signified the presence of water.

Brite's end of the cavalcade caught up eventually. The cattle had bunched in a meadow that surely would hold them all night, but at this hour they were weary and only a few were grazing.

Reddie swung the *remuda* off to a bend in the creek. Brite rode on up to the head of the swale, where Moze had halted. Only two drivers remained with the herd, each solitary on opposite sides of it. They drooped in their saddles. A scattering of low trees afforded a fairly good site for camp. All the other drivers were dismounted. Brite got off, and stumbled around on cramped legs until he located Pan Handle and Texas Joe off to one side under a tree.

Brite's heart contracted when he espied Joe lying with a bloody bandage round his head. He heard Pan Handle say: "Tex, it's kinda low down of yu."

"All's fair in love an' war. I'm crazy aboot her an' I reckon she doesn't care a damn—"

"Heah comes the boss," interrupted Pan Handle, warningly. Brite had heard enough, however, to get an inkling of what the wily cowboy was up to. He decided he would hide his suspicion.

"Tex, old man, I shore hope yu ain't bad hurt," he burst out, in alarm, as he hurried up.

"Aboot goin' to cash, boss."

"My Gawd! Man, this is terrible. Let me see."

"Rustle Reddie over heah," replied Texas, in an awful voice.

Reddie was unsaddling her black on the other side of camp. She heard Brite's call, but showed no inclination to hurry. Her face flashed in their direction.

"Reckon I'd better go prepare her, Tex," said Brite, conceiving a loyal idea in the girl's behalf.

"Fetch her pronto," called Texas, after him.

Brite lost no time reaching Reddie, and when she turned he was amazed to find her white and shaking.

"Dad—I saw! Tex has—been shot!" she whispered, with a gasp. "For pity's sake—don't tell me—"

"Reddie, the damn cowboy ain't hurt atall," retorted Brite. "He 'pears bloodied up some. But I've a hunch he wants to scare yu."

Reddie's face warmed, and slow comprehension drove the horror from her telltale eyes.

"Honest Injun, Dad?" she asked, hoarsely.

"I'll swear it."

She pondered a moment, then jerked up, all spirit. "Thanks, Dad. But for yore hunch I'd shore have given myself away."

"Lass, yu turn the tables on thet tricky hombre," suggested Brite.

"Watch me! Come a-runnin'," she replied, and fled toward where Texas lay. Brite thumped after her as best he could, arriving just in time to see Reddie fall on her knees with a poignant cry.

"Oh, Pan—he's been shot," she cried, in horrified tones.

Pan Handle confirmed that with a gloomy nod. Texas lay with the bloody yellow scarf across his forehead, just shading his eyes. Devil as he was, perhaps he could not risk exposing them to her perception.

"Wal, I should smile I have, Reddie," he drawled, in a husky whisper. "But no matter. Pan an' me got the herd back."

"But, Jack!—Jack!—You're not—not—" she wailed in accents that must have tricked the lover into ecstasy.

"Reckon—I'm gonna—cash."

"*Not die!*—Jack?—Oh, my heaven!"

"Yes, girl. I'm gonna die—oot heah on the lone prairie."

"Jack, darlin'!" she sobbed, covering her face with her hands and rocking to and fro over him.

"Awl . . . Then yu'll be sorry?" asked Texas, in a tender voice.

"My heart will break. . . . It will kill me!"

Texas Joe manifested a peculiar reaction for a man about to depart from life at such a harrowing moment. Reddie, too, appeared about to go into convulsions.

"Kiss me—good-by," whispered the villain, determined to carry the subterfuge as far as possible.

Suddenly Reddie uncovered her face, which was rosy, and convulsed, too, but in smiles. She snatched the scarf off Texas' forehead, exposing the superficial scalp wound over his temple.

"Yu deceitful, lyin' cowboy!" she burst out. "Yu may have fooled a lot of pore girls in yore day. But yu cain't fool this one."

"Dog-gone!" ejaculated Texas, his eyes popping. "Yu air smart!"

"The minute I seen yu I was on to yu," she replied, mockingly, as she arose.

"Yeah? . . . All right, Miss Reddie," he replied, in grim discomfiture. "Pan said it was a low-down trick. An' it was, I reckon, but next time there won't be no foolin'."

Always, at the last, Texas Joe was not only a match for Reddie, but a master at finesse. Her dark eyes changed startlingly. It was indeed easy to see when this complex range-rider was in earnest. Reddie sobered instantly, and drooping her head, she hastened away.

"Boss, did yu double-cross me?" demanded Texas, with those piercing eyes shifting to Brite.

"Land's sake! How could I?" ejaculated the boss.

"Wal, yu're a pretty smart old hombre," growled Texas. Then he brightened. "Dog-gone! She had me most oot of my haid. Pan, ain't Reddie just the wonderfulest girl thet ever was?"

"I haven't seen 'em all," drawled Pan Handle. "But she shore would be hard to beat. . . . Tex, I don't believe she gives a dam' aboot yu."

"Aw!"

"No girl could have done thet with yu lyin' there all bloody. An' yu're a natural liar an' actor. My idee is thet yu found oot what you wanted to know so powerful bad."

"Wal, thet's some good, anyhow," rejoined Texas, sitting up with a change of manner. "Boss, did yu take a look oot there?"

He pointed with long arm and his gesture had impressiveness.

"Boy, I been lookin' my eyes oot," responded Brite. "Shore don't know how to thank you an' Pan. Or what to say. I'll wait till yu tell me aboot it."

"There, Pan, what yu make of thet? He's an old Texas cattleman, too."

"Mr. Brite, if yu had looked the herd over carefully yu'd have seen thet we have fifteen hundred haid of long-horns more'n when we started."

"What!" ejaculated Brite, astounded.

"It's a fact, boss," added Texas. "Our good luck is matchin' our bad. Thet Hite ootfit had a herd of their own, stole, I reckon, from other drivers. Must have had them just this side of the Little Wichita."

"Wal, I'm stumped. What's the brand?"

"We saw a lot of X Two Bar an' some Circle H. Do yu know them brands?"

"Reckon I don't."

"New branded over an old mark, we figger. Wilder'n hell, too. As if we hadn't had enough hard work. . . . Get Pan to tell yu aboot last night."

Texas strode off, muttering to himself, and went down toward the creek, evidently to wash his bloodstained scarf, which he carried in his hand. Brite waited for the somber-faced gunman to speak, but was disappointed. Whereupon Brite, pretending tasks to do, moved about the camp fire, where the trail drivers were congregated, talking low. The advent of Reddie and Ann entirely silenced them. If Brite had expected his boys to be elated, he made a mistake. Perhaps they were keeping something from him and the girls. Mr. Hardy was holding his own, considering the serious nature of his wound, but he had developed a fever and was a pretty sick man. Williams said if they could get him to Doan's Post on the Red River that he had a fighting chance for his life. Presently Moze called them to supper, which turned out to be a more than usually silent meal.

San Sabe and Little rode in, after being relieved, and reported Indians with the buffalo several miles to the west.

"Thet bunch been keepin' along with us all day," said Williams. "But it ain't a very big one, so I reckon we needn't set up huggin' ourselves all night. Howsomever, we won't keep no fire burnin'."

"I gotta get some sleep," complained Texas Joe. "Pan Handle is an owl. But if I don't get sleep I'm a daid one."

Just before dark Texas called Brite aside, out of earshot of camp.

"Gimme a smoke, boss. Funny, me bein' nervous. . . . Did Pan tell yu what come off last night?"

"Not a word."

"Humph! Dam' these gunmen, anyhow," growled Texas. "Yu just cain't make one of 'em talk. I'll say Pan talked last night, though, with his gun. . . . Boss, thet was the strangest deal I was ever up against. If we'd known there was ten or eleven men instead of six we might have been a little leery."

"Tell me as much as yu like, Texas," replied Brite, quietly. "It's enough for me to know yu're safe an' we got our cattle back."

"Ahuh. . . . Wal, Hite wasn't standin' guard, so we reckoned after it was over. . . . Luck was with us, boss. We rode oot an' located before the storm busted. So when the lightnin' began to flash we didn't have far to go. As we worked up on the herd we seen one guard ride off hell bent for election. He'd seen us shore. Just after thet the rain hit us somethin' fierce. We split as planned an' started round the herd. They was millin' around in a bunch, lowin' an' crackin' their horns, an' gettin' restless. Wind an' rain, an' lightnin' too, were all at my back. An' thet shore was lucky. I hadn't gone far when I heahed a shot. The wind was comin' off an' on, so when it lulled a bit I could heah. Thet was how I come to heah one of Hite's guards yell: 'Thet yu, Bill? Yu heah a shot?' . . . I yelled yes an' kept on ridin'. It was black as coal 'cept when the flashes came. I got close to this guard when all the sky 'peared to blaze. He yelled: 'Hell! Who—!' . . . An' thet was all he had time for. I rode on, sort of feelin' my way, bumpin' into cattle off an' on. If they'd stampeded then they'd run me down. It didn't rain. It just came down in bucketsful. I couldn't see more'n twenty steps, an' could heah nothin' but wind an' rain an' thunder. Then I seen another guard. Seen him clear. But the next flash was short an' when I shot it was in the dark. When it lighten'd again I seen a hawse down an' the guard gettin' to his feet. It went dark again quick just as I shot. An' he shot back, for I saw the flash an' heahed his gun. He missed, though. An' so did I. Couldn't see him next time, so I rode on ahaid. . . . Wal, after thet I had it most as light as day, for seconds at a time. But I didn't meet no more guards. A long time after I expected to I seen the white flag wavin' from Pan's hat, an' I was shore glad. We met an' yelled at each other, then the long-horns took it in their haids to run. Right at us! We had to ride to get oot of the way. But the lightnin' kept flashin', an' the rain slowin' up, so we kept tab on them easy. They must have run ten miles. The storm passed an' they quit to settle down."

"How'd yu get thet bullet crease in yore haid?" queried Brite.

"Thet was this mawnin' a little after daybreak," concluded Texas. "We hung around the herd, watchin' an' listenin'. But nobody come. In the mawnin', however, four hawsemen charged us. They had only one rifle. An' we had our buffalo guns. So we stopped them an' held them off. I got this cut first thing. So far as we could tell we didn't hit one of them. Finally they rode off over the ridge. Pan an' me both recognized Ross Hite. He had the rifle, an' he was the one who bloodied me up. Hope I run into him again."

"I hope yu don't," returned Brite, bluntly.

"Wal, so does Pan Handle," drawled Texas. "Do yu know, boss, I reckon Pan an' Hite have crossed trails before. Because Pan said I didn't want to be meetin' Hite before he did. An' after thet I needn't never look for him again. What yu make of thet?"

"Humph," was all Brite replied. His brevity was partly actuated by the approach of Reddie and Ann.

"Better go to bed, girls," advised Texas. "Thet's shore what I'm aboot to do."

"Won't you let us bandage your head?" asked Ann, solicitously. "Reddie says you had a terrible wound."

"Shore. But thet's not in my haid, Ann," drawled Texas. "I got a scratch heah. It's stopped bleedin'."

"Texas, air yu goin' to tell us aboot last night?" queried Reddie, curiously. "Pan Handle seems all strange an' froze. We shore left him pronto."

"Nothin' much happened, Reddie," replied Texas. "We scared thet Hite ootfit an' stampeded the herd. An' heah we air."

"Scared my eye!" quoth Reddie. "Do yu reckon me an' Ann air kids to give guff to?"

"Wal, if guff is taffy, I say shore."

"Yu shot some of Hite's men," declared Reddie, with force. "I saw some daid—"

"Aw, yu mean them guards thet was struck by lightnin' last night," went on Texas, coolly. "Talk aboot retribushun! Why, girls, the Lawd was on our side last night. It's common enough for lightnin' to kill a trail driver or cowhand now an' then. But to strike three or four men in one storm an' all close together—thet's somethin' supernatural."

In the gathering dusk the girls regarded the nonchalant cowboy with different glances—Ann's wide-eyed and awed—Reddie's with dark disdain.

"Wal, there's shore a lot supernatural aboot yu, Texas Jack," she drawled.

Brite slept with one eye open that night. It passed at length without any disruption of the quiet camp. The trail drivers got off slowly and not until the sun burst red over the ridge top.

Orders were for the wagons and *remuda* to keep close to the herd. Watchful eyes circled the horizon that day. Far over on each side of the trail black lines of buffalo showed against the gray. Their movement was imperceptible. Brite often turned his glass upon them, but more often on the distant knolls and high points, seeking for Indian signs.

Eight or ten miles a day was all the trail drivers risked for their herds. Even this could not always be adhered to, especially with the obstacles of flooded rivers ahead, buffalo all around, and the menace of the savages, if not sight of them, ever present. Brite had begun to feel the strain of suspense, but had not noted it in any of his men.

At length, about mid-afternoon, it was almost a relief actually to sight a band of mounted Indians on a high top back from the trail. Uncertainty ceased for Brite, at least. By trying he ascertained that he could not make out this band with his naked eye. Perhaps the blurred figures might be clearer to his keen-sighted scouts. With the glass, however, Brite could see well enough to recognize the Indians as Comanches, and in sufficient force to cause more than apprehension.

Whereupon he rode forward to acquaint Hash Williams with his discovery. The hunter halted his team, and taking up the glasses without a word, he searched the horizon line.

"Ahuh, I see 'em. About forty, or so," he said, and cursed under his breath. "Looks like Comanches to me. If thet's Nigger Hawse we're shore flirtin' with the undertaker. Ride on ahaid an' tell Shipman to keep on goin' till he finds a place where we'd have some chance if attacked."

Brite was to learn that Texas had already espied the Indians.

"Up to deviltry, I reckon," he said. "I was thinkin' thet very thing Williams advises. Don't tell the girls, boss."

When Brite dropped back behind the *remuda* again, he was accosted by Reddie, who suspected that something was amiss. Brite told her, but advised not letting Ann know.

"Gosh! I don't know what good bein' an heiress would be if I lost my hair!" she exclaimed.

"Lass, yu wouldn't be anythin' but a good daid girl," replied Brite.

At last, at almost dusk, the herd was halted out on a flat near which a thread of water ran down a shallow gully.

Camp was selected on the north bank in the shelter of rocks. Moze was ordered to make his fire in a niche where it would be unseen. The riders came and went, silent, watchful, somber. Night fell. The wolves mourned. The warm summer air seemed to settle down over the camp as if it bore no tidings of ill. But the shadows in the rock cracks and caverns harbored menace.

Three guards kept continual watch around camp all night and six guards stayed with the herd. Two of the drivers were allowed to sleep at one time. So the night passed and the gray dawn—always the perilous hour for Indian attack— and the morning broke without incident.

But that day was beset with trials—barren ground for the cattle, hard going on the horses, ceaseless dread on the part of the trail drivers for the two girls and the injured man in their party. Several times during the day the Comanches were sighted watching them, riding along even with their position, keeping to the slow pace of the herd. How sinister that seemed to Brite! The red devils knew the trail; they were waiting for a certain place, or for something to happen, when they would attack.

Buffalo increased in numbers on all sides, still distant, but gradually closing up gray gaps in their line. That black line extended north as far as eye could see. The fact became evident that Brite's outfit was driving into the vast herd, leisurely grazing along. The situation grew hourly more nerve-racking. To swerve to either side was impossible, to stop or go back meant signal failure, defeat, and loss. The drivers absolutely had to stick to the trail and keep going.

The Chisholm Trail had again taken a decided slant to the northwest. And probably somewhere ahead, perhaps across the Red River, it would bisect the vast herd of buffalo. The alarming discovery was made that the following herd of long-horns had come up in plain sight, and ten miles behind it another wavered a long, dark line on the gray. Brite asked his men why these pursuing trail drivers were pressing him so hard. And the answer was Indians, buffalo, and the two hundred thousand head of cattle that had started and must keep on. To turn or slow down meant to fall by the wayside.

Texas Joe drove late that day and made dry camp. All night the guards sang and rode to keep the herd bedded down. Morning disclosed the endless stream of buffalo closer. But Indians were not in sight. Smoke signals, however, arose from two distant hills, one on each side of the trail.

Loss of sleep and ceaseless vigilance by night, and the slow march by day wore upon the drivers. Brite had ceased to count the camps. Every hour was fraught with dread expectation. Yet at last they reached the Red River. The buffalo were crossing some miles above the trail, but a spur of the prodigious herd kept swinging in behind. Texas Joe pointed the cattle across and took the lead himself, magnificent in his dauntlessness.

The Red was midway between high and low water stages —its most treacherous condition. Four hours were consumed in the drive across and more than a hundred long-horns were lost. All the drivers were needed to get the wagons over, a desperate task which only such heedless young men would have undertaken.

Night found them in camp, some of them spent, all of them wearied, yet cheered by the fact that Doan's Post was within striking distance on the morrow.

Texas Joe drove the remaining ten miles to Doan's before noon of the next day. All the drivers wanted to get a few hours' release from the herd, to drink, to talk, to get rid of one danger by hearing of another. But when Brite called for volunteers to stand guard with the herd for a few hours they all voiced their willingness to stay.

"Wal, I'll have to settle it," said Brite. "Ackerman, yu drive the Hardys in. Tex, yu an' Pan Handle come with me. . . . Boys, we'll be back pronto to give yu a chance to ride in."

Doan's Post gave evidence of having more than its usual number of inhabitants and visitors. Horses were numerous on the grass plain around the post. Half a dozen wagons were drawn up before the gray, squat, weather-beaten houses. A sign, DOAN'S STORE, in large black letters, showed on the south side of the largest house. This place, run by Tom Doan, was a trading post for Indians and cattlemen, and was in the heyday of its useful and hazardous existence.

Mounted men, riders with unsaddled horses, Indians lounging and squatting before the doors, watched the newcomers with interest. Arriving travelers were the life of Doan's Post. But the way Pan Handle and Texas Joe dismounted a goodly distance from these bearded watchers and proceeded forward on foot surely had as much significance for them as it had for Brite. The crowd of a dozen or more spread to let the two slow visitors approach the door. Then Brite came on beside the Hardy wagon. Reddie, disobedient as usual, had joined them.

"Howdy, Tom," called Brite, to the stalwart man in the door.

"Howdy yoreself," came the hearty response. "Wal, damme if it ain't Adam Brite. Git right down an' come in."

"Tom, yu ought to remember my foreman, Texas Joe. An' this is Pan Handle Smith. We've got a sick man in the wagon heah. Hardy, by name. Thet's his daughter on the seat. They're all thet's left of a wagon train bound for California. Can yu take care of them for a while, till Hardy is able to join another train?"

"Yu bet I can," replied the genial Doan. Willing hands lifted Hardy out of the wagon and carried him into the Post. Ann sat on the wagon seat, her pretty face worn and thin, her eyes full of tears, perhaps of deliverance, perhaps of something else, as she gazed down upon the bareheaded cowboy.

"We've come to the partin' of the trail, Miss Ann," Deuce was saying, in a strong and vibrant voice. "Yu're safe heah, thank God. An' yore dad will come around. I'm shore hopin' we'll make it through to Dodge. An'—I'm askin' yu—will it be all right for me to wait there till yu come?"

"Oh yes—I—I'd be so glad," she murmured, shyly.

"An' go on to California with yu?" he concluded, boldly.

"If yu will," she replied; and for a moment time and place were naught to these two.

"Aw, thet's good of yu," he burst out at last. "It's just been wonderful—knowin' yu. . . . Good-by. . . . I must go back to the boys."

"Good-by," she faltered, and gave him her hand. Deuce kissed it right gallantly, and then fled out across the prairie toward the herd.

CHAPTER **14** REDDIE JUMPED off her horse beside the Hardy wagon, on the seat of which Ann sat still as a stone, watching the cowboy. Ackerman turned once to hold his sombrero high. Then she waved her handkerchief. He wheeled and did not look back again.

"Ann, it's pretty tough—this sayin' good-by," spoke up Reddie. "Let's go in the Post, away from these men. I'm shore gonna bawl."

"Oh, Reddie, I—I'm bawling now," cried Ann, as she clambered down, not sure of her sight. "He was so—so good—so fine. . . . Oh, will we ever meet—again?"

Arm in arm the girls went toward the door of the Post, where Brite observed Ann shrink visibly from two sloe-eyed, gaunt, and somber Indians.

"Let's get this over pronto, Tex," said Brite. "I'll buy what supplies Doan can furnish."

"All right, boss. Pan an' I will come in presently," replied Texas. "We want to ask some questions thet mebbe Doan wouldn't answer."

Brite hurried into the Post. It was a picturesque, crowded, odorous place with its colorful Indian trappings, its formidable arsenal, its full shelves and burdened counters. When Doan returned from the after quarters, where evidently he had seen to Hardy's comfort, Brite wrote with a stub of a lead pencil the supplies he needed.

"What you think? This ain't Santone or Abilene," he said gruffly. "But I can let you have flour, beans, coffee, tobacco, an' mebbe—"

"Do yore best, Tom," interrupted Brite, hastily. "I'm no robber. Can yu haul the stuff oot to camp?"

"Shore, inside an hour."

"Thet's all, then, an' much obliged. . . . Any trail drivers ahaid of me?"

"Not lately. You've got the trail all to yourself. An' thet's damn bad."

Brite was perfectly well aware of this.

"Comanches an' Kiowas particular bad lately," went on Doan. "Both Nigger Horse an' Santana are on the rampage. Let me give you a hunch. If thet old Comanche devil rides into camp, you parley with him, argue with him, but in the end you give him what he wants. An' for thet reason take grub to spare an' particular coffee an' tobacco. But if thet Kiowa chief stops you don't give him a thing 'cept a piece of your mind. Santana is dangerous to weak outfits. But he's a coward an' he can be bluffed. Don't stand any monkey business from the Kiowas. Show them you are heavily armed an' will shoot at the drop of a hat."

"Much obliged, Doan. I'll remember your advice."

"You're goin' to be blocked by buffalo, unless you can break through. I'll bet ten million buffalo have passed heah this month."

"What month an' day is it, anyhow?"

"Wal, you have been trail-drivin'. . . . Let's see. It's the sixteenth of July."

"Yu don't say? Time shore flies on the trail. . . . I'd like to know if Ross Hite an' three of his ootfit have passed this way lately?"

"Been several little outfits by this week," replied the trader, evasively. "Travelin' light an' fast. . . . I don't know Hite personally. Heerd of him, shore. I don't ask questions of my customers, Brite."

"Yu know yore business, Doan," returned Brite, shortly. "For yore benefit, though, I'll tell yu Hite's ootfit raided us twice. He had all of my herd at one time."

"Hell you say!" ejaculated Doan, sharply, pulling his beard. "What come of it?"

"Wal, we got the stock back an' left some of Hite's ootfit along the trail."

Reddie Bayne came stumbling along, wiping her eyes.

"Wait, Reddie. I'll go with yu," called Brite. "Where can I say good-by to the Hardys?"

She pointed to the open door through which she had emerged. Brite went in quickly and got that painful interview over.

"Just a minute, Brite," called Doan, as the cattleman hurried out. "I'm not so particular aboot Indians as I am aboot men of my own color. But I have to preserve friendly relations with all the tribes. They trade with me. I am goin' to tell you, though, that the two bucks standin' outside are scouts for some Comanche outfit, an' they've been waitin' for the first trail herd to come along. You know all you trail drivers do. Pack the bucks back to the next herd, if you can. It's a mistaken policy. But the hunch I want to give you is to stop those two Comanches."

"Stop them?"

"Shore. Don't let them come out an' look over your outfit— then ride to report to their chief. Like as not it's Nigger Horse, himself."

"That *is* a hunch. I'll tell Texas," replied Brite, pondering, and went out with Reddie.

"Gee!" she whispered, with round eyes. "He's givin' us a hunch to shoot some more Comanches."

" 'Pears thet way. Yet he shore didn't give us any hunch aboot Ross Hite."

Texas Joe and Pan Handle appeared to be in a colloquy with two men, and Williams and Smiling Pete were engaged with the remainder of the white men present.

"Williams, yu'll ride over to say good-by?" queried Brite.

"Shore we will. For two bits I'd go on all the way with yu," he replied.

"Wal, I'll give yu a lot more than thet. . . . Yu've been mighty helpful. I couldn't begin to thank yu."

"Pete wants to hunt buffalo," rejoined Williams. "An' thet sticks us heah."

Brite got on his horse. "Tex, we're goin'. Come heah."

Texas strode over, and giving Reddie a gentle shove as she mounted, he came close to Brite.

"Texas," whispered Brite, bending over. "Those two Comanches there are scouts for a raidin' bunch, so says Doan. Dam' if he didn't hint we ought to do somethin' aboot it. He cain't, 'cause he has to keep on friendly terms with all the reddies."

"Wal, boss, we got thet hunch, too, an' heahed somethin' aboot Hite. I'll tell yu when we come back to camp."

Reddie had put her black to a canter, and had covered half the distance back to camp before Brite caught up with her.

"Save yore hawse, girl. What's yore hurry?"

"Dad, I just get sick inside when I see thet look come to Texas Jack's eyes," she replied.

"What look?"

"I don't know what to call it. I saw it first thet day just before he drawed on Wallen. Like thet queer lightnin' flash we saw durin' the storm the other night."

"Reddie, yu ought to be used to hard looks of trail drivers by now. It's a hard life."

"But I want Texas Jack to quit throwin' guns!" she cried, with surprisingly poignant passion.

"Wal! Wal!" exclaimed Brite. "An' why, lass?"

"Pretty soon he'll be another gunman like Pan Handle. An' then, sooner or later, he'll get killed!"

"I reckon thet's true enough," replied Brite. "Come to think aboot thet, I feel the same way. What air we goin' to do to stop him?"

"Stop Tex? It cain't be done, Dad."

"Wal, mebbe not oot heah on the trail. But if we ever

end this drive—then it could be done. *Yu* could stop Tex, lass."

She spurred the black and drew away swift as the wind. Brite gathered that she had realized how she could put an end to the wildness of Joe Shipman.

The cattle were grazing and in good order. Westward along the river, clouds of dust rolled aloft, and at intervals a low roar of hoofs came on the still hot air. The buffalo were crossing the Red River. Brite and Reddie took the places of San Sabe and Rolly Little at guard, and the two cowboys were like youngsters just released from school. They raced for town. Several slow dragging hours passed by. The herd did not move half a mile; the *remuda* covered less ground. Brite did not relish sight of a mounted Indian who rode out from the Post and from a distance watched the camp.

A little later Brite was startled out of his rest by gunshots. He leaped up in time to see the Indian spy riding like a streak across the plain. Texas and Pan Handle, two hundred yards to the left, were shooting at the Comanche as fast as they could pull triggers. Probably their idea was to frighten him, thought Brite, in which case they succeeded amply. No Indian could ride so well as a Comanche and this one broke all records for a short race. It chanced that he took down the plain in a direction which evidently brought him close to the far end of the herd, where one of the cowboys was on guard. This fellow, either Holden or Bender, saw the Indian and opened up on him with a buffalo gun. From that instant until the Comanche was out of sight he rode hidden on the far side of his mustang.

Texas Joe was using forceful range language when he rode in, and manifestly had been irritated by something.

"What ails yu, Tex?" asked Brite. "I'm feelin' cheerful, myself."

"Yu're loco. Do yu know what we did? We hired them cowhands to hawg-tie the two Comanches an' to keep 'em in Doan's storehouse for a couple of days. Great idee! But all for nothin'. This buck we was shootin' at had counted our wagons, hawses, cattle, an' drivers. We was shore shootin' at thet redskin to kill. But he was oot of range. What'n hell was eatin' yu men thet yu didn't see him long ago?"

Brite maintained a discreet silence.

"Boss, the supplies will be oot pronto," went on Texas as he dismounted. "Reddie, if yu have another hawse handy I'll relieve one of the boys."

"Same heah," spoke up Pan Handle.

"Throw some grub pronto, Moze. . . . Boss, our man Hite rode through heah day before yestiddy mawnin'. He had three fellars with him, one crippled up serious an' had to be tied in the saddle. Hite was spittin' fire, an' they all was ugly."

"Did they stop at Doan's?"

"Shore, accordin' to Bud. They was oot of grub an' ammunition. Had only two pack hawses. We shore won't see no more of Hite till we get to Dodge. He hangs oot at Hays City, so Bud said, an' comes often to Dodge."

"Let Hite go, boys. No sense huntin' up trouble," advised Brite, tersely.

"Boss, yu're a forgivin' cuss," drawled Texas, admiringly. "Now I just cain't be thet way. An' Pan, heah, why, he'll ride a thousand miles to meet thet Ross Hite again. An' I'm goin' with him."

"Yu air not," spoke up Reddie, tartly, a red spot in each cheek.

"Wal, dog-gone! There's the kid, bossy as ever. Brite, if I get plugged on the way up yu let Reddie boss the ootfit."

Texas Joe had found a way to make Reddie wince, and he was working it on every possible occasion. The chances were surely even that the daring cowboy would lose his life one way or another before the end of the trail, and Reddie simply could not stand a hint of it without betraying her fear. Probably, to judge from her flashing eyes, she would have made a strong retort had it not been for the arrival of Williams and Smiling Pete.

"Wal, heah we air to set in our last supper on Moze," said Williams, genially. "I shore hate to say good-by to this ootfit. Folks get awful close on such drives as we had comin' up."

"Reddie Bayne, don't yu want to stay behind with us?" asked Smiling Pete, teasingly. "We shore won't boss yu aboot like thet Texas fellar."

"Ump-umm. I like yu, Smilin' Pete," replied Reddie, in the same spirit. "But I'm strong for Santone an' Dad's ranch."

"Dad?" echoed the hunters, in unison.

"Shore. I've adopted Mr. Brite as my dad."

"Haw! Haw! The lucky son-of-a-gun. He ain't so old, neither. Mebbe Hash an' me will have to send our cairds to yore—"

But Reddie ran away behind the chuck-wagon.

"Come heah, yu men, an' be serious," said Brite. "We want all the hunches yu can give us for the rest of this drive north."

Brite's outfit left Doan's Post before sunrise next morning with just short of six thousand long-horn cattle. The buffalo herd had apparently kept along the Red River.

In the afternoon of that day a band of Comanches rode out from a pass between two hills and held up the cavalcade. Brite galloped ahead in some trepidation, yelling for Reddie to leave the *remuda* and follow him. When he arrived at the head of the herd, he found Texas Joe and Pan Handle, with the other drivers, lined up before about thirty squat, pointed-faced, long-haired Indians.

"Boss, meet Nigger Hawse an' his ootfit," was Texas's laconic greeting.

"Howdy, Chief," returned Brite, facing Nigger Horse. This Comanche did not look his fame, but appeared to be an ordinary redskin, stolid and unofficious. He did not altogether lack dignity. To Brite he was a surprise and a relief. But his basilisk eyes might have hid much. Brite wished the buffalo-hunters had come on with them.

"How," replied Nigger Horse, raising a slow hand.

"What yu want, Chief?"

"Beef."

Brite waved a magnanimous hand toward the herd.

"Help yoreself."

The Comanche spoke in low grunts to his redmen.

"Tobac," he went on, his dark, inscrutable eyes again fixing on Brite.

"Plenty. Wagon come," replied Brite, pointing to Moze, who had the team approaching at a trot. Nigger Horse gazed in the direction of the chuck-wagon, then back at the vast herd, and lastly at the formidably armed drivers solidly arrayed in a line.

"Flour," resumed the chief. His English required a practiced ear to distinguish, but Brite understood him and nodded his willingness.

"Coffee."

Brite held up five fingers to designate the number of sacks he was willing to donate.

"Beans."

"Heap big bag," replied Brite.

Manifestly this generosity from a trail driver had not been the accustomed thing.

"Boss, the old devil wants us to refuse somethin'," put in Texas.

"An' he'll keep on askin' till yu have to refuse," added Pan Handle.

Moze arrived with the chuck-wagon, behind which the Comanches rode in a half circle, greedy-eyed and jabbering. Moze's black face could not turn pale, but it looked mighty strange.

"Pile oot, Moze," ordered Brite. "Open up yore box, an' get oot the goods we selected for this missionary business."

"Yas s-suh—y-yas, suh," replied the Negro, scared out of his wits.

"Sack of flour first, Moze," said Brite. "An' throw it up on his hawse. Make oot it's heavy."

Obviously this last was not necessary. Either the sack was heavy or Moze had grown weak, for he labored with it and almost knocked Nigger Horse off his mustang. The Indian let out what sounded like: "Yah! Yah!" But he surely held onto the flour. Then Brite ordered Moze to burden the Comanche further with the generous donation of tobacco, coffee, and beans.

"There yu air, Chief," called out Brite, making a show of friendliness.

"Flour," said Nigger Horse.

"Yu got it," replied Brite, pointing to the large sack.

The Indian emphatically shook his head.

"Greasy old robber!" ejaculated Texas. "He wants more. Boss, heah's where yu stand fast. If yu give in he'll take all our grub."

"Brite, don't give him any more. We'd better fight than starve," said Pan Handle.

Whereupon Brite, just as emphatically, shook his head and said: "No more, Chief."

The Comanche yelled something in his own tongue. Its content was not reassuring.

"Heap powder—bullet," added Nigger Horse.

"No," declared Brite.

The Indian thundered his demand. This had the effect of rousing Brite's ire, not a particularly difficult task. Brite shook his head in slow and positive refusal.

"Give Injun all!" yelled the chief.

"GIVE INJUN HELL!" roared Brite, suddenly furious.

"Thet's the talk, boss," shouted Texas. "Yu can bluff the old geezer."

"Brite, stick to thet," broke in Pan Handle, in ringing voice. "Listen, all of yu. If it comes to a fight, Tex an' I air good for Nigger Hawse an' four or five on each side of him. Yu boys look after the ends."

"Reddie, yu duck back behind the wagon an' do yore shootin' from there," ordered Texas.

Then ensued the deadlock. It was a critical moment, with life or death quivering on a hair balance. How hideously that savage's lineaments changed! The wily old Comanche had made his bluff and it had been called. Probably he understood more of the white man's language than he pretended. Certainly he comprehended the cold front of those frowning trail drivers.

"Boys, yu got time to get on the ground," called the practical Texas, slipping out of his saddle and stepping out in front of his horse. In another moment all the men, except Brite, had followed suit. Texas and Pan Handle held a gun in each hand. At such close range they would do deadly work before the Comanches could level a rifle or draw a bow. Nigger Horse undoubtedly saw this—that he had bluffed the wrong outfit. Still, he did not waver in his savage dominance.

Brite had an inspiration.

"Chief," he burst out, "we do good by yu. We give heaps. But no more. If yu want fight, we fight. . . . Two trail herds tomorrow." Here Brite held up two fingers, and indicating his cattle, made signs that more were coming up the trail. "Heap more. So many like buffalo. White men with herds come all time. Two moons." And with both hands up he opened each to spread his fingers, and repeated this time and again.

"Ugh!" ejaculated Nigger Horse. He understood, and that tactful persuasion of Brite's was the deciding factor. He let out sharp guttural sentences. Two of his followers wheeled their ponies toward the herd, fitting arrows to their bows. Then Nigger Horse, burdened with his possessions, not one parcel of which would he relinquish to eager hands, rode back without another word, followed by his band.

"Close shave!" breathed Brite, in intense relief.

"Shore. But closer for thet bull-haided Comanche an' his ootfit," declared Texas. "He made a mistake an' got in too close. We'd cleaned them oot in ten seconds. Hey, Pan?"

"I'd like to have broke loose," replied Pan Handle, in a queer voice.

"Let wal enough alone, yu fire-eaters," yelled Brite.

"Boss, we'll hang together till the *remuda* passes," returned Texas.

"Whoopee! We're a hot ootfit!" shouted Deuce Ackerman, lustily, his head thrown back, his jaw corded. The relaxation of the other drivers showed in yells or similar wild statements.

"I doan' know aboot this heah ootrageous luck," observed

Whittaker, softly, as if to himself. He was the quietest of the drivers.

"Somebody'd had to shoot quick to beat me borin' thet dirty old redskin," spoke up Reddie, coolly.

"My Gawd! The girl's ruined!" ejaculated Texas.

"Haw! Haw! Haw!" roared the tenderfoot Bender. But a second look at the hulking, fierce-eyed, black-faced, young Pennsylvanian convinced the cattleman that Bender's tenderfoot days were passed. He himself felt the cold, hard, wild spirit rise.

"On, boys," he ordered. "Once across the Canadian we'll be halfway an' more to Dodge."

"We'll drive 'em, boss," replied Texas Joe, grimly. "No more lazy, loafin', fattenin' mossy-horns this trip!"

They made ten miles before night, ending the longest drive since they had left San Antonio. The night fell dark, with rumble of thunder and sheet lightning in the distance. The tired cattle bedded down early and held well all night. Morning came lowering and threatening, with a chill wind that swept over the herd from the north. Soon the light failed until day was almost as dark as night. A terrific hailstorm burst upon the luckless herd and drivers. The hailstones grew larger as the storm swept on, until the pellets of gray ice were as large as walnuts. The drivers from suffering a severe pounding passed to extreme risk of their lives. They had been forced to protect heads and faces with whatever was available. Reddie Bayne was knocked off her horse and carried senseless to the wagon; San Sabe swayed in his saddle like a drunken man; Texas Joe tied his coat round his sombrero and yelled when the big hailstones bounced off his head; bloody and bruised, the other drivers resembled men who had engaged in fierce fistic encounters.

When this queer freak of nature passed, the ground was covered half a foot deep with hailstones. Dead rabbits and antelope littered the plain, and all the way, as far as Brite could see to the rear, stunned and beaten cattle lay on the ground or staggered along.

"I told yu-all things were gonna happen," yelled Texas to

his followers as they made camp that night, sore and beaten of body. "But I'm not carin', if only the buffalo will pass us by."

Next day they were visited by members of a tribe of Kiowas supposed to be friendly with the whites. They had held "heap big peace talk" with Uncle Sam. Brite did not give so much as he had in the case of the Comanches, yet he did well by them.

During the night these savages stampeded the south end of the herd. How it was done did not appear until next day, when among the scattered cattle was found a long-horn here and there with an arrow imbedded in his hide. Some of these had to be shot. The herd was held over until all the stampeded steers and cows could be rounded up. It took three days of strenuous riding by day and guarding by night. Texas Joe and his trail drivers passed into what San Sabe described as being "poison-fightin' mad!"

Bitter as gall to them was it to see two trail herds pass them by and forge to the front. After seven weeks or more of leadership! But Brite did not take it so hard. Other herds now, and both together not so large as his, would bear the brunt of what lay ahead.

That fourth day, when they were off again, buffalo once more made their appearance. Soldiers from Fort Cobb, a post forty miles off the trail to the east, informed Brite that they had been turned back by the enormous, impenetrable mass of buffalo some miles westward. They had been trailing a marauding bunch of Apaches from the Staked Plain.

Brite's men drove on, and their difficulties multiplied. Stampedes became frequent; storms and swollen creeks further impeded their progress; the chuck-wagon, springing leaks in its boat-like bottom, had almost to be carried across the North Fork of the Red. Sometimes it became necessary to build pontoons and riders had to swim their horses alongside, holding the pontoons in place. But they kept on doggedly, their foreman cool and resourceful, all bound to this seemingly impossible drive.

Pond Creek, which headed sixty miles northwest of Fort Cobb, was an objective Texas Joe spoke of for twenty-four hours and drove hard one long day to reach.

Brite had his misgivings when at sunset of that day he rode to the top of a slope and saw the herd gaining momentum on the down grade, drawn by sight and scent of water after a hot, dry drive.

This creek, usually only a shallow run, appeared bank-full, a swift, narrow river extremely dangerous at that stage for beast and man. There had been no rain that day anywhere near the region the herd had traversed. Texas Joe had been justified in thinking Pond Creek was at normal height, and he had let the herd go over the ridge without first scouting ahead, as was his custom. It was too late now unless the herd could be stopped.

Brite spurred his horse down the slope, yelling over his shoulder for Reddie to hurry. Drivers on each side of the herd were forging to the front, inspired, no doubt, by the fiercely riding Texas Joe. It was bad going, as Brite found out to his sorrow, when he was thrown over the head of his falling horse, thus sustaining a mean fall. Reddie was quick to leap off and go to his side.

"Oh, Dad! Thet was a tumble!" she cried. "I thought yu'd break yore neck. . . . Set up. Air yu all heah? Let me feel."

"I reckon—nothin' busted," groaned the cattleman, getting up laboriously. "If thet ground hadn't been soft—wal, yu'd—"

"My Gawd, Dad! Look!" cried Reddie, frantically, leaping on her horse. "They're stampedin' down this hill."

Brite got up to stand a moment surveying the scene. A tremendous trampling, tussling, cracking roar, permeated by a shrill bawling sound, dinned in his ears.

"Red, it's only the back end thet's stampedin'," he shouted.

"Yes. But they're rushin' the front down."

"Rustle. We can help some, but don't take chances."

They galloped down along the flank of the jostling cattle to the short quarter of a mile of slope between the point of the herd and the river. The drivers were here in a bunch, yelling, riding, shooting, plunging their mounts at the foremost old mossy-horns. Brite and Reddie rode in to help, keeping close to the outside.

Then followed a hot-pressed, swift, and desperate charge on the part of the trail drivers to hold the front of the herd. It was hazardous work. Texas Joe yelled orders through pale lips, but no driver at any distance heard them. The bulls and steers had been halted, but as pressure was exerted in the rear they began to toss their great, horned heads, and to bawl and tear up the ground. The mass of the herd, up on the steeper slope, maddened now to get to the water, could not be bolstered back by the front line.

"Back!" yelled Texas, in stentorian voice, waving wide his arms to the drivers. All save San Sabe heard or saw, and ran their horses to either side. Deuce, Texas, Reddie, Whittaker, and Bender reached the open behind Brite just as a terrible groan ran through the herd.

Texas Joe's frantic yells and actions actuated all to join in the effort to make San Sabe hear. His position was extremely perilous, being exactly in the center of the straining herd. His horse was rearing. San Sabe, gun in each hand, shot fire and smoke into the very faces of the leaders. Pan Handle, Holden, and Little, flashing by on terrorized horses, failed to attract him. How passionate and fierce his actions! Hatless and coatless, his hair flying, this half-breed *vaquero* fronted the maddened herd with an instinct of a thousand years of cattle mastery.

The line of horned heads curved at each end, as if a dam had burst where it joined the banks. Suddenly then the center gave way with that peculiar grinding roar of hoofs, horns, and bodies. Like a flood it spilled down upon San Sabe. His horse gave a magnificent leap back and to the side, just escaping the rolling juggernaut. The horse saw, if San Sabe did not, that escape to either side was impossible. On the very horns of the running bulls he plunged for the river.

But he did not gain a yard on those fleet long-horns, propelled forward by thousands of rushing bodies behind. To Brite's horror it appeared that the limber cattle actually gained on San Sabe. His horse tripped at the brink of the bank and plunged down. The rider was pitched headlong. Next instant a live wall of beasts poured over the brink with resounding hollow splash, and as if by magic the river bank became obliterated.

CHAPTER **15** SPELLBOUND, Brite gazed at the thrilling and frightful spectacle. A gigantic wave rose and swelled across the creek to crash over the opposite bank. In another moment the narrow strip of muddy water vanished, and in its place was a river of bristling horns, packed solid, twisting, bobbing under and up again, and sweeping down with the current. But for that current of deep water the stream bed would have been filled with cattle from bank to bank, and the mass of the herd would have plunged across over hundreds of dead bodies.

In an incredibly short space the whole herd had rolled into the river, line after line taking the place of the beasts that were swept away in the current. From plunging pell-mell the cattle changed abruptly to swimming pell-mell. And when the last line had gone overboard the front line, far down the stream, was wading out on the other side.

The change from sodden, wrestling crash to strange silence seemed as miraculous as the escape of the herd. Momentum and current forced the crazy animals across the river. Two hundred yards down all the opposite shelving shore was blotted out by cattle, and as hundreds waded out, other hundreds took their places, so that there was no blocking of the on-sweeping tide of heads and horns. It was the most remarkable sight Brite had ever seen in connection with cattle.

Texas Joe was the first to break out of his trance.

"—— thet fool!" he thundered, with a mighty curse and with convulsed face, eyes shut tight, and tears streaming from under the lids, with lips drawn and cheeks set in rigid holes, he seemed to gaze up blindly at the sky, invoking help where there was no help, surrendering in that tragic moment to the inevitable and ruthless calling of the trail driver.

Pan Handle rode down to the scored bank where San Sabe had disappeared. His comrade Holden followed slowly. Rolly Little bestrode his horse as if stunned.

Brite remembered Reddie, and hastened to her side. With bowed head and shaking shoulders she bent over, hanging to the pommel of her saddle.

"Brace up, Red," said Brite, hoarsely, though deeply shaken himself. "We got to go through."

"Oh—we'd grown—like one family," cried the girl, raising her face.

"Reddie, drive yore *remuda* in," shouted Texas, in strident voice. "Deuce, take Holden an' foller the herd. Rest of yu, help me with the wagon."

Night settled down again, silent except for the rush of the sliding river and the strange back-lashes of sand-laden water. Moze bustled silently around the camp fire. Several of the drivers were eating as if that task, like the others, had to be done. Texas, Pan Handle, Deuce, and Rolly were out on guard, hungry and wet and miserable. Reddie had gone supperless to bed. Brite sat drying his legs, fighting his conscience. Three young faces appeared spectrally in the white embers of the fire!

Next day it was as if the trail drivers had never weakened and almost cracked. Obstacles heightened their spirits and deadened their memories. Deer Creek was bone dry. The stock got through the following day without water. A third drive over miles of wasteland and dragging sand put horses as well as cattle in a precarious condition. All night long the herd milled like the ceaseless eddy of a river, bawling and lowing. No sleep or rest that night for any of Brite's outfit! If next morning they found a branch of the South Canadian dusty and dry, that would be the end.

Indians stopped with Moze that night. "No water!" they said. Buffalo had ranged to the West.

At dawn the drivers pointed the herd and goaded them on ruthlessly. The sun rose red in a copper sky. The heat veils floated up from the sand. Miles from the branch of the Canadian the old mossy-horns scented water. The riders could not hold them. Nothing could stop the thirst-maddened brutes. When the leaders launched out, the whole herd stampeded as one. The trail drivers had a wild run, but without hope of checking the stampede. They rolled on, a sweeping, thundering clatter, shaking the earth and sending aloft a great yellow cloud of dust.

The river checked that stampede and saved Brite incalculable loss. Once across the South Branch into grassy level range again, the trail drivers forgot the past and looked only ahead. Day after day passed. At Wolf Creek they encountered the long-looked-for buffalo herd, the ragged strings of which reached out to the east. Texas Joe rested his outfit and stock a day at this good camp site.

A sultry night presaged storm. But the interminable hours wore to dawn, and the torrid day passed without rain. Texas Joe, sensing another storm, drove the herd into the head of a narrow valley, steep-walled and easy to guard.

"I doan' like this heah weather," said Whittaker, breaking a somber silence around the camp fire.

"Wal, who does?" rejoined Texas, wearily. "But a good soakin' rain would help us oot."

"Shore, if it rained rain."

"My hair cracks too much to suit me," said another.

"Reddie, how's the *remuda?*"

"Actin' queer," she replied. "Sniffin' the air, poundin' the ground, quiverin' all over."

Brite feared that the peculiar condition of earth, atmosphere, and sky presaged one of the rare, awe-inspiring, and devastating electric storms that this region was noted for. He recalled what trail drivers had told which seemed too incredible to believe. But here was the strange red sunset, the absolutely still and sultry dusk, the overcast sky that yet did not wholly hide the pale stars, the ghastliness of the unreal earth.

"World comin' to an end!" ejaculated Texas Joe. Like all men of the open, used to the phenomena of the elements, he was superstitious and acknowledged a mysterious omniscience in nature.

"Fine night to be home sparkin' my girl," joked Rolly Little.

"Rolly, boy, yu'll never see home no more, nor thet flirtin' little redhaid," taunted Deuce Ackerman, fatalistically.

"Come to think of thet, all redhaids are flirty an' fickle," philosophized Texas.

Reddie heard, but for once had no audacious retort. She was obsessed with gravity.

"Tex—Dad—it ain't natural," she said, nervously.

"Wal, lass, whatever it is, it'll come an' pass, an' spare us mebbe, please God," rejoined the cattleman.

"Boss, is it gonna be one of them storms when electricity runs like water?" queried Texas.

"I don't know, Tex, I swear to goodness I don't. But I've heahed when the sky looks like a great white globe of glass with a light burnin' inside thet it'll burst presently an' let down a million jumpin' stars an' balls an' ropes an' sparks."

Texas got to his feet, dark and stern. "Fork yore hawses, everybody. If we're goin' to hell we'll go together."

They rode out to join the four guards already on duty.

"What's comin' off?" yelled Less Holden, as the others came within earshot.

"We're gamblin' with death, cowboy," returned Texas Joe.

So indeed it seemed to Brite. The weird conditions imperceptibly increased. It became so light that the faces of the drivers shone like marble in moonlight. There were no shadows. Darkness of night had been eliminated, yet no moon showed, and the stars had vanished in the globe overhead.

"We can hold 'em in heah onless they stampede," said Texas. "What's the stock doin', Less?"

"Not grazin', thet's shore. An' the *remuda* is plumb loco."

Brite followed Reddie over to the dark patch of mustangs, huddled in a compact drove under the west wall. This embankment was just steep and high enough to keep the mustangs from climbing. A restless nickering ran through the mass. They trooped with low roar of hoofs away from the approaching riders.

"Just a little fussy, Dad," said Reddie, hopefully.

"Cain't yu sing them quiet, Reddie?" asked Brite.

"I'll try, but I shore don't feel like no nightingale tonight," replied Reddie. "I haven't heahed any of the boys."

In low and quavering tones Reddie began "La Paloma," and as she progressed with the song, her sweet and plaintive voice grew stronger. The strange atmosphere appeared to intensify it, until toward the close she was singing with a power and beauty that entranced the listening cattlemen. When she finished, Texas Joe, who seldom sang, burst out with his wild and piercing tenor, and then the others chimed in to ring a wonderful medley down that lonely valley. The *remuda* quieted down, and at length the great herd appeared chained to music.

The trail drivers sang in chorus and in quartets, duets and singly, until they had repeated their limited stock of songs, and had exhausted their vocal powers.

When they had no more to give, the hour was late, and as if in answer, from far down the range rumbled and mumbled low thunder, while pale flashes of lightning shone all over the sky.

The drivers sat their horses and waited. That they were uneasy, that they did not smoke or sit still, proved the abnormality of the hour. They kept close together and spoke often. Brite observed that Reddie seldom let her restless black move a rod away.

The rumble of thunder and the queer flashes might have presaged a storm, but apparently it did not come closer. Brite observed that the singular sheen became enhanced, if anything. The sultry, drowsy air grew thicker. It had weight. It appeared to settle down over stock and men like a transparent blanket.

Suddenly the sky ripped across with terrific bars of lightning that gave forth a tearing, cracking sound. Rain began to fall, but not in any quantity. Brite waited for the expected clap of thunder. It did not materialize. Then he recognized for a certainty the symptoms of an electrical storm such as had been described to him.

"Boys, we're in for a galvanizin'," he called. "We're as safe heah as anywheres. We cain't do nothin' but take our chance an' try to hold the cattle. But if what's been told me is true they'll be scared still."

"We're heah, boss," boomed Texas, and a reassuring shout came from Pan Handle.

"Oh, Dad!" cried Reddie. "Run yore hand through yore hawse's mane!"

Brite did as bidden, to be startled at a cracking, sizzling sweep of sparks clear to the ears of his horse. He jumped as if he had been shot. Brite did not attempt that again. But he watched Reddie. Electric fluid appeared to play and burn with greenish fire through the black's mane, and run out on the tips of his ears and burst. The obedient horse did not like this, but he held firm, just prancing a little.

"Lass, the air is charged," said Brite, fearfully.

"Yes, Dad, an' it's gonna bust!" screamed Reddie as the whole range land blazed under the white dome.

Hoarse shouts from the drivers sounded as if wrenched from them. But after that one outburst they kept mute. Brite had involuntarily closed his eyes at the intense flare. Even with his lids tightly shut he saw the lightning flashes. He opened them upon an appalling display across the heavens. Flash after flash illumined the sky, and if thunder followed it was faint and far off. The flashes rose on all sides to and across the zenith, where, fusing in one terrible blaze, they appeared to set fire to the roof of the heavens.

The *remuda* shrank in a shuddering, densely-packed mass, too paralyzed to bolt. The cattle froze in their tracks, heads down, lowing piteously.

No longer was there any darkness anywhere. No shadow under the wall! No shadow of horse and rider on the ground! Suddenly the flash lightning shifted to forked lightning—magnificent branched streaks of white fire that ribbed the sky. These were as suddenly succeeded by long, single ropes or chains of lightning.

Gradually the horses drew closer together, if not at the instigation of their riders, then at their own. They rubbed flanks; they hid their heads against each other.

"My Gawd! it's turrible!" cried Texas, hoarsely. "We gotta get oot of the way. When this hell's over, thet herd will run mad."

"Tex, they're struck by lightnin'," yelled Holden. "I see cattle down."

"Oot of the narrow place heah, men," shouted Brite.

They moved out into the open valley beyond the constricted neck, and strange to see, the *remuda* followed, the whole drove moving as one horse. They had their heads turned in, so that they really backed away from the wall.

The chain lightnings increased in number, in brilliance, in length and breadth until all in a marvelous instant they coalesced into a sky-wide canopy of intensest blue, too burning for the gaze of man. How long that terrifying phenomenon lasted Brite could not tell, but when, at husky yells of his men, he opened his eyes, the terrific blue blaze of heaven had changed to balls of lightning.

Here was the moment Brite believed he was demented. And these fearless cowhands shared the emotion which beset him. They gaped with protruding eyes at the yellow balls appearing from nowhere, to roll down the walls, to bounce off and burst into crackling sparks. It appeared that balls of fire were shooting in every direction to the prolonged screams of horses in terror.

Brite took the almost fainting Reddie into his arms, and held her tight. He expected death at any instant. Zigzag balls of lightning grew in size and number and rapidity until the ground was criss-crossed with them. They ran together to burst into bits or swell into a larger ball. Then to Brite's horror, to what seemed his distorted vision, these fiendish balls ran over the horses, to hang on their ears, to drop off their noses, to roll back and forth along the reins, to leap and poise upon the rim of his sombrero. Yet he was not struck dead, as seemed inevitable.

All at once Brite became aware of heat, intense sulphurous

heat, encompassing him like a hot blanket. Coincident with that, the rolling, flying balls, like the chains of lightning before them, coalesced with strange sputtering sound into a transparent white fog.

The air reeked with burnt sulphur and contained scarcely enough oxygen to keep men and beasts alive. By dint of extreme will power Brite kept from falling off his horse with Reddie unconscious in his arms. The men coughed as if half strangled. They were bewildered. The herd had been swallowed up in this pale mysterious medium. The hissing, crackling sound of sparks had ceased.

Slowly that fog lifted like a curtain to disclose to Brite's eyes the dark forms of horses and riders. Cooler air took the place of the heat. A vast trampling stir ran through the herd. It seemed likewise to revivify the trail drivers.

"Pards, air we in hell?" shouted Texas, huskily. "Or air we oot? . . . Boys, it's passed away. We're alive to tell the tale. . . . Ho! Ho! Brite's ootfit on the Canadian! . . . The herd's millin', boys! Bear in! Ride 'em, cowboys! . . . By Gawd! our luck is great! Not bad, but great! . . . An' shore we're drivin' on to Dodge. . . . Ride 'em, men! Charge an' shoot to kill! . . . The night's gone an' the day's busted."

"Hi! Hi! Hi! Hi!" screamed the drivers as they drove the leaders back.

In the gray of dawn Brite supported the swaying Reddie in her saddle back to camp.

"Oh, Dad—my *remuda!*—where air they?" she sobbed.

"Inside, lass, inside thet line of fire-eaters," replied the old cattleman. "An' they'll hold!"

Only the reality of the sunrise, the calm morning with its sweet clarified air, the solid earth under their feet and the grazing stock, could ever have dispelled the nightmare of those hours of brimstone.

Texas Joe rode in to fall off his horse and limp to the camp fire. He stretched wide his long arms, as if to embrace the fresh sweetness of the dawn.

"On our way, men! The herd's pointed," he called, his voice thick and shaky. "Gimme aboot a gallon of coffee if there ain't any likker." He fell on a pack, favoring his lame leg. "Wal, my sins air shore wiped oot. All the hell I ever deserved I got last night."

Five watchful, strenuous, endless days later Brite's outfit drove across the North Fork of the Canadian River to camp on Rabbit Ear Creek.

The day before they had passed Camp Supply in the middle of the morning. Texas Joe was too wise to make a halt. Brite rode in with the chuck-wagon.

This camp was teeming with soldiers, Indians, cowhands, and bearded men of no apparent occupation. It was also teeming with rumor of massacre of the wagon train Hardy had hoped to join at Fort Sill, of trail herds north and south, of bands of rustlers operating in Kansas and rendezvousing in the Indian Territory, of twenty million buffalo between the Canadian and Arkansas rivers, of hell itself let loose in Dodge and Abilene. Brite had kept all this to himself. The boys were somber enough, and somehow they might make the drive through.

"Aboot what time is it?" asked Whittaker, dreamily, as some of them sat in camp.

"Sundown, yu locoed galoot," retorted Ackerman.

"Shore. But I mean the month an' day."

"Gawd only knows. . . . An' I don't care."

"I'll bet my spurs Holden can figger it oot. He's a queer duck. But I like him heaps. Don't yu?"

"Cain't say thet I do," returned Deuce, gruffly. Brite had noted more than once how devoted the Uvalde cowboys had been to each other, and how Ackerman appeared jealous of his partner Little, now that the others were gone. Loss of San Sabe had been hard on Deuce.

"Wal, I'll ask him, anyhow," went on Whittaker. "Less," he shouted, "can yu figger oot what day this is?"

"Shore. I'm a walkin' calendar," rejoined Holden, with self-satisfied air, as he pulled a tobacco-pouch from his pocket.

"But don't tell Tex. He says to hell with when an' where it is." He emptied a handful of pebbles out of the bag and began carefully to count them. When he had concluded he said: "Gosh, but they add up! Fifty-six. . . . Fifty-six days oot an' today makes fifty-seven. Boys, we're just three days shy of bein' two months on the trail."

"Is thet all!" ejaculated Whittaker.

"Then it's near August?" queried Ackerman, ponderingly. "We ought to make Dodge by the end of August. . . . I wonder aboot thet Fort Sill wagon train. . . . Boss, I forgot to ask yu. Did yu heah any word of thet wagon train Doan expected from Fort Sill?"

Brite could not look into the lad's dark, eager eyes and tell the truth.

Next day, halfway to Sand Creek, Texas Joe stood up in his stirrups and signaled the news of buffalo. Day after day this had been expected. Somewhere north of the Canadian the great herd would swing across the Chisholm Trail.

Soon Brite saw the dark, ragged, broken lines of buffalo. They appeared scarcely to move, yet after an interval, when he looked again, the straggling ends were closer. Texas Joe halted for dry camp early in the day. What little conversation prevailed around the fire centered on the buffalo.

"Nothin' to fear drivin' along with the buffs," vouchsafed Bender.

"Thet's all yu know."

"Wal, mebbe they'll work back west by mawnin'."

"But s'pose they keep on workin' east—acrost our trail?"

"Trail drivers never turn back."

"An' we could be swallered up by miles of buffalo—cattle, hawses, chuck-wagon, riders an' all?"

"I reckon we could. . . . Boss, did yu ever heah of thet?"

"Of what?" asked Brite, though he had heard plainly enough.

"Ootfit gettin' surrounded by buffalo."

"Shore I have. Thet happens often. Stock grazin' right along with the buffalo."

"Ahuh. Wal, what'd happen if the buffalo stampeded? . . . Thirty million buffalo all movin' at once?"

"Hell, cowboy! It ain't conceivable."

"I'll bet my last cigarette it happens."

So they talked, some of them optimistically, others the opposite, all of them reckless, unafraid, and unchangeable. Morning disclosed long black strings of buffalo crossing the trail ahead.

All day Brite's herd had shaggy monsters for company, short lines, long thin strings, bunches and groups, hundreds and twos and fours of buffalo, leisurely grazing along, contented and indifferent. Sand Creek offered a fine camp site and range for cattle. The mossy-horns appeared as satisfied as their shaggy brothers. They bedded down early and offered no trouble. The guards slept in their saddles.

All next day the trail followed Sand Creek. The drivers were concerned about the booming of needle guns to the east and south. Hunters on the outskirts of the herd or trail drivers coming! That day a long, black, thick line of buffalo crossed behind Brite's herd, and turning north crept along parallel with it. This line had no break. Behind and to the west the black wave, like a tide of broken lava, rolling imperceptibly, slowly augmented and encroached upon the cattle herd. How insignificant and puny that herd of six thousand long-horns now! It was but a drop in the bucket of the Great Plains.

But the west and north remained open, at least as far as eye could see. Brite thought he had crossed directly in front of the mass of buffalo. They might travel that tranquil way for days; and again the whirl of a dust-devil, the whip of a swallow on the wing, might stampede them into a stupendous, rolling avalanche.

Sand Creek merged into Buffalo Creek, a deep, cool, willow-bordered stream where all the luxuriant foliage of the prairie bloomed. Texas made camp at the point where the creeks met.

"We'll rest up heah a day or two," he said. "Somebody knock over a buffalo. Rump steak would shore go great. . . . Reddie, do yu want to kill a buff?"

"No. I'm too tender-hearted," she replied, musingly. "I see so many cute little buffalo calves. I might shoot one's mother."

"Tender-hearted? Wal, I'm dog-goned!" drawled Texas, mildly. He had greatly sobered these late days of the drive and seldom returned to his old raillery. "We-all had it figgered yu was a killer."

"Aw, I don't count redskins, greasers, stampeders—an' now an' then an occasional cowhand."

"I savvy. But I meant a killer with yore gun—not yore red curls, yore snappin' eyes, yore shape thet no boys' pants could hide."

Reddie promptly vanished physically and vocally into the empty air. That was all the pleasantry in camp on this night.

"I wish thet Hash Williams had stuck with us," Texas mused.

"But, Tex, what the hell difference does it make now?"

"Wal, a lot, if we knowed what the pesky buffs would do."

"Ump-umm! I say, since we gotta drive on, to keep goin'."

"But mebbe the buffalo might drift by."

"What? Thet herd? Never this summer. They are as many as the tufts of gramma grass."

"What yu think, boss?" queried the foreman, showing that he needed partisanship to bolster up any of his judgments.

"Wait till mawnin'," advised the cattle-owner.

Certainly the morning brought to light fewer buffalo and wider space, yet to east and south and west the black lines encroached upon the green. Only the north was clear.

"Point the herd!" ordered Brite, driven by fears and hopes.

"I was gonna do thet, anyhow," drawled Texas Joe. "We can only die once, an' if we have to die let's get it over. This dyin' by days an' hours is like tryin' to win a woman's love."

If Joe had but known it—if he could have seen the light in Reddie's eyes as Brite saw it—he would have learned that that could be attained by the very things he thought so little of.

So they drove on and the buffalo closed in black all around

them. Herd, *remuda,* and riders occupied the center of a green island surrounded by rugged, unbroken waves. This island was a couple of miles long by about the same in width, almost a circle. It kept that way for hours of suspense to the drivers.

Long-horns had no fear of buffalo. Brite remembered how the mossy-horned old bulls bawled and tossed their mighty horns at sight of buffalo coming close. But to the vast herd these cattle and horses were grains of dust under their feet.

About noon there came a change. Something quickened the buffalo. Brite felt it, saw it, but could give no solution. Buffalo were beyond understanding.

"Oh, Dad, I heah somethin' behind!" called Reddie, fearfully.

"What?"

"I don't know. It's like the wind in the pines."

Brite strained his ears to hear. In vain! The noonday hour was silent, oppressive, warm with the breath of midsummer. But he saw Texas halt his horse, to turn and stand in his stirrups, gazing back. He, too, had heard something. Brite looked behind him. The buffalo were a mile in the rear, ambling along, no longer nipping the grass. The shaggy line bobbed almost imperceptibly.

"Dad, I heah it again," cried Reddie.

Pan Handle rode around the rear of the cattle, to gallop ahead and join Texas. They watched. Other cowboys turned their faces back. Something was amiss. The cattle grazed along as if buffalo were not encompassing them. But the little Spanish mustangs evinced uneasiness. They trotted to and fro, stood with pointed ears, heads to the south. They had the heritage of two-hundred years of prairie life. At sight of them Brite's heart sank. He tried to stem the stream of his consciousness and not think.

"There it comes, stronger," declared Reddie, who had ridden to Brite's side.

"What yu make of it, lass?"

"Like low thunder now. . . . Mebbe a storm brewin'."

The sky, however, was cloudless, a serene azure vault,

solemn and austere, keeping its secrets. Miles back, low down over the black horizon of shaggy, uneven line, a peculiar yellow, billowy smoke was rising. Dust clouds! Brite would rather have been blind than have been compelled to see that.

"Look! Dust risin'!" cried Reddie, startled She pointed with shaking hand.

"Mebbe it's nothin' to worry aboot," said Brite, averting his eyes.

"An' heah comes Tex. Look at thet hawse!"

The foreman swerved in round the rear of the herd to meet the three riders who rode toward him. After a short consultation one of these galloped off to the east, to round the herd on that side. Texas then came on at a run.

He reined in before Brite and Reddie, who had stopped involuntarily. Texas Joe's face was a bronze mask. His amber eyes were narrow slits of fire.

"Heah anythin', boss?" he queried, sharply.

"Nope. But Reddie does. I see some dust rollin' up behind."

"*Stampede!*" flashed the cowboy, confirming Brite's suspicion.

"Oh, my Gawd!" burst out Reddie, suddenly realizing. "We're trapped in a circle. . . . Jack, what will we do?"

"It's been comin' to us all this drive," replied Texas. "An' I reckon now it's heah. If thet stampede back there spreads through the whole herd we've got about one chance in a thousand. An' thet chance is for our cattle to run bunched as they air now, square an' broad across the rear. Ride behind thet, Mr. Brite, an' good luck to yu. . . . Reddie, if the buffs close in on yu, take to the wagon. A big white heavy wagon like ours might split a herd thet'd trample over hawses."

"Oh, Jack—don't go—till I—" she flung after him. But Texas only turned to wave good-by, then he rode on to meet Moze. That worthy was coming at a stiff trot. They met, and Texas must have imparted alarming orders, for the Negro put the team to a lope that promised shortly to overtake the *remuda*. Texas wheeled back to the left.

Brite and Reddie drove the *remuda* to the rear of the herd, just back of the riders. Soon Moze came lumbering up. Then all accommodated their paces to the movement of the cattle and maintained their position. All of the seven guards now rode at the rear of the herd.

As soon as this change was established Brite took stock of the buffalo. Apparently the immense green oval inside the herd was just as big as ever. But had it narrowed or shortened? He could not be sure. Yet there was a difference. On all sides the buffalo line bobbed at a slow walk. All still seemed well. Brite tried to get his nerve back. But it had been shaken. A terrible peril hung over them. At the last word he did not care particularly about himself, though the idea of being ridden down and pounded by millions of hoofs into a bloody pulp was horrible, but he suffered poignantly for Reddie, and her lover, and these tried and true men who had stood by him so loyally. But God disposed of all. Brite framed a prayer for them, and then like a true Texan prepared to fight to the last bitter gasp.

This enabled him to look back to make out what to expect and how soon. No change in the buffalo. But that yellow, rolling cloud had arisen high, to blot out the sky halfway to the zenith.

All of a sudden Brite realized that for a moment or perhaps longer he had been aware of a filling of his ears with distant sound.

"Reddie!" he yelled. "I heah it!"

To his amazement, the girl had gravitated toward Texas Joe, who had ridden around the *remuda* to approach her. They met, and his forceful gesture sent Reddie back alongside the wagon.

There was no more need for words. Still Brite's stubbornness refused to yield to the worst. Had not some vital, unforeseen chance saved them more than once on this fatal drive? "*Quién sabe?*" he muttered through his teeth.

On each flank the buffalo had markedly changed in aspect. Where before they had wagged along, now they bobbed. Far ahead the forward mass had not yet caught this acceleration. From behind, the low roar gradually increased. Brite's mustang snorted and balked. He had to be spurred. All the horses betrayed a will to bolt. The *remuda* pranced at the heels of the herd, held in on each flank by the riders.

That state of action and sound stayed the same for moments. It was Texas' strange throwing up of his hands that acquainted Brite with a transformation. The buffalo had broken into a lope. An instant later that low roar perished in an engulfing sound that would have struck terror to the stoutest heart. The gap between the rear of the herd and the oncoming buffalo began rapidly to close. Louder grew the roar. On each side of the cattle, far ahead, the buffalo closed in, so that the shape of a great triangle was maintained. It would be impossible for the cattle to mix with the buffalo. An impenetrable, shaggy wall moved on all sides.

Before the advancing mass behind had caught up to Brite the nimble-footed long-horns broke into a swinging lope. That seemed well. It evened matters. The *remuda* appeared less likely to bolt. Moze kept the chuck-wagon rolling at their heels.

Above the steady roar of hoofs all around swelled a sound that swallowed it—the deafening thunder of the stampede in the rear. It had started the herd into action. But now its momentum forced the buffalo ahead again to break their pace. Like a wave rolling onward in the sea it caught up with the cattle, passed through the buffalo on each flank and raced forward to the leaders.

Brite realized the terrible instant when the stampede spirit claimed the whole mass. He felt the ground shake with his horse and his ears cracked to an awful rumble. It ceased as suddenly. He could no longer hear. And as if of one accord, the long-horns and the horses broke into a run.

Brite looked back. A thousand hideously horned and haired heads close-pressed together formed the advance line fifty yards or less behind him. Only gradually did they gain now. Before this moment the pursuing buffalo had split to go on each side of the cattle herd.

For miles the fleet long-horns evened pace with the shaggy monsters of the plains. And in that short while the circle closed. Cows raced buffalo and did not win. The wicked long-horned bulls charged the black wall of woolly hides, to be bowled over and trampled underfoot.

The conformation of the land must have changed from level to grade. Brite's distended eyes saw a vast sea of black ahead, a sweeping tide, like a flood of fur covering the whole prairie. No doubt it was the same on each side of him and for miles behind. Even in that harrowing moment he was staggered by the magnificence of the spectacle. Nature had staged a fitting end for his heroic riders. Texas Joe, on one side of the chuck-wagon, Pan Handle on the other, rode with guns belching fire and smoke into the faces of bulls that charged perilously close. Moze's team was running away, the *remuda* was running away, the six thousand cattle were running away. But where? They were lost in that horde of bison. They were as a few grains of sand on the sea shore.

When the buffalo filled all the gaps, dust obscured Brite's vision. He could see only indistinctly and not far. Yet he never lost sight of Reddie or the wagon. Any moment he expected the wagon to lurch over or to lose a wheel in one of its bounces, and to see Moze go down to his death. But that would be the fate of them all.

Only the *remuda* hung together. Except Pan Handle, Texas, and Reddie, all the riders were surrounded by buffalo. Brite's stirrups rubbed the hump-backed monsters; they bumped his mustang on one side, then on the other.

Bender on his white horse was a conspicuous mark. Brite saw him forced to one side—saw the white horse go down and black bodies cover the place. Brite could feel no more. He closed his eyes. He could not see Reddie sacrificed to such a ghastly fate and care to endure himself.

The hellish stampede went on—a catastrophe which perhaps a gopher had started. A violent jolt all but unseated Brite. He opened his eyes to see a giant bull passing. Yielding to furious fright, Brite shot the brute. It rolled on the ground and the huge beasts leaped over or aside. Sometimes Brite could see patches of ground. But all was yellow, infernal haze, obscuring shadows, and ceaseless appalling motion. It must have an end. The cattle could run all day, but the terrorized horses would fall as had Bender's.

Yet there were Reddie and Texas, sweeping along beside the wagon, with buffalo only on the outside. Farther on through the yellow pale, Brite made out white and gray against the black. A magenta sun burned through the dust. Sick and dizzy and reeling, Brite clung to his saddle-horn, sure that his end was near. He had lived long. Cattle had been his Nemesis. If it had not been for Reddie—

Suddenly his clogged ears appeared to open—to fill again with sound. He could hear once more. His dazed brain answered to the revivifying suggestion. If he was no longer deaf, the roar of stampede had diminished. The mustang broke his gait to allow for down grade. Rifts of sky shone through the yellow curtain. A gleam of river! Heart and sense leaped. They had reached the Cimarron. All went dark before Brite's eyes. But consciousness rallied. The terrible trampling roar was still about him. His horse dragged in sand. A rude arm clasped him and a man bawled in his ear.

Brite gazed stupidly out upon the broad river where strings of cattle were wading out upon an island. To right and left black moving bands crossed the water. The stampede had ended at the Cimarron where the buffalo had split around an island.

"How—aboot—Reddie?" whispered the cattleman as they lifted him out of the saddle.

"Heah, Dad, safe an' sound. Don't yu feel me?" came as if from a distance.

"An'—everybody?"

"All heah but Bender an' Whittaker. They were lost."

"Aw! . . . I seen Bender—go down."

"Boss, it could have been wuss," said Texas, gratefully.

"Oh, Dad! Did yu see me go down?" cried Reddie. "I got pitched ahaid—over my hawse. . . . Thet cowboy snatched me up—as if I'd been his scarf."

"Which cowboy?" queried Brite.

"Texas—Jack. . . . Thet's the second time—shore."

"Boss, we're stuck," reported the practical Texas, brushing Reddie aside. "Some of our cattle went with the buffalo. The rest is scattered. Our *remuda* half gone. . . . But, by Gawd! we're heah on the Cimarron! When these cussed buffs get by we'll round up our stock an' drive on."

Before dark the last straggling ends of the buffalo herd loped by. Meanwhile camp had been made on high ground. Two of the riders were repairing the wagon. Moze was cooking rump steak. Pan Handle labored zealously at cleaning his guns. Texas Joe strode here and there, his restless eyes ever seeking Reddie, who lay on the green grass beside Brite. The outfit had weathered another vicissitude of the Trail.

It took Brite's remaining riders four days to round up five thousand head of cattle. The rest were lost, and a hundred head of the *remuda*. And the unbeatable cowboys kept telling Brite that he had still five hundred more long-horns than the number with which he had started.

Trail herds crossed the Cimarron every day, never less than two, and often more, and once five herds. The rush was on. Good luck had attended most of the drivers. A brush with Nigger Horse, a few stampedes, a bad electrical storm that caused delay, hailstones that killed yearling calves—these were reports given by the passing drivers.

A huge cowhand, red of face and ragged of garb, hailed the members of Brite's outfit in camp.

"On the last laig to Dodge! I'll be drunker'n hell soon," he yelled, and waved his hand.

Brite got going again on the fifth day, with cattle and *remuda* rested, but with his cowboys ragged as scarecrows, gaunt and haggard, wearing out in all except their unquenchable spirit.

They had company at every camp. Snake Creek, Salt Creek, Bear Creek, Bluff Creek, and at last Mulberry Creek only a few miles out of Dodge.

That night the sun went down gloriously golden and red

over the vast, level prairie. Ranchers called on the trail drivers.

"Dodge is shore a-hummin' these days," said one. "Shootin', drinkin', gamblin'! They're waitin' for yu boys—them painted women an' black-coated caird sharps."

"WHOOPEE!" yelled the cowboys, in lusty passion. But Deuce Ackerman was silent.

Texas Joe took a sly look at the downcast Reddie, and with a wink at Brite he drawled: "Gosh! I'm glad I'm free. Just a no-good cowhand in off the Trail with all the hell behind! Boss, I want my pay pronto. I'll buck the tiger. I'll stay sober till I bore thet rustler Hite. Then me for one of them hawk-eyed gurls with a pale face an' painted lips an' bare arms an'——"

"Yes, yu *air* a no-good cowhand," blazed Reddie, furiously. "Oh, I—I'm ashamed of yu. I—I hate yu! . . . To give in to the bottle—to some vile hussy—when—when all the time our boys—our comrades lay daid oot there on the prairie. How can yu—do—it?"

"Thet's why, Reddie," replied Texas Joe, suddenly flayed. "It shore takes a hell of a lot to make a man forget the pards who died for him. . . . An' I have nothin' else but likker an' a painted—"

"Oh, but yu have!" she cried, in ringing passion. "Yu fool! Yu fool!"

CHAPTER **16** DODGE CITY was indeed roaring. Brite likened the traffic in the wide street, the dust, the noise, the tramp of the throng to a stampede of cattle on the trail.

After the drive in to the pastures, and the count, Brite had left the cowboys and the wagon, and had ridden to town with Reddie. He had left her asleep in her room at the hotel, where she had succumbed at sight of a bed. He hurried to the office of Hall and Stevens, with whom he had had dealings before. He was welcomed with the eagerness of men who smelled a huge deal with like profit.

"Brite, you're a ragamuffin," declared the senior member of the firm. "Why didn't you rid yourself of that beard? And those trail togs?"

"Tomorrow is time enough for thet. I want to sell an' go to bed. What're yu payin' this month?"

"We're offerin' twelve dollars," replied the cattle-buyer, warily.

"Not enough. My count is five thousand an' eighty-eight. Call it eighty even. Fine stock an' fairly fat."

"What do you want?"

"Fifteen dollars."

"Won't pay it. Brite, there are eighty thousand head of cattle in."

"Nothin' to me, Mr. Hall. I have the best stock."

"Thirteen dollars."

"Nope. I'll run over to see Blackwell," replied Brite, moving toward the door.

"Fourteen. That's my highest. Will you sell?"

"Done. I'll call tomorrow sometime for a certified check. Meanwhile send yore cowhands down to take charge."

"Thanks, Brite. I'm satisfied if you are. Cattle movin' brisk. How many head will come up the Trail before the snow flies?"

"Two hundred thousand."

Hall rubbed his hands. "Dodge will be wide open about the end of August."

"What is it now? I'm goin' to get oot quick."

"Won't you need some cash to pay off?"

"Shore. I forgot. Make it aboot two thousand five hundred. Good day."

Brite wrestled his way back to the hotel, landing there out of breath and ready to drop. He paid a Negro porter five dollars to pack up a tub of water. Then he took a bath, shaved, and went to bed, asleep before he hit the pillow.

What seemed but a moment later a knocking at his door awakened him.

"Dad, air yu daid?" called a voice that thrilled him.

"Come in."

Reddie entered, pale, with hollow eyes and strained cheeks, but sweet to gaze upon. She sat down upon the bed beside him.

"Yu handsome man! All clean shaved an' nice. Did yu buy new clothes?"

"Not yet. I left thet till this mawnin'."

"It's ten o'clock. When did yu go to bed?"

"At four. Six hours! Oh, I was daid to the world."

"Where is—air the boys?"

"Also daid asleep. Don't worry. They'll straggle in late today, lookin' for money."

"Dad, do me a favor?"

"Shore. Anythin' yu want."

"Don't give the cowboys—at least Texas Jack—a-any money right away."

"But, honey, I cain't get oot of it," protested Brite, puzzled. "Soon as he comes heah."

"Will he want to—to get drunk—as he bragged an'—an'—" She dropped her head to the pillow beside Brite's.

"Shore. They'll all get drunk."

"Could I keep Jack from thet?" she whispered.

"I reckon yu could. But it'll cost a lot. Do yu care enough aboot him, lass?"

"Oh! . . . I—I love him!"

"Wal, then, it'll be easy, for thet fire-eatin' hombre loves the ground yu ride on."

"Have I yore consent?"

"Why, child!"

"But yu're my Dad. I cain't remember my real one."

"Yu have my blessin', dear. An' I think the world of Texas Joe. He's the salt of the earth."

"Could yu let him quit trail drivin'? Because if he drove I'd have to go, too."

"Reddie, I got a fortune for thet herd. Which reminds me I still have ninety-two hawses to sell."

"But yu cain't sell mine."

"We'll leave him with Selton, to be sent south with the first ootfit."

She leaped up, flushed and happy, with tears like pearls on her tanned cheeks and eyes of sweet, thoughtful shadows.

"Hurry. Get up an' dress. Take me oot to buy things. A girl's! Oh, I will not know what to buy. It's like a dream. . . . Hurry, Dad. I wouldn't dare go alone."

"I should smile yu wouldn't."

When she ran out Brite made short work of getting into his torn and trail-stained rags. Soon they were on their way down the main street of Dodge. It presented a busy scene, but the roar was missing. Too early in the day! Reddie was all eyes. She missed nothing. Cowboys, gamblers, teamsters, Negroes, Mexicans, Indians, lined the street, waiting for something to begin.

Brite took Reddie into Denman's big merchandise store, where he turned her over to a woman clerk to give her the best of everything and not consider expense. Then he hastened to purchase an outfit for himself. That did not require long, but he encountered a trail driver, Lewis by name, and in exchanging experiences time flew by. Hurrying back, he found Reddie dazed and happy, sitting amid a circle of parcels. They had a merry and a toilsome job packing their purchases back to the hotel. Reddie barred herself in with her precious possessions.

Some time later a tap on Brite's door interrupted the finishing touches of his dressing.

"Come in," he answered.

Texas Joe entered, his lean, handsome face shining despite its havoc.

"Mawnin' boss," he drawled. "My, but yu're spruced up fine."

"Yes, an' yu'll be feelin' like me pronto. How's the boys?"

"I don't know. Asleep I reckon. They come in town to go to bed. I'll find them some place."

"Where's Pan Handle?"

"Sleepin' to quiet his nerves. Boss, he'll be lookin' for Hite before the day's oot."

"Tex, if I asked yu as a particular favor, would yu give up goin' on a debauch an' take first stage with me an' Reddie?"

"Boss, yu're askin' too much. Somethin' turrible, or mebbe wonderful, has gotta come between me an' thet hell-rattlin' drive."

"I understand. But do this for me. Go with me to Hall's office, then to the bank. An' I'll take yu to the store where I bought this ootfit."

"Thet's easy. I'll stick to yu shore till I get my money. Clean broke, boss. Not a two-bit piece. An' I had some money when we left Santone. My Gawd! will I ever see thet town again?"

"Shore yu will. Come on."

They went out into the street. "Boss, would yu mind walkin' on my left side. I might have to clear for action, yu know. If we meet Hite—wall our pard Pan is gonna be left."

But nothing happened on their several errands. Upon returning to the hotel, Texas engaged a room and proceeded to get rid of the stains and rags of the Chisholm Trail. Brite went to Blackwell, where he sold the *remuda* for twenty dollars a head. He was treading the clouds when he got back to the hotel. Cattlemen he knew engaged him in spirited inquiry about the resourcefulness of Texas. Men and women, some of them flashily dressed, passed through the lobby to the dining-room. Brite noted a very pretty young lady, in gaily colorful array, pass to and fro as if on parade. He observed that she had attracted the attention of a frock-coated gambler. And when he accosted her, Brite decided he had better make sure the girl wanted this kind of attention. When he strode over, what was his amaze and consternation to hear the girl say in a sharp familiar voice: "Heah, Mr. Flowery Vest, if I was packin' my gun I'd shoot yore laig off!"

"*Reddie!*" burst out Brite, beside himself.

"Hello, Dad. An' yu didn't know me! Lend me yore gun."

The gambler fled. Brite gazed speechless at his adopted daughter, unable to believe his own sight.

"Reddie, darlin', is it yu?"

"Shore it's me. Thet is, I think an' feel it is 'cept when I look in thet mirror. . . . Oh, Dad! I feel so strange—so tormented—so *happy*. Thet woman was smart. She picked oot all these things for me. . . . Do I look—nice?"

"Nice! Reddie, yu air the sweetest thing I ever seen. I am knocked flat. I am so glad I could bust. An' to think yu're my lass."

"I'd hug yu—if we was anywhere else. . . . Dad, will *he* like me—this way?"

"He! Who?"

"Texas Jack, of course."

"Like yu? He'll fall on his knees if yu give him a chance."

"Oh!" She started, with dark bright eyes widening. "There's Texas now. Oh, I hardly knew him. . . . Dad, stand by me now. I wouldn't say my happiness is at stake—or all of it—but my love is. . . . If I've only got—the nerve—"

"Remember Wallen, honey, an' thet day of the stampede," was all Brite had time to say, when Texas Joe transfixed him and Reddie in one lightning flash of falcon eyes.

"Boss!—Who—who—"

"Jack, don't yu know me?" Reddie asked, roguishly. Brite marveled at the woman of her—so swift to gain mastery over her weakness.

"For Gawd's sake!" gasped Texas.

"Come, Jack," she cried, clasping his arm and then Brite's, and dragging them away. "We'll go up to Dad's room. I've somethin' to say—to yu."

All the way up the stairs and down the hall Texas Joe seemed in a trance. But Reddie talked about the town, the people, the joy of their deliverance from the bondage of the Trail. Then they were in Brite's room with the door shut.

Reddie subtly changed. She tossed her dainty bonnet on the bed as if she had been used to such finery all her life.

"Jack, do yu like me?" she asked, sweetly, facing him with great dark eyes aglow, and she turned round for his benefit.

"Yu're staggerin' lovely, Reddie," he replied. "I'd never have knowed yu."

"This ootfit is better then them tight pants I used to wear?"

"Better! Child, yu're a boy no more," he said, wistfully. "Yu're a girl—a lady. An' no one who knowed yu would want to see yu go back now."

"Yu'd never dare spank me in this dress, would yu?"

Texas flushed red to the roots of his tawny hair. "Gawd, no! An' I never did spank yu as a girl."

"Yes, yu did. Yu knew me. Yu saw me bathin' in the creek thet day. . . . Naked! Don't yu dare deny thet."

It was a torturing moment for Texas and he seemed on the rack. "Never mind. I forgive yu. Who knows? Mebbe but for thet. . . . Jack, heah is what I want to say. Will yu give up goin' on a drunk?"

"Sorry, Miss Bayne, but I cain't. Thet's a trail driver's privilege. An' any human bein' wouldn't ask him not to drown it all."

"Not even for me?"

"I reckon—not even for yu."

She slowly drew close to him, as white as if sun and wind had never tanned her face, and her dark purple eyes shone wondrously.

"If I kiss yu—will yu give it up? . . . Once yu begged for a kiss."

Texas laughed mirthlessly. "Funny, thet idee. *Yu* kissin' *me!*"

"Not so funny, Jack," she flashed, and seizing his coat in strong hands she almost leaped at his lips. Then she fell back, released him, sank momentarily against him, and stepped back. Texas Joe, with corded jaw in restraint, bent eyes of amber fire upon her. They had forgotten Brite or were indifferent to his presence.

"Wal, yu did it. Yu kissed me. An' I'm ashamed of yu for

it. . . . Reddie Bayne, yu cain't buy my freedom with a kiss."

"Oh, Jack, it's not yore freedom I want to buy. It's yore salvation."

"Bah! What's life to me?" he retorted, stern-lipped and somber-eyed. "I want to carouse, to fight, to kill, to sleep drunk—drunk—drunk."

"I know, Jack. Oh, I think I understand. Wasn't I a trail driver, too? An' do I want these awful things? No! No! An' I want to save yu from them. . . . Yu madden me with yore cold. . . . Jack, spare me an' end it—quick."

"I'm sparin' yu more'n yu know, little lady," he replied, darkly passionate.

"Shore *somethin'* will coax yu oot of this hell-givin' idee. . . . What? I'll do anythin'—anythin'—"

He seized her in strong arms and lifted her off her feet against his breast.

"Yu'd marry me?"

"Oh yes—yes—yes!"

"But why, girl? *Why?*" he demanded in a frenzy of doubt.

Reddie flung her arms around his neck and strained to reach and kiss his quivering cheek. " 'Cause I love yu, Jack— so turrible!"

"Yu love me, Reddie Bayne?"

"I do. I do."

"Since—when?" he whispered, playing with his joy.

"Thet day—when Wallen came—an' yu—saved me."

He kissed her hair, her brow, her scarlet cheek, and at last the uplifted mouth.

"Aw, Reddie! Aw! It was worth goin' through—all thet hell—for this. . . . Girl, yu've got to kill the devil in me. . . . When will yu marry me?"

"Today—if yu—must have me," she whispered, faintly. "But I—I'd rather wait—till we get back to Dad's—to Santone, my home."

"Then we'll wait," he rang out, passionately. "But we must

leave today, darlin'. . . . This Dodge town is brewin' blood for me."

"Oh, let's hurry," she cried, and slipping out of his arms, she turned appealingly to Brite. "Dad, it's all settled. We've made up. When can yu take us away?"

"Today, an' pronto, by thunder," replied Brite, heartily. "Pack yore old duds an' go to the stage office at the east end of the street. We've got plenty of time. But go there pronto. It's a safer place to wait. I will pay off an' rustle to meet yu there."

Brite spent a fruitless hour trying to locate the cowboys. Upon returning to the hotel, with the intention of leaving their wages, as well as their share of the money found on the stampeder Wallen, he encountered Pan Handle, vastly changed in garb and face, though not in demeanor.

"Hullo, Pan. Lookin' for yu. Heah's yore wages as a trail driver an' yore share—"

"Brite, yu don't owe me anythin'," returned the gunman, smiling.

"Heah! None of thet or we're not friends," retorted Brite, forcing the money upon him. "I'm leavin' in an hour by stage with Tex an' Reddie. They made it up, an' we're all happy."

"Fine! I'm shore glad. I'll go to the stage to see yu off."

"Pan, hadn't yu better go with us, far as Abilene, anyway?"

"Wal, no, much as I'd like to. I've somebody to see heah yet."

"Wal, I'm sorry. Will yu take this wad of bills an' pay off those fire-eaters of mine."

"Shore will. But they're heah, just round on the side porch."

"Let's get thet over, pronto," said Brite, fervently. Strange how he wanted to see the last of these faithful boys!

Holden sat on the porch steps, while Ackerman and Little leaned arm in arm on the rail. They still wore their ragged trail garb, minus the chaps, but their faces were clean and bright from recent contact with razor and soap.

"Howdy, boss. Got any money?" asked Rolly, lazily, with a grin.

"Shore. I have it heah waitin' for yu—wages, an' bonus, too. Thet share of Wallen's money amounts to more'n all yore wages."

"Boss, I'm gonna take ten to blow in, an' want yu to put the rest in somebody's hands to keep for me," said Ackerman, keenly. "Yu know I'm not trailin' back to Texas."

"We'll miss yu, Deuce."

Less Holden stood up, lithe and clean cut, with warm glance on the money about to be handed to him.

"Dog-gone yu! Rolly, gimme thet quirt," drawled Deuce, mildly.

"Darn if I will," rejoined Little, holding the quirt behind his back.

"It's mine, yu son-of-a-gun!" They wrestled like boys in play, but before Deuce could obtain the quirt from his friend, Holden snatched it.

"I reckon findin's keepin's," he laughed.

With a shout the two cowboys flung themselves upon him. Brite sat down to watch the fun. Pan Handle looked on dubiously. The boys were sober. They had not had a drink. They were just full of lazy glee. As the three of them tugged at the quirt their warm young faces flashed into sight, one after the other. And they grunted and laughed and tugged.

"Aw, Less, thet hurt. Don't be so gol-durned rough," complained Rolly as Holden wrenched the quirt away from the other two. Little looked askance at the blood on his hand. But he was too good-natured to take offense. Deuce, however, suddenly changing from jest to earnest, wrenched the quirt in turn from Holden.

"Heah, Rolly. It's yores. Let's quit foolin'," said Deuce.

But Holden leaped for the quirt, and securing a grip, he tore at it. He flung Rolly off his balance. Like a cat, however, the agile cowboy came down on his feet. The playful violence succeeded to something else. Holden, failing to secure the quirt, let go with his right and struck Rolly in the face.

"*Aw!*" cried Rolly, aghast. Then as fierce wild spirit

mounted he slashed at Holden's darkening face with the quirt. Blood squirted.

"*Heah, boys! Stop!*" yelled Pan Handle.

But too late. Holden threw his gun and shot. Rolly doubled up, his face convulsed in dark dismay, and fell. Like tigers then Holden and Ackerman leaped to face one another, guns spouting. Holden plunged on his face, his gun beating a tattoo on the hard ground. Brite sat paralyzed with horror as Deuce sank down, his back to the porch.

The demoniac expression faded from his dark face. His gun slipped from his hand to clatter on the steps, blue smoke rising from the barrel. His other hand sought his breast and clutched there, with blood gushing out between his fingers. He never wasted a glance upon the prostrate Holden, but upon his beloved comrade Rolly he bent a pitying, all-possessing look. Then his handsome head fell back.

Pan Handle rushed to kneel beside him. And Brite, dragging up out of his stupor, bent over the dying boy. He smiled a little wearily. "Wal, old—trail driver, we pay," he whispered, feebly. "I reckon—I cain't—wait for—little gray-eyed—Ann!"

His whisper failed, his eyes faded. And with a gasp he died.

An hour later Brite met Pan Handle and with him left the hotel.

"Pan, I'll never drive the trail again," he said.

"Small wonder. But yu're a Texan, Brite, an' these air border times."

"Poor, wild, fire-hearted boys!" exclaimed Brite, still shaken to his depths. "All in less than a minute! My God! . . . We must keep this from Reddie. . . . I'll never forget Deuce's eyes—his words. 'Old trail driver, we pay!' . . . I know an' God knows he paid. They all paid. Oh, the pity of it, Pan! To think thet the grand game spirit of these cowboys—the soul thet made them deathless on the trail—was the cause of such a tragedy!"

Dodge was not concerned with auditing a few more deaths. It was four in the afternoon and the hum of the cattle metropolis resembled that of a hive of angry bees.

Saddle horses lined the hitching-rails as far as Brite could see. Canvas-covered wagons, chuck-wagons, buckboards, vehicles of all Western types, stood outside the saddle horses. And up one side and down the other a procession ambled in the dust. On the wide sidewalk a throng of booted, belted, spurred men wended their way up or down. The saloons roared. Black-sombreroed, pale-faced, tight-lipped men stood beside the wide portals of the gaming-dens. Beautiful wrecks of womanhood, girls with havoc in their faces and the look of birds of prey in their eyes, waited in bare-armed splendor to be accosted. Laughter without mirth ran down the walk. The stores were full. Cowboys in twos and threes and sixes trooped by, young, lithe, keen of eye, bold of aspect, gay and reckless. Hundreds of cowboys passed Brite in that long block from the hotel to the intersecting street. And every boy gave him a pang. These were the toll of the trail and of Dodge. It might have been the march of empire, the tragedy of progress, but it was heinous to Brite. He would never send another boy to his death.

They crossed the intersecting street and went on. Brite finally noticed that Pan Handle walked on the inside and quite apart. He spoke briefly when addressed. Brite let him be, cold and sick with these gunmen—with their eternal watchfulness, their gravitating toward the violence they loved.

Dodge roared on, though with lesser volume, toward the end of the main thoroughfare. Brite gazed with strange earnestness into the eyes of passers-by. So many intent, quiet, light eyes of gray or blue! Indians padded along in that stream, straight, dusky-eyed, aloof, yet prostituted by the whites. No more of the gaudy butterfly girls! Young men and old who had to do with cattle! The parasites were back in that block of saloons and dance-halls and gambling-dens. They passed Beatty and Kelly's store, out from under an awning into the light. A dark-garbed man strode out of the barbershop.

"*Jump!*" hissed Pan Handle.

Even as Brite acted upon that trenchant word his swift eye swept to the man in front of the door. Sallow face, baleful eyes, crouching form—Ross Hite reaching for his gun!

Then Brite's dive took him out of vision. As he plunged off the sidewalk two shots boomed out, almost together. A heavy bullet spanged off the gravel in the street.

Lunging up, Brite leaped forward. Then he saw Pan Handle standing erect, his smoking gun high, while Hite stretched across the threshold of the barbershop door.

A rush of feet, excited cries, a loud laugh, then Pan Handle bent a little, wrenching his gaze from his fallen adversary. He sheathed his gun and strode on to join Brite. They split the gathering crowd and hurried down the street. Dodge roared on, but in lessening volume.

Breathless with haste and agitation, Brite reached the stage office.

"Waitin' for yu, boss," drawled Texas Joe from inside the big stage-coach. "Wal, yu're all winded. Yu needn't have rustled. I'd kept this stage-driver heah."

"Oh, Dad, I was afraid," cried Reddie, leaning out with fair face flushed.

"Dog-gone! Heah's Pan Handle, too," exclaimed Texas. "Shore was fine of yu to come down to say good-by."

Pan Handle coolly lighted a cigarette with fingers as steady as a rock. He smiled up at Reddie.

"Lass, I shore had to wish yu all the joy an' happiness there is in this hard old West."

"Thank yu, Pan," she replied, shyly. "I wish—"

"All aboard thet's goin'," yelled the stage-driver from his seat.

Brite threw his bag in and followed, tripping as he entered. The strong hand that had assisted him belonged to Pan Handle, who stepped in after him. Then the stage-coach lurched and rolled away.

"Wal now, Pan, where's yore baggage?" drawled Texas Joe, his falcon eyes narrowing.

"Tex, I reckon all I've got is on my hip," replied Pan Handle, his glance meeting that of Texas Joe.

"Ahuh. . . . Wal, I'm darn glad yu're travelin' with us."

"Oh, Dad, yu didn't forget to say good-by to the boys for me, especially to Deuce, who'll never come back to Texas?"

"No, Reddie, I didn't forget," replied Brite.

"I hope Ann can coax Deuce never again to be a trail driver," concluded Reddie, happily, as she smiled up at Texas Joe. "I'd shore like to tell her how."